FIRST SEMESTER

FIRST SEMESTER

FIRST SEMESTER

ISBN-13: 978-0-373-83082-4
ISBN-10:   0-373-83082-3

www.KimaniTRU.com

Printed in U.S.A.

FIRST SEMESTER

Cecil R. Cross II

KIMANI
tru™

KIMANI tru

FRESH. CURRENT. AND TRUE TO YOU.

Dear Reader,

What you're holding is very special. Something fresh, new and true to your unique experience as a young African-American! We are proud to introduce a new fiction imprint—Kimani TRU. You'll find Kimani TRU speaks to the triumphs, problems and concerns of today's black teens with candor, wit and realism. The stories are told from your perspective and in your own voice, and will spotlight young, emerging literary talent.

Kimani TRU will feature stories that are down-to-earth, yet empowering. Feel like an outsider? Afraid you'll never fit in, find your true love or have a boyfriend who accepts you for who you really are? Maybe you feel that your life is a disaster and your future is going nowhere? In Kimani TRU novels, discover the emotional issues that young blacks face every day. In one story, by attending a historically black college, a young man struggles to get out of a neighborhood that holds little promise. In another, a young woman's life drastically changes when she goes to live with the father she has never known and his middle-class family in the suburbs.

With Kimani TRU, we are committed to providing a strong and unique voice that will appeal to *all* young readers! Our goal is to touch your heart, mind and soul, and give you a literary voice that reflects your creativity and your world.

Spread the word...Kimani TRU. True to you!

Linda Gill
General Manager
Kimani Press

KIMANI PRESS™

I dedicate this novel to my grandmother Velma Vinson who watched me scoot before I could stand. She ran her course. Now it's my turn. I know she's watching from heaven.

Acknowledgment

First of all, I would like to thank God for blessing me with the ability and creativity to write this novel, and the opportunity to share it with the world. Without Him, I am an inkless pen. With Him, nothing is impossible. I would like to thank my parents, Cecil and Vera, for guiding me, encouraging me and always believing in my dreams. Thanks for coming up with the title, Mom! To my sister, Ebony, I thank you for being my number one fan. I'm yours, too! When the movie drops, you're starring in it! My brother, Dre, thanks for introducing me to the "A" and teaching me how to stick to the script! Grandma Mabel, you are truly heaven-sent. Thanks for being my angel in the physical form. Keunna, Kahlana and Katrice, thanks for your sense of humor, style and strength. "D Baby," thanks for equipping me with the heart of an entrepreneur. Nana, thanks for putting a pen and pad in my hand on "the trip." It's still paying off! To my agent, Regina Brooks, thanks for recognizing my talent, always keeping it real and consistently pushing for perfection.

Mark, my brotha from anotha motha, thanks for staying down since day one. We on our way! Rodo, thanks for being my college roommate, a loyal friend, and for helping me launch *LOOK Magazine,* an idea bigger than us. Doc, thanks for your mentorship, and for convincing me that I can do all things through Christ, who strengthens me. To the rest of my cousins, aunts, uncles and extended fam, thanks for your love and continued support.

To my favorite professor, Ms. Shawn Evans-Mitchell, thanks for being the first to read and edit this project, and for giving me the confidence to shop it. Special shout-outs to Ish, for schooling me about the Bay, the Chill Factor click, for putting me up on G in the Chi, Bobby V, for showing me how fast dreams can become reality, Jon and Kev, for keeping my pen moving with *RedZone Magazine,* my CIA boys, for your prayers, and my Plush Blue fam, for grinding with me and keeping my pockets laced while I was waiting for this book to drop. To my frat brothers in Kappa Alpha Psi, thanks for your support. Keep on achieving! To Oprah, thanks for having your questions ready. I'm coming for that couch! Big ups to all the bookstores, radio stations and newspaper and magazine editors for helping put *First Semester* on the map!

Last but not least, I would like to thank all of the Ramen-noodle-eating, long-registration-line-standing, dorm-room-living college students who spent their refund-check money to buy this book. You were my inspiration.

PROLOGUE

LOOKING BACK

They say hindsight is twenty-twenty. But sometimes, by the time you look back, it's too late.

If somebody would've told me that one test score would determine whether or not I was allowed to stay in college in Atlanta or be sent back to the streets of Oakland, I probably would've done things a little differently. Especially since I knew I only had one chance.

After all, "You never get a second first semester."

CHAPTER 1

THE CRIB

No matter how hard I tried to enjoy myself on graduation night, I couldn't party the way I wanted to. I walked across the stage, heard my name called on the loudspeaker, shook the principal's hand, got my diploma, turned my tassels and threw my cap in the air. I even took pictures with my family afterward. Yet a small part of me still felt like a failure.

Maybe sitting at the kitchen table guzzling shots of Hennessey with my boy T-Spoon had something to do with my moment of introspection. But for some reason, I just wasn't in the partying mood. For mostly everybody else at the party, this was the end of the line. Just getting a high school diploma was the biggest accomplishment they would ever know. T-Spoon was a fifth-year senior who bounced around four different high schools before finally giving up and getting his GED a couple of months ago. He was probably more excited than anybody just to have his GED, especially since he had a baby on the way. I've known T-Spoon since elementary school, and I must admit, I never even thought he would go for his GED. He was one of my boys who I'd grown up with, but knew to keep at a distance, because he was a live wire. With T-Spoon you never knew what to expect. Although we hadn't talked much over the last couple months, I knew that for T-Spoon, getting his GED was equivalent to anybody else getting their Ph.D. But the more we drank, the more his sentences were filled with a hopeless hood mentality all too common where I'm from.

"You know you my nigga, right?" he asked in a drunken slur as he tore the plastic off a Swisher Sweet cigar wrapper. "I bet you never thought your boy would've graduated, huh?"

By "graduated" I took it he meant got his GED. Instead of asking for clarification, I just flowed with it.

"You're doing your thing, blood," I said, taking another swallow of Hen.

"Doing my thing, huh?" he asked. "Man, what's up with you tonight? You seem like you're somewhere else, blood."

"I'm just tripping on how fast time is flying, bro," I said. "I'm looking around at cats we done played Little League with, football with—they're grown men now. Breezies we used to play hide-and-get-it with at recess are walking around pregnant."

"Somebody finally got it," he said, laughing.

"I guess so," I said.

"But that's called life," he said, as he split the cigar in half and dumped its tobacco in the garbage can. "And I don't know about you, but I'm enjoying mine. A nigga just came up on a quarter pound of some of that purp we robbed from the white boys out in Vallejo last weekend."

"Y'all hit 'em up for a *quarter pound?*"

"And got out of there like a thief in the night, pimpin'. But like I was sayin', I'm figna make a couple dumps, get this money and smoke like Bob Marley. If I get all this weed off in the next week, I'll have enough to go up on a half pound by myself, and still have enough to throw some dubs on the Caprice."

"Then what?"

"What you mean, then what?"

"Say you get off all that fire in a week, you get your half a powwow and you hook up your car. Then what?"

"Then I do it all over again," he said as he whipped a fat dime sack out of his pocket and began to break down the weed on the kitchen table. "You know a nigga got a seed on the way, so I gotta grind."

"That's exactly what I'm talking about, blood," I said. "I didn't sit through all these classes for four years just to grind. And neither did you. A nigga's tired of trying to make ends meet slangin' these dope sacks. There's gotta be more to life than this."

"For some people there is," he mumbled as he licked the blunt and rolled it to give it an airtight seal. "That's why I got my GED, so I'll have something to fall back on. But last time I checked, Microsoft ain't hiring people with GEDs. So until they start, I'm hustling, blood. But you got your diploma. You should be straight. That's your ticket."

"You would think so, right?"

"You ain't got into college yet?" he asked as he cuffed his hand around the lighter and sparked his blunt.

"I ain't got accepted to no *real* schools," I said, downing another shot. "It's to the point where you would think a high school diploma ain't good enough to get in college no more."

"What you mean *real* school?" he asked.

"Schools outside of Cali."

"What!" he asked excitedly, exhaling a large cloud of smoke. "Don't tell me my nigga is trying to leave the Town! You ain't never even been no further than L.A., and you're trying to leave Cali?"

"Who's trying to leave Cali?" a familiar voice asked.

When I turned around to see who it was, my boy Todd had already extended his hand to give me our hood handshake. After gripping me up, then T-Spoon, he asked again, "So, who's bouncing?"

"Go ahead and tell him, blood," T-Spoon said, taking a long pull of the blunt before passing it to me. "Tell him about your plan to go to a real college."

"Oh!" Todd yelled. "My nigga got into a college!"

"Nah, blood," I said, taking a slow drag. "You know how T-Spoon be jumping to conclusions."

"So, what happened?" Todd asked.

"Nothing," I said as I damn near coughed up a lung. "We were just talking about life, and how niggas gotta make some grown-man decisions right about now."

"It's one thing to make a grown-man decision," T-Spoon said, gulping down another shot of Hen. "But leave Oakland? I don't know about that one, blood."

"I mean, why not?" I asked. "Don't get me wrong. You know I've got love for the Town. But I ain't never left California in my life, blood."

"Me neither," T-Spoon said. "You say that to say what?"

"I don't know," I said. "I mean, if you're content with being stuck in the Town your whole life, then I guess that's cool for you. But I just feel like there's got to be something else out here for me. It's time for me to see some new shit."

"I can dig it," Todd said, reaching for the blunt. "I don't know about y'all, but I'm gone."

"You too?" T-Spoon asked.

"Your boy got accepted to Crampton last week," Todd said. "I'm outta here."

"I applied there too," I said.

"How come you didn't get in?" T-Spoon asked.

"Probably because he waited until the very last second to send in his application," Todd said. "You know J.D. is good for waiting to do everything."

"Hey, you know I do my best work with my back against the wall," I said.

"I don't know about all that," T-Spoon said between laughs. "I still remember the first time me and my mom came by your crib to pick you up for our first football game."

"Ahh, shit, here you go," I said.

"We were already running hella late," T-Spoon continued. "And when we got there, he was just waking up, trying to figure out how to put his pads in his pants. He tried to grab all of his stuff and rush out of the house. But he forgot to bring..."

"One cleat and one thigh pad," I said, cutting him off.

"Hold on," Todd said, laughing even harder. "I remember that game. You forgot your helmet too, nigga."

"You sure did," T-Spoon said. "Man, we had some fun growing up. I can't believe y'all are talking about bouncing. Where is Crampton anyway?"

"It's an historically black college in Virginia," Todd said.

"Now, that's what's crackin'!" I said.

"I don't know nothin' about no historically black college," T-Spoon said, picking up the fifth of Hen, leaning his head back and downing the last couple of swigs. "But there's some historically fat asses in that party downstairs. I don't know about y'all, but I'm tryin' to get behind one of 'em."

"I'm feeling that," Todd said as he held the dwindling remains of the blunt in between his fingers, trying to get one last pull. "Ah, I almost burnt my finger trying to smoke with y'all. C'mon, blood." He grabbed me by my shoulder. "Don't even trip on that school shit. You'll be straight."

"Oh yeah, blood, I almost forgot," T-Spoon said, stumbling back into the kitchen. "When you get into that *real* college... and you *will* be getting in...do something I never did."

"What's that?" I asked.

"Don't bullshit, man. Take it serious. Finish."

"If I get in, I got you," I said.

"You mean, *when* you get in, right?" Todd asked.

"Yeah, blood," I said, still sounding unsure. "When I get in."

The floor was sticky and the walls were dripping with perspiration. The small red lightbulb hanging from the ceiling vibrated with every thud of the bass. Smoke clouded the room, and damn near everybody at the party was holding a drink. Girls were bent over with hands on their knees, backing it up on guys who stood their ground behind them, bouncing to the beat while holding their hands high in the air, as if they were being robbed. The shoulder-to-shoulder crowd had to have exceeded fire code regulations hours ago, but no one cared. What was supposed to be an invitation-only, postgraduation get-together in my homeboy Jerrell's basement had turned into the most crackin' party of the year. It was almost too good to be true. Parties in Oakland never lasted long. I was just waiting for a fight to break out, or the rollers to swing through and shut the joint down.

It didn't take long for my intuition to materialize.

Just when I spotted my girlfriend, Keisha, in the mix, and was on my way to dance with her, some stocky, dark-skinned dude with dreads, trying to smoke a blunt and get low at the same time, accidentally bumped into me while he was dancing, charring the sleeve of my fresh white T with the ashes. Obviously he was too drunk to know that he'd almost burned a hole through my shirt, so I let it slide. But when he stumbled on T-Spoon's brand-new white-on-white Air Force Ones, I knew he'd gone too far. Within seconds, T-Spoon, who'd probably had one too many himself, pushed the guy so hard he tripped over someone else and fell flat on his back. If the fall wasn't embarrassing enough, everyone in the party laughed so loud they drowned out Tupac's "Ambitionz of a Ridah" blaring through the speakers. T-Spoon, wearing a drunken grin from ear to ear, bent down, picked the guy's blunt up off the floor, took a puff and waved it high in the air.

"Anybody wanna hit this?" he asked obnoxiously.

"This fool is crazy, blood," Todd said, laughing.

"I could've told you that," I said as I downed the last of my Hennessey.

Suddenly, a shot rang out, shattering the lightbulb dangling overhead. Complete darkness sent a chill through the room. It resumed with three more shots, aimed in my direction. I felt the second shot drill a hole through the wall just beside me, and grabbed my ear in agony as the third bullet whistled by. After the last shot, I heard a groan, then felt a hand try to grasp my shoulder, only to slide away limply.

"Help me, J.," T-Spoon said as his lifeless body crumbled to the floor, landing at my feet. In the midst of the stampede for the stairs, I could hear loud cries and shrieks echoing from the stairwell. But I just crouched down, holding my boy T-Spoon, in silence.

Two weeks had gone by since I'd decided I'd had enough of the city that I could never have imagined leaving before. Growing up in East Oakland, I was no stranger to violence. In the last four years, I'd seen a dude get beat into a coma, witnessed a pregnant girl get her front teeth kicked out and lost countless homeboys to senseless drive-bys. But until T-Spoon got killed at Jerrell's party, I'd become immune to all of it. Until then, it was just a way of life. But now I was sick of it.

Over the last couple of weeks, whenever I wasn't with Keisha, I spent most of my time at Todd's crib, playing video games. Sometimes, Keisha would come with me. At that point, I was doing any and everything to keep my mind off the fact that one of my boys had recently died in my arms. I'd had so many nightmares about it that sometimes just going to sleep seemed like torture.

Though I had trouble sleeping, just being around Todd made things a whole lot easier for me. That's why he was my best friend. He was the only one who stayed in the basement with me until the paramedics arrived. Todd always found a way to keep his cool, even though he was going through the same strife. He grew up in the hood like everyone else, but Todd was the one everybody expected to make it out. When he wasn't catching touchdown passes for our high school football team, he was making speeches as class president. He was even voted homecoming king. He kicked it with the rest of us on weekends, but somehow always managed to get his homework done. I was tight with a lot of guys in the hood, but none were closer to me than Todd. Although I never said it, at times I looked up to him.

In Oakland, we were inseparable. Wherever I went, Todd wasn't far behind, and vice versa. We did everything together—hit up parties, played basketball, went to the movies. Hell, our senior year, we even opened our mail together. And everybody knows that there's no better feeling than opening your own mail as a high school senior. But sometimes, opening my mail over at Todd's crib was a catch-22. Although I loved to see him get accepted to virtually every school he applied to, most of the time the letters I received from colleges were rejection letters. Of the six schools I'd applied to, I'd received letters from five of them. All of them started off the same way: "Mr. Dawson, we have reviewed your application. This year, we had an overwhelming number of qualified applicants. Unfortunately, we were unable to accept you into our institution."

I never really read further than that. The first couple of times I read the letters, I could barely swallow. I hated rejection. The only school I hadn't heard from was University of Atlanta. Everyone kept telling me not to worry about getting in, because it was a black college, and they let everybody in. I knew that wasn't true, because Todd had just gotten rejected from Boward a week ago—and he had a 3.2 grade point average. The digits in my GPA were the same, just the other way around. So, as far as I was concerned, that notion about historically black colleges and universities accepting everybody was for the birds.

I told people I didn't care if I got in or not, but I did. I wanted to see the girls in Atlanta that everybody kept talking about, and see the city that hosted Freaknik, which I'd heard so many stories about. I wanted to check out some of the bands I'd seen on the movie *Drumline,* and go to some of those parties I'd seen on all those *Girls Gone Wild* commercials. But most of all, I knew that if I stayed I would just end up chillin' on the block smoking weed all day with my homies, and working a dead-end job. I would probably start off at a community college, but end up in jail with the rest of the O.G.s from the hood. Or worse, six feet deep like some of my boys I played ball with who never made it to our senior prom. I had come to terms with the possibility of staying in the hood, but I wanted out.

If anybody knew how bad I wanted to get out of Oakland, it was Todd. After a while, he could see that I was annoyed by the whole mail-opening ritual we'd started, so once he decided Crampton was the school for him, he stopped opening letters from other colleges. Instead, he just balled them up and tossed them in the trash, without even looking to see if he'd been accepted. I'd always go dig the letters out of the trash and read them out loud anyway. He always got in. Keisha usually changed the subject to lighten the mood.

"So, you guys heard about that album release party The Game is supposed to be throwing this weekend?" she said, after I read yet another one of Todd's acceptance letters aloud.

"Yeah," Todd said, changing the subject. "It's supposed to be crackin'."

"Speaking of parties," I said. "Ever since that party the other week, I've been having this crazy dream."

"What kind of dream, blood?" he asked.

"It's kind of hard to explain. But it always starts out with me walking down this long hallway. Some dude is walking in front of me."

"Who?" he asked.

"I don't know. I can never make out his face. Anyway, I finally get to this room that I'm about to go into, and smoke is coming from under the door. For some reason, I go in anyway. Then this girl opens the door—"

"What girl?" Keisha asked, arching her eyebrows and folding her arms.

"I don't know. I can never make her face out."

"I'm gonna need to know these things, J.D.," she said with an attitude.

"Anyway, that ain't even important. Like I was saying, as soon as the door swings open, I hear a gunshot."

"Then what?" Todd asked, as if he were waiting for the punch line.

"Nothing. Then the dream is over."

"You been sleeping with a night-light?" he asked jokingly.

"C'mon, blood, I'm serious."

"You need to quit watching all them Freddie Kruger reruns on the USA channel."

"You're probably just reliving what happened at that party, boo," Keisha said.

"Nah, Keesh, I'm telling you, this dream is different."

"Didn't the doctor say you were going to go through post-traumatic stress?" she asked.

"I don't know. All I know is that I keep having this damn dream. I need to do something to take my mind off of it. Let me open up my couple little letters and see what I'm working with," I said, turning toward Keisha. "Pass me those envelopes over there on that chair please, boo."

"What's all this crap?" she asked.

"They call that mail, baby."

"Duh," she said, rolling her eyes. "Why you always gotta be so damn sarcastic all the time? I was talking about these Jehovah's Witnesses leaflets and this restaurant coupon book."

"I don't know. I didn't sift through everything. I was in a rush. I just grabbed what was in the mailbox and bounced. Here's something with my name on it, though," I said, opening a white envelope.

It was from my aunt Sonya. A couple of weeks ago, my mom told me that the company her fiancé works for had its stock go public or something like that, and they went from broke to multihundred thousandaires overnight. When I saw her name on the envelope, my eyes lit up. They immediately drooped back to size when I focused on the other letter addressed to me. It was from University of Atlanta—my last hope. I figured I might as well take the good news first, so I tore into the letter from my aunt Sonya. I stood the card right side up and gave it a shake to loosen the dough. Nothing fell out. I re-checked the front of the envelope to make sure I had the right aunt. Yep, it was her all right, but no dough. The card said something about "all of her blessings" and "best wishes." Ironically, a brotha sure did *wish* she could've *blessed* me with some of that bread.

"Damn, that's cold," Keisha said. "She could've sent a brotha a little sumptin' sumptin'."

"For real, blood," Todd added, with a snicker. "That's no bueno."

"You've still got one more letter here with your name on it," Keisha said, reaching for it. "And hey, look, it's from University of Atlanta. Why are they sending you mail?"

I quickly snatched it back.

"I know who it's from," I said.

"Well, hurry up and open it, blood," Todd said.

"I might not want to open it, right now. I think I'm gonna just wait till later."

"Later? Man, please. That's the letter we've been waiting on," Todd said. "If you don't open it, I will." He reached for the envelope.

I held him off with one hand, while holding the envelope up and away from him as he tried to reach for it.

"Y'all look like some little kids playing possum," Keisha said, with a giggle. "Would *somebody* please open the letter? I don't care who it is."

Truthfully, I was stalling for a reason. I was afraid of what was inside.

"Okay, I'll do it," I said as I took a deep breath and walked over to the window. As I looked across the street into an alley, I could vaguely see a few of the homies from the hood having a smoke session. Another was down the block making a sale to a crackhead. I just shook my head, then slowly opened the envelope. I could feel Keisha looking over my shoulder. It started off the same way as the rest of the rejection letters I'd received:

"Mr. Dawson, we have reviewed your application. This year we had an overwhelming number of qualified applicants."

But the next sentence changed my life.

It read: "We are delighted to inform you that you have been accepted to University of Atlanta."

"Oh, my God, dog!" I said as the letter dropped from my hand to the floor.

Keisha quickly bent down to pick it up.

"What?" Todd asked.

"He got in!" Keisha screamed. "My baby got accepted to college!"

"Yeeeeaaaahhh, booooy!" he said, in his best Flavor Flav impression as he pumped his fist in the air and opened his arms to give me a big hug.

"Here," he said, passing me his cordless phone. "Call your mom and tell her. I know she's going to be proud."

He was right.

CHAPTER 2

LEAVING HOME

I had been on the phone with Keisha for over an hour, but I was getting nowhere, fast. I just couldn't understand why she would want to break up with me, two days before I was supposed to leave for college. I was frustrated because it seemed there was nothing I could say to change her mind.

"As hard as this is for me to say, I think it's best you just do you, J.D.," she said, sniffling.

"Do *me*? What are you talking about, Keesh? Where is all this coming from?"

"C'mon, J.D., don't play dumb. I mean, I love you and all, but I'm not stupid. You're going to be thousands and thousands of miles away from me in Atlanta."

"So what?"

"So you're probably going to be down there trying to sow your wild oats!"

"What makes you think that?"

"Think about it. I helped you write your admission essay for most of your college applications, and you didn't even tell me that you were applying to U of A, so there's no telling what other secrets you might be hiding."

"Secrets? C'mon now, I told you the only reason I didn't tell you that I was applying there was because I didn't want to be embarrassed if I didn't get in."

"Yeah, whatever. If I was that important to you, you wouldn't keep anything from me."

"I'm not trying to keep anything from you! Why are you sounding so insecure all of a sudden?"

"All of my girls told me that when their boyfriends left for college, they ended up getting cheated on. And I'm not even trying to go that route."

"Oh, so you're gonna break up with me over some shit your *girls* told you?"

"It's not even all about that. Let's be real, J.D., you have a hard enough time keeping your zipper up out here, so there's no telling what you'll be doing down there, or who you'll be doing it with. I'm cool."

"*You're cool?* What's that s'posed to mean?"

"It means I'm not trying to hold you back. And I'm not trying to be hurt in the end. So you do your thing out there, I'll do my thing out here at Oakland State and if it's meant for us to be together, then I guess we'll see. But for now, I think it's best we just go our separate ways."

Keisha didn't come with me to the airport. In fact, I hadn't talked to her since she broke up with me three days ago. After calling her and leaving messages for two days straight, I finally just gave up. Once it sank in that I would be moving to Atlanta and she would be going to Oakland State University, closer to home, she thought I would be moving on with my life—without her.

No matter how hard I tried, I couldn't understand how she could possibly break up with me just because I decided to do something positive with my life. But the more Todd told me about all of the fine-ass girls he'd seen on campus when he went on the Black College Tour, the better being single in Atlanta sounded. Still, I wish I could've seen her before I left.

It's hard to explain the emotions going through my head as I boarded the airplane to Atlanta. I knew that I wanted to get away from Oakland to see what the rest of the world had to offer, but a part of me wanted to stay.

Aside from thinking about whether or not Keisha would find someone else and move on with her life, I thought about living without Todd for the first time. We'd gone to school together since second grade. When I needed to cheat on a test, he slid me his notes. When I needed the low-down dirty scoop on a chick I'd met, he was the first one I'd call. He even helped me make our high school football team by intentionally missing a pass in tryouts, just so I could look good making an interception. He was the closest thing I had to a brother, and I'd never gone more than a few weeks without kicking it with him. Starting college without him would be weird.

I thought about T-Spoon's baby mama screaming at the grave site, when they lowered his casket into the ground. I thought about how his son would grow up fatherless, like I did. I thought about staying, and getting revenge.

I thought about the look on my little sister Robyn's face when the airport security guard told her she couldn't escort our mom and me all the way to the gate. My cheeks were still wet from all the tears that poured down her face as she kissed me goodbye. She was only sixteen, but she was beautiful. Her caramel complexion, pretty smile and shoulder-length hair were enough to spark any high schooler's hormones. But to make matters worse, she had the body of a grown woman. The guys in my hood couldn't care less if she was still in high school— they were scavengers. Who would look out for her now? Would some of my so-called homies try her now that they knew I was away at school?

My mind told me to return my ticket and get my money back, but my legs wouldn't correspond. Plus, my ticket was nonrefundable. The one-way, standby ticket I copped from AirTran was only fifty-five dollars. As I stood in line behind a white guy who was wearing a pair of slacks, a dress shirt and a pair of loafers, holding a book entitled *Rich Dad, Poor Dad* in one hand, and his laptop shoulder bag with Georgia Tech embroidered on the side with the other, I thought that maybe I was in a little over my head. The guy couldn't have been more than a couple of years older than me, but I figured if he was a college student, there was no way I belonged on a campus anywhere in the vicinity. I just wouldn't fit in. For the first time since I'd applied to college, I questioned my motives. I wondered whether I was really cut out for college life.

I thought about just charging the ticket to the game and taking an "L." Just then, I turned around and looked into my mom's eyes. She was so excited you would've thought *she* was going off to college herself, instead of coming along to help me get settled in. The joyful expression on her face, combined with the thought of living on my own for the first time with no rules or regulations, made my decision a little easier. But I was still unsure. As I weighed my options, I heard the lady working the ticket check-in desk invite all standby passengers to board the plane.

The thick Bay Area fog caused our flight to be delayed, so our plane waited behind two others on the runway. I'm not the type to hit up the church house on a regular basis. I'm more of the Christmas and Easter Sunday type of churchgoer. Honestly, I can't even remember praying over my food since last Thanksgiving dinner. But I know there's a time and a place for everything. And I knew that this was both the time and the place for a quick prayer. I clasped my hands, closed my eyes and asked the Lord to allow my plane to make it to Atlanta safely.

As I finished, I heard the wheels at the rear of the plane retract as we left the earth's surface. Before the plane got lost in the charcoal clouds, I pressed my forehead against the small window I was seated next to. I knew that it would be a long time before I'd catch another glimpse of the city I'd inherited my game from. I spotted the Bay Bridge, and I could vaguely see Oakland Coliseum. But Interstate 580 and Lake Merit were clear as day. Most people call Oakland "the Town," others "the House," and some "the O." But I called it home. I became teary-eyed as I thought about the memories and family members I was leaving behind. I loved Oakland, and as much as I would miss it, we needed time away from each other.

Although I had no idea what college life was all about, I knew it was time to flip a new switch. I didn't have any friends who could give me a firsthand account of what I was getting myself into, and I couldn't ask my dad or either of my grandfathers about their college experiences, because they had none. Aside from my mother, nobody in my family had ever been to college. And she didn't graduate. This was my opportunity to break the generational curse. Nobody expected me to go to college. But succeeding in college was my way to prove all of them wrong.

My future was as cloudy as the sky our airplane disappeared into, but my vision was clear. I knew this was my chance to make something of myself, and I was determined to make the most of it.

CHAPTER 3

REGISTRATION

My uncle Leroy met us outside Hartsfield-Jackson Airport. You would've thought he'd be happy to see us, but he was heated for two reasons. First of all, it was ninety-five degrees outside, and the air conditioner in his Lincoln Mercury had stopped working the day before he picked us up. Secondly, our bags took forever to come off the conveyer belt, so he'd been circling the terminal for nearly an hour. I didn't mind the wait, because it seemed like all of the women in Atlanta were two steps past dimes—they looked like silver dollars. It took my mom forever to drag me from the airport.

"If you snap your neck to look at one more of these little fast girls you're gonna need a neck brace," she said. "You better get your mind right. These little girls ain't going nowhere."

By the time we came outside, Uncle Leroy said that he'd driven around the airport a dozen times. My mom's brother was only about five foot eight, but he had to be pushing three hundred pounds. He was a true heavyweight. I tried to avoid the puddles of sweat gathered under his armpits when he got out of the car to give me a hug, but he got me. I accidentally misjudged the heat from the sun beaming down on his leather car seats, and scorched my calves when I jumped in the backseat. I hadn't even seen a fraternity yet, but I felt like I'd already been branded.

"Dizamn!" I said, instinctively jumping out of his whip. "Don't you have some kind of towel or something I can put back here?"

"I was just about to get that out of the trunk when you jumped in, nephew," he said, laughing. "You didn't even give me time to look at you. Boy, you done shot up. You're taller than your uncle now, huh? What are you now, about six foot?"

"Six-two, to be exact," I said confidently.

"It looks like you done put on a little weight too," he said, grabbing me by my biceps. You've got to be at least a hundred and thirty-five pounds now."

"Try a hundred and seventy-five," I said, flexing my muscles. "You feel these guns?"

"I see you got a little sumptin' sumptin', but you know you're still no match for your uncle on the hoop court. I post up young guys like you in the gym all the time."

"No offense, but I think your glory days are just about over, Unc, on and off the court," I said.

"Well, since I have to pass the torch to somebody, I guess your glory days are just about to get started," he said.

"Leroy, your torch burnt out a long time ago," my mom said. "Now, would you hurry up? It's burning up out here!"

After checking in at the Best Western in College Park, a residential area near the airport, my uncle dropped us off in front of the Student Center on Atlanta University's campus.

"Don't do nothing I wouldn't do, young buck," he said.

"Farting in public elevators and looking around like it was somebody else ain't my style," I said.

"Well, do you, then. Ain't that what y'all young folk say? Do you."

Before I planted both feet outside the car, a female wearing a short skirt and a cut-up shirt with her belly ring showing walked up to me and passed me a flyer. The females on the flyer were dressed sexier than the girl who gave it to me. All of them were showing their tattoos. The girl who gave me the flyer had a huge tattoo of a butterfly just above her ass. I peeped it as she walked away.

I heard my uncle mutter, "Mmm, mmm, mmm. Hate to see ya go, but I love to see ya walk away, sweet thang," as he pulled off.

I read the flyer as my mom and I walked toward the Student Center. It said something about a back-to-school tattoo party. On the back of the flyer, it said everyone showing their tattoos would get in free before midnight. Ladies showing their body paint would be admitted free of charge all night. The flyer had my undivided attention. Nobody had ever just walked up and dropped a flyer on me like that before. My mom's voice snapped me out of my trance.

"You need to be worried about getting your classes straight, not a *rattoo* party."

"It's a tattoo party, Mom."

"Ain't gonna be nothin' but some hood rats in there showing their tattoos. Sounds like a *rattoo* party to me. Just get registered for your classes, boy."

"Fa sho. First things first. But this party still sounds like it's gonna be crackin'."

"You just need to be cracking the books," my mom said as we walked toward the main entrance to the Student Center. "I'm not spending all this money for you to come out here and play games, J.D."

I laughed.

"I'm serious," she said. "This ain't high school. You're really going to have to buckle down."

"Don't trip, Mom. I'ma handle my business."

"I know you will, baby. I believe in you. But you know I gotta keep it real."

The sun was beaming. Walking outside felt like doing jumping jacks in a sauna. The air-conditioning in the center felt almost as good as the females inside it looked. The Student Center was crawling with dimes. There were a couple of nickels in the crowd, but my eyes bypassed them like hitchhikers on the side of the road. It seemed like I saw about fifteen girls for every dude. The ratio was lovely.

"Now, this is what I call an institution of higher learning," I mumbled.

She looked like she was from some exotic island. Her long, wavy hair fell from her head like it was running from her eyebrows, hiding behind her shoulders. She looked like she could've been smuggling Osama bin Laden under that booty. She was wearing a pair of hip-hugging shorts and a red T-shirt that had the letters O.G. stitched in huge letters across the front. There were at least a hundred others walking around campus wearing the exact same shirt, but she stood out. For some reason, she kept looking me up and down. But every time I looked her way, she bashfully glanced down toward my shoes. After we exchanged looks for a third time, she finally walked over toward me, her caramel thighs rubbing together as she made her way across the room.

"Excuse me," she said, looking deep into my eyes. Somewhere between staring at her perky nipples and her moist lips, I lost the rest of her sentence, trying to think of a smooth intro to hit her with.

"...and I'll be your orientation guide," she said. "What's your name?"

I didn't catch her name but I'd heard all I needed to hear. All that mattered was that she was speaking to me.

"J.D.," I answered, in my deeper-than-usual, supersuave voice that I usually saved for late-night phone calls with cuties. "I'm from Cali."

"You came a long way. You don't want to miss registration. Just take those steps and you'll see everybody in line," she said as she turned to walk away.

Just when I was thinking of a reason to get her to talk to me again, and a smooth segue into a more meaningful conversation, she came back.

"I almost forgot to give you your registration packet," she said, handing me a manila envelope with U of A on the front. "And I think there's something you might want to know."

"You're reading my mind, girl," I said. "What's your phone number? I definitely need to know that."

"Oh no, it's not like that," she said, pulling me closer and standing on her tippy toes to whisper in my ear. "You've got some tissue stuck to the bottom of your shoe."

As she giggled, walking away, all I could do was smile and discreetly use my left shoe to remove it from under my right foot. Times like that, you just have to laugh to keep from crying. I was convinced that my next encounter with her couldn't be any more embarrassing, so I looked forward to it. Besides, at least she'd remember me.

I made eye contact with my mom, who was reclining on a couch across the room, and gave her the "let's go" signal with my eyebrows.

The registration booths were inside the auditorium, but the line stretched all the way into the hallway. It took us an hour just to make it to the door. It wasn't all bad though. It gave my mom and me some time to talk. My mom was a jokester. She had me cracking up when she was telling me about the two times Robyn failed her driver's license test.

"The first time she was so nervous she forgot to buckle up and crushed two cones while trying to parallel-park with her hazard lights on instead of her turn signal. The second time she did everything right, except for riding with the emergency brake on the entire time."

I laughed so hard I almost started crying. Laughing at my mom's jokes took my mind off waiting in that long line. The registration advisers were only letting ten people inside the room at a time. By the time we made it inside the huge auditorium, I was just happy to finally be able to sit down in a chair.

"We gon' be in here forever," I mumbled as I slumped into my seat.

The administrators had turned the auditorium into a movie theater. They were showing *Malcolm X* on a projector the size of a movie screen. When we got to the scene where Malcolm's hair started burning from the lye, I felt somebody tap my arm. I turned around to see who it was, and I had to do a double take. It was a white dude with braids and a goatee.

"That barbershop right there is in my hood, yo," he said, pointing to the screen, as if I'd asked him.

I nudged my mom with my knee, and tried not to burst out laughing in his face. He had on an orange, white and blue New York Knicks headband with the authentic Patrick Ewing throwback jersey to match. He had a phat chain with an icy basketball pendant hanging off it. I couldn't believe what I was seeing.

"You from N.Y.?" I asked.

"Boogie down Bronx all day, kid," he said in a thick, Jay-Z-ish accent.

I heard my mom snicker. I tried to change the subject to keep my mind off of how black this cat sounded. "That jersey is tight. Where did you flip that?"

"I copped this right on Lenox Avenue, son. Them Js you got on are hot, though. You're killing 'em, yo. Where you staying?"

"Marshall Hall," I said.

"Word is bond? Me too. What floor you on, B?"

"First floor."

"Say word? Holla at ya, boy! They're gonna have some major flavor on that ground floor, yo. I say we should just call ourselves the G-Unit."

Just as I was about to tell him that was the corniest shit I'd ever heard in my life, we had to get up and move up a row. "I'ma holla at you, though," I said.

"Word. I'll holla at you once you get settled in."

I couldn't stop shaking my head. That was crazy. Dude sounded blacker than me. Three hours, one orientation packet and the entire Antoine Fisher movie later, we had snaked our way to the front row. But I couldn't stop thinking about that white dude.

"You think the kids at white colleges have to go through all this just to register?" I asked my mom.

"What they eat don't make you shit, does it?" she said sarcastically.

"Nah," I said, laughing.

"Then why you worried about it? That's them. This is you. I doubt it, though. This is crazy. We still have to unpack. Let me call Leroy and tell him to bring all your bags up here since we're almost to the front."

By the time we made it to the front counter, I felt almost as drained as the woman standing in front of me looked. Her kitchen was frazzled. It looked like she had just come from an Ozzy Osbourne concert. She got straight to the point.

"ID, Social Security number and award letter please," she said, without ever looking up. I fumbled through my pockets looking for my award letter, but I couldn't find it.

"I know exactly where I left it," I said. "On the coffee table at the crib."

My mom was shaking her head.

"I'm going to need the application number off your award letter before I can process anything," the lady said, with an attitude. She tried to cover it up by flashing a smile that said she hadn't been to lunch all day and she was ready to quit at any moment.

I asked my mom if I could use her cell phone.

"It's out of juice," she said. "It cut off after I told Leroy to bring your stuff up here. Boy, I swear you'd lose your head if it wasn't connected to your neck."

"I ain't got all day!" the lady behind the counter squealed.

Before I could look around, I felt a cell phone antenna tap me on my shoulder. It was the white dude. I was surprised at how tall blood was. He had to be at least six foot five.

"Good lookin' out," I said.

"No doubt," he said. "I know how they always trying to hold a brotha down. Take your time, kid."

I called my sister and she gave me the application number. I gave the phone back to the white dude and asked him what his name was.

"Dub-B," he said.

"I appreciate that, blood."

Ten minutes later the lady behind the counter told me that my Federal Plus loan hadn't posted on my account yet, so my mom and I had to sign a promissory note. The lady retreated to a copy machine and came back with two copies—one for me and one for my mom. My copy had my class schedule stapled to it.

The lady behind the counter flashed a genuine smile and said, "Welcome to University of Atlanta, Mr. Dawson. According to your paperwork, it looks like you are on academic probation this semester. That means you will have to maintain a 2.5 GPA in order to return. So, good luck, and stay focused. You never get a second first semester."

CHAPTER 4

MOVING IN

The door to Marshall Hall was propped wide open. There were eight dorms on campus, but Marshall Hall was the only all-male dorm. I would have preferred to stay in the coed dorms, but they were for upperclassmen. The small parking lot outside the four-level brick building was full of cars with their trunks popped. All of the parents were helping their kids move in. When I spotted my uncle, he was leaning up against his car, staring like a pervert at some girl walking up the steps. I grabbed a box from the trunk, and looked at him like he was R. Kelly at an eighth grade winter ball. His eyes were still fixed on the girl with the ridiculously large ba-dunk-a-dunk, walking up the steps.

"Help a brotha out, Unc," I said. "Grab a box."

"Man, if I was about ten years younger—"

My mom cut him off. "Leroy, if you were ten years younger you would be an overweight thirty-two-year-old with a GED, and still old enough to be that little girl's daddy. Now grab a box and come on."

"Sugar daddy," he said under his breath with a chuckle as he grabbed my stereo from his trunk.

I looked in my pocket to check my room number on the sheet

of paper the lady in the registration line had given me. Room 112—where the players dwell. When we got inside Marshall Hall, a relatively buff brotha wearing a purple T-shirt with Bloody Beta Psi sketched in gold across the front was waiting at the front desk. He was sitting behind a sign-in sheet and motioned for us to come over.

"How y'all doing?" he asked.

"Hot!" my uncle said. "It feels like somebody's got the heat set on Africa outside."

"Well, we try to keep it pretty cool in here," he responded, while laughing. "My name is Varnelius Mandel. I'm a graduate student here at U of A and the head resident assistant in Marshall Hall. And you are?"

"James," I said.

"James who?" he asked with an authoritative tone.

"James Dawson."

"And you, ma'am?" he asked my mom.

"I'm Valerie Bremer, J.D.'s mother."

"Who are you, the police?" I mumbled under my breath.

"What was that?" he asked in that same fatherly tone.

I didn't think he'd heard me. I had to think of something quick.

"This is a relief," I said. "I've been waiting to get down here and get settled in since I found out I got in."

"Well, I'm going to do everything in my power to make sure you stay in. This little asterisk next to your name means that you're on academic probation. Is that correct?"

"Yeah," I said.

"Well, that's supposed to be a little indication to let me know that I don't have to put up with any crap from you. But truthfully, I don't expect any. I mean, in my eyes, you've got a clean slate. But your teachers will have this asterisk next to your name on their roll books as well, so they will be paying extra-close attention to you. But so long as you stay out of trouble, me and you ain't got no problems. And if you maintain a 2.5 for the entire year, you won't even have to worry about that whole academic probation thing anymore. Cool?"

"Cool."

"All right. Well, Mr. Dawson, here's your key. Find your name on that list and sign next to it."

I couldn't pinpoint exactly what I didn't like about Varnelius, but right away something told me he was a couple of tacos short of a combo. Besides, I figured anybody named Varnelius was bound to have some self-esteem issues. I signed my name and grabbed my envelope off the counter.

"Take a right, go down the hall and room 112 is the last door on your left-hand side. If you need anything, just let me know."

"Thanks for your help," my mom said.

I picked up my box and took a couple of steps forward, apprehensively looking around. There were red signs everywhere that read Distinguished Men of Marshall Give Respect to Get Respect. It looked like something out of Spike Lee's *School Daze*. By the time I made it to my room my arms felt heavy. I let the box thud to the floor, and grabbed my key out of the envelope I'd stuffed in my back pocket. I had taken two steps inside when I felt something scatter across my foot. I dropped my box, jumped onto the bed and screamed. My mom jumped back.

"What is it?" she asked in a high-pitched voice.

Just as I was about to sound like I'd lost my mind and say "I don't know," it came out. It was a roach about the size of Texas. It was so big I was waiting for it to bark at me.

"That ain't cool," I said as my knees shook uncontrollably.

I had never seen an insect that big in my life. And the way it just aggressively sashayed to the middle of the floor like it was auditioning for *America's Next Top Model* made it look even more intimidating. My mom stood outside the door laughing at me.

"That ain't nothing but a little roach. You'd better get used to it. You're down South now. I know big, bad J.D. ain't scurred," she said as she cracked up. "Wait till I tell your sister about this!"

As she was laughing like she was watching *The Kings of Comedy,* my uncle walked into the room with my stereo hoisted over his eyes. He was clutching a honey bun in between his teeth, and he was headed straight for the roach. I wanted to say something, but I couldn't. He took about three steps before it sounded off.

Crack!

My uncle gently sat my stereo on the bed and looked at my mom. She was laughing so hard, tears began to fall.

"What's so funny?" he said, looking around.

He took one more step, looked down, and saw bug guts stretching from his elevated foot to the floor. That roach was a goner.

"That's cold," my uncle said as he opened his honey bun. "Y'all could've said something."

I went to the bathroom and got a soapy paper towel to clean it up with. After finishing the despicable chore, I followed my uncle to his ride to get the rest of my things from his trunk. While I went back and forth to the car, my mom was busy unpacking my things and rambling on and on about me staying focused.

She'd been in my shoes before, so I tried to listen without letting it go in one ear and out the other. Plus, she was kind of young. My mom was only thirty-eight. She had me when she was twenty. She was in her first semester as a junior at Florida A&M University when she found out she was pregnant with me. Her parents had just moved from Arkansas to Oakland to find better jobs. When she went there to give birth to me, she ended up moving in with them. With my pops nowhere to be found, she had to work full-time to take care of me and never got a chance to finish college. Since I was basically the man of the house, my mom and I had grown close and shared a special bond. I could talk to her about anything. She was cool like that. She always warned me about how sneaky and conniving girls could be. When she talked, I listened.

"I just don't want you to make the same mistakes I did," she said. "Don't be down here doing the most, letting these little girls run over you. I seen the way they were looking you up and down. If you're gonna be running up in these girls down here, do it safely," she warned. "I bought you an economy-size box of Trojan condoms. That doesn't mean I want you running around like Deuce Bigalow the male gigolo. I'd just rather you have 'em and not need 'em than need 'em and not have 'em. All of them come with spermicide on them, so there ain't gonna be no little James juniors running around. You ain't got no excuses, and neither do them little fast-ass girls. If they tell you they're on the pill or on the shot, don't believe them."

"C'mon now, that's common sense."

"Hey, if common sense was so common, everybody would have it."

I laughed.

"I'm serious, J.D. You know what I always tell you, opportunity knocks once—"

"But temptation leans on the doorbell," I said, helping her finish her favorite quote. "I know. You've said that a million times."

"Well, I'm glad you know it," she said. "Now all you've got to do is act like it. This is a great opportunity for you, but there's going to be a lot of temptation along the way. And I don't want you coming home with nothing but a good report card. You hear me?"

"Yeah," I said.

I heard a knock at the door. It was weird because my door was wide open. Why would anyone knock? It was my roommate and his parents. I wondered how long they'd been standing there. My roommate's mom looked like she'd seen a ghost, so I figured they'd heard my mom's little sex-ed spill.

"Lawd, have mercy," my roommate's mom said as she walked into the room with a bottle of blessing oil. She was wearing one of those large church hats with the huge brim and hella flowers scattered all over it, and a purple dress. She looked like she had just gotten out of Sunday morning service. My roommate's father was checking the number above the door to make sure he had the right room.

My roommate's mom extended her hand to my mother's. "My name is Sister Betty and this is my husband, Pastor Timothy McGruden the Second," she said, pointing toward the man in the black and gold Alpha Mu Alpha T-shirt. "And this is our son, Timothy the Third."

He looked as nervous as a prisoner meeting his cell mate for the first time. I was just waiting for the urine to trickle down the side of his pants.

"Yes, my name is Timothy, and you must be James," he said in a second grader's voice.

"You know it," I said.

"Hello," he said, sounding like a kindergartner meeting his school bus driver for the first time.

I stretched out my balled-up fist to give him a pound, and he slapped it like he was trying to give me a high five. It was an awkward exchange, but I could tell he was an awkward type of cat.

"It was nice to meet you," my mom said in her fake PTA voice.

"God bless you," Mrs. McGruden said.

I thought her reply was a little odd, but I shrugged it off. My mom and I walked to the car, waking my uncle from his slumber on the couch on the way out.

The parking lot was more packed when we came out than before we went inside, and it was hot enough to cook a Thanksgiving turkey on the concrete. I missed the Bay Area breeze already. My uncle cranked up his car as my mom leaned against the side of it. She was nervously fidgeting with the strap on her Louis Vuitton purse.

"Want to spend tonight at the hotel?" she asked, although she already knew the answer.

"Nah," I said, looking around at the parking lot full of fine girls I'd never seen in my life. "I'm straight."

"I bet you are," my mom said, flashing a fake smile. "Forget you, then. I'm going out with one of my girlfriends anyway."

As far as I knew, she had no girlfriends in Atlanta. I knew she wanted to cry. After I thought about what I had just said, I did too. You could've heard an ant burp. I tried to smooth over the awkwardness of the moment.

"I need to just go ahead and get settled in here," I said. "I might as well get used to it. Feel me?"

"I feel you," my mom said, switching her purse from her left shoulder to her right. "I guess you're all set up now. You don't need your mama no more. Did you hang up that suit that I bought you?"

"Yep."

"What about that Rocawear polo I got for you?"

"Yes."

"Do you have the Bible your grandmother gave you?"

"Got it."

"Well, don't forget to take your earrings out and clean those lobes with some alcohol every once in a while. I didn't buy you diamond earrings for your birthday for you to smear earwax all over them."

"I got you."

"And don't stop going to church just because you're out here in school. You find a good church to go to, and don't be out in the clubs so late on Saturday you can't get up Sunday morning."

"Uh-huh," I said, looking around. There were more prospects in the parking lot than a McDonald's high school All-American basketball game. I saw this girl wearing a skirt so short it looked like a belt. I figured her parents must've been gone already. Just as I had estimated her bra size, my mom's voice interrupted my lustful trance.

"And make some new friends too," she said. "Start hanging around some ambitious guys who have dreams, and guys who take school seriously. Don't be hanging around that same riffraff you got caught up with back home. You see where they can get you. I mean, look what happened to T-Spoon."

"Mom, I got you," I said, cutting her off.

"Okay, okay," she said. "Just making sure."

"Clean my ears, go to church and make new friends. I got it."

"I know that's right. My baby boy is a big college man now. These next four years are supposed to be the best years of your life, so you have some fun too," she said, pulling me close. "I'm so proud of you. I love you, J.D." She hugged me as tight as a boa constrictor for what felt like five minutes straight. I heard her sniffle. I was trying to maintain some sense of coolness when I heard my uncle yell from the car.

"You hug that boy any tighter you ain't gonna have to worry about no GPA," he said. "You gonna have to give him CPR!"

"Shut up, Leroy," my mom said, brushing away tears from her eyes. "Well, let me go. You know I gotta get back to Oakland and keep your sister in line. So I guess I'll be seeing my college student on Christmas."

She gave me another hug and told me she loved me again.

"I love you too," I said. "Call me as soon as you make it home."

"I will, baby."

"Thanks for your help, Uncle Leroy," I said as he tried to maneuver out of the cramped parking lot.

"Thank me by doing good in school, young buck," he said. "And remember, you've got to get in a girl's head before you let her get in your bed!"

"Leroy!" my mom yelled, poking him in his side.

"What? He needs to hear that."

"No, he doesn't," my mom said. "The only thing he needs to be worried about getting into is the books."

"Hey, nobody knows where the nose goes when the doors close," he said.

"You ain't got no sense, Leroy," my mom said as she stuck her hand out the window, giving her signature homecoming queen wave as they left the parking lot.

I turned to walk back toward my room to check the agenda the cutie in the O.G. T-shirt had given me earlier. There were a couple of girls talking to a few guys sitting on the steps leading to my dorm. I felt a few of their eyes wander my way, but I didn't pay them any attention. That was all part of my game. I had girls all figured out. The less attention you showed them, the more interested they became. It was a mind thing. I acted as if they weren't even there and kept walking.

When I opened my door, the sweet smell of the incense I had lit earlier flooded the hallway. I started to step inside my room, but I noticed the McGrudens holding hands in a circle having a family prayer, so I stayed outside. I leaned my back against the wall and started to nervously nibble on my fingernails. I was reminiscing about my old hood when I heard a thick Atlanta accent coming my way. It was my next door neighbor.

"Say, shawty, what kind of incense you burning?" he asked.

"It's the one that comes in the blue box. I forget the name of it. But it smells hella good."

He came closer, flashing his gold fronts with his balled-up fist outstretched to give me some dap. I gave him a pound.

"That's that good-good right thurr', shawty. You'll let ya boy hold one of 'em?"

I wanted to let him hold a pack of Certs and a bottle of Scope. His breath smelled like he had just polished off a bowl of uncleaned chitterlings.

"I ain't tripping, family," I said, as Timothy's parents walked out of the room. His father stopped right in front of me.

"Have you accepted the Lord Jesus Christ as your personal savior, son?" he asked.

"Yeah," I answered.

"Keep God first and all of your needs will be supplied. You're welcome to come to church with Timothy the Third any Sunday. Have a blessed day."

"You too," I said.

I looked at the dude from Atlanta. He looked back at me. We

both shook our heads. The McGrudens were something else. I walked into my room and saw Timothy typing diligently on his computer. If he had typed any faster someone would need a fire extinguisher to put out the smoke from his keyboard. That must've been some e-mail, because he never even looked up. I grabbed my agenda, a stick of incense, and stepped back outside.

"What your name is anyway, shawty?" he asked.

"James, but everybody calls me J.D."

I noticed what looked like a bullet wound on the right side of his chest. He had a tattoo of Jesus's clasped hands and R.I.P. tattooed on his right shoulder. I tried to make out the name underneath but couldn't. I started to ask about it, but I left it alone.

"What's yours?" I asked.

"Lawry," he said in a Southern drawl.

"Larry?"

"No, sir. L-a-w-r-y. You must be from Cali," he said, laughing.

"How'd you know I was from Cali?"

"Y'all talk so proper, shawty, it's easy to tell you ain't from 'round here. Plus, y'all always say 'hella' when y'all talk."

"What part of Atlanta you from?"

"Ret here in da SWAT, shawty."

"What's the SWAT?"

"Southwest Atlanta."

"How come you don't just stay at the crib, instead of paying to stay in the dorm?"

"Since I don't have to pay tuition, my pops said he would pay for me to stay on campus."

"How you got it like that, where you don't have to pay tuition?"

"My mom works for the school."

"So that means you go to school for free?"

"Yes, sir."

"That's what's up," I said. "What your mama do for the school, blood?"

"She's the director of student enrollment."

"Oh, so you're in there like booty hair, then, huh?" I asked.

"I guess you could say that, shawty," he said, laughing.

Any time he used words that started with th or took a lot of breath to pronounce, I became woozy. He was hella cool, but this cat's breath smelled like a fish tank that hadn't been cleaned in a year.

"If my mom had known that, I know she would've filled out an application for a job here," I said.

"If it wasn't for my mom working here, I probably wouldn't even be going here. Not at eight thousand dollars a semester! I couldn't even do it."

"Who you tellin', blood? I'm figna come out owing about fifty g's in student loans. And that's not a good look."

"Neither was summer school."

"What you mean, summer school?"

"Since I don't have to pay tuition, my mom made me go to summer school so I could get a jump on my classes. I guess it was straight because I got to meet some of the females before y'all got here. Plus, I already got thirty credits on my transcript."

"What you mean, you guess, blood? You already got a head start on everybody else with the breezies *and* you didn't even have to pay for it? I would've signed up for that in a heartbeat."

"When I was sitting up in the hot-ass classes all summer, I wasn't even thinking about all that, shawty. Now that I think about it, you got a point. But enough about classes. What you figna get into?"

"I can't call it, family," I said, glancing at my agenda. "It says we're supposed to meet the O.G.s in front of the Student Center for a tour of the campus in ten minutes."

"I don't know about all that," he said.

"I know. It does seem kind of lame, huh? But I know there's gonna be some sexy young brizzles out there, so I'ma see what's up with it."

"You ain't lying, shawty. You see ol' baby with the short skirt on?"

"Did I? I didn't know it was going down like that down here, blood."

"I'ma go on and get out there with ya. Let me light this incense and throw a shirt on."

I wanted to tell him to add brushing his teeth to his to-do list. I stepped inside his room, and the first thing I noticed was a slightly musty stench. He definitely needed the incense. Aside from the smell, his room was a disaster. He had boxes of just about every flavor of ramen noodles you could think of laid out on his bed, and clothes and shoes were strewn all over the floor. I figured his roommate had made it in already. I knew that one person couldn't have junked up a room this bad by himself.

"My roommate ain't made it in yet," he said. "I wonder what kinda nigga he is. I made it here first so I could pick which side of the room I wanted."

By the looks of things, he hadn't made up his mind yet.

"I see you rooming up with Urkel, huh? He must have that HOPE scholarship too because I seen him in a couple of my classes this summer. He's lame to death. But shawty is hilarious! I swear, we must've laughed at that fool every day."

"Yeah, he's an L-seven."

"What the hell is an L-seven, shawty?"

"Make an L with your left hand, a seven with your right and put your fingertips together."

He dropped the stick of incense on his bed and followed my directions. But he still didn't get it. "What the hell is you talking 'bout, shawty?"

"He's a square, blood. A square."

"Damn sure does make a square. I like that right there. L-seven. I'ma have to use that one."

"You 'bout to make us late, blood. Throw on a shirt so we can make this move."

Lawry searched through the rubble on his floor, mumbling something about not being able to find anything to wear.

I said, "If you cleaned this joint up you'd probably be able to find something. You got it looking like Ground Zero in here."

"Everybody ain't have they mama come make up they bed for 'em, shawty," he said, throwing on some blue denim shorts and slipping out of his wife beater. When he turned around, my jaw damn near hit the ground. He had fresh, red lacerations and whip marks from the top of his shoulders to the bottom of his spine. The first thing that came to mind was *Roots* and Kunta Kinte. Then, *The Passion of the Christ*.

"Dizamn!" I said, at a loss for words. "What happened to your back, blood?"

"Oh, that ain't nothin'," he said, playing it off. "We got into it with these cats at the club a few days ago. A nigga cracked me in the back with a Moët bottle. But it ain't no thang, shawty. C'mon, let's get out of here."

With that, he flicked off the lights, and I followed him outside. I knew there had to be more to his explanation, but I figured it was probably best for me not to know what really happened, unless he wanted to tell me. When we made it outside, we walked past a group of girls sitting on the steps leading to our dorm. At best, the finest one was a six, and that's being generous. But the way Lawry got at her would've made you think she was Halle Berry.

"Say, shawty, what yo' name is?" he asked.

The girls kept talking like he hadn't said a thing.

"I say, what yo' name is, shawty?" he said, looking right at Halle Scary.

Her eyes got big and her head swiveled frantically, like she had just noticed her cell phone was missing from her pocket, and she had to find it. She kept looking around, with her "I know this nigga ain't talking to me" face on, before finally saying, "You can't be talking to me," in a high-pitched voice.

"Why can't I be?" he asked in an even higher pitch, flashing his golds. The other girls chuckled.

"Don't no nigga approach me like that. I ain't ashy, I'm classy. Come at me with some respect next time and I might entertain your thoughts and tell you my name."

She didn't have to blast him like that. I felt kind of sorry for him. I could tell he wasn't going to let her have the last word.

"No, this scallywag didn't," he said, turning back toward me. "All the horses missing hair around here on account of you, and you got the nerve to have a stank attitude."

"Not as stank as your breath," she said.

That one hurt. Her friends laughed like they were watching *In Living Color* reruns. Lawry looked like he was lost for words. For a second, I thought he was going to hit her.

"I didn't want your phone number anyway, shawty," he said as he walked away, sparking a Black & Mild cigar.

Lawry had kind of played himself with that last line. She hadn't even said anything about him trying to get her number, so you could tell he was a little shaken up. Both of us laughed as we walked across the street to the Student Center. He laughed to keep himself from feeling embarrassed, and thought I was laughing at his joke. But I was laughing at him.

"I ain't trippin' on her anyway, shawty," Lawry said. "If anything, she would've just been good for some late-night cut. I got a girl."

"Oh yeah?" I asked, still laughing. "What's her name?"

"Well, she's not *officially* my girlfriend just yet, but it's only a matter of time."

"I can dig it, blood," I said. "What's her name?"

"She's fine as hell too," Lawry said, completely ignoring my request for her name. "She's a petite redbone, with long hair. Everybody says she looks like Alicia Keys."

"That's what's up," I said. "But what's her name?"

"And she's from the D.C. area, so you know she's got that sexy East Coast accent," he said.

"That's nice," I said. "Does she have a name?"

"Oh, her name is Jasmine."

"Oh, okay," I said. "Alicia Keys, huh?"

"That's what they say. She lives right next door in Tubman Hall. You'll see her."

Judging by the way he'd just gotten shot down, for me to believe him, I'd have to.

CHAPTER 5

O.G. SCHOOLING

We walked across the street to the Student Center just in time. The last tour group was about to leave. There had to be at least two hundred people waiting for a tour of the campus. Half of them were students. Of the hundred students, at least seventy-five of them were females. The odds were definitely in my favor. There were six orientation guides leading the tour groups. Five of them wore the red T-shirts with O.G. written on the front. The other one was a short, stocky guy with a tattered Afro, who was wearing a pair of blue Dickies, a white T-shirt, and blue Chucks. He looked older. I could tell he was from the West Coast, but I couldn't figure out why he was leading the tour. He threw his hands up in the air.

"Everybody staying in Marshall Hall, come with me," he said.

I didn't want to leave the group of females, but I followed directions. About twenty other guys huddled around him.

"Y'all can probably already tell I ain't your average tour guide. I ain't hella bootsie like the rest of the orientation guides. Plus, I'm not really feeling the color scheme. My name is Terrell but everybody calls me Fats. I'm the only *real* O.G. out here, cuz. I've been at U of A for a while now, so I know the ins and

the outs and the outs and the ins of this yard. I know these professors like the back of my hand, cuz. I stayed in Marshall Hall
too. It seems like just yesterday I was getting off the plane from
L.A. and moving in. It's crazy how fast seven years can fly by.
I could've damn near had a Ph.D. by now, but I ain't been on
my p's and q's. I didn't even sign up to be an orientation guide.
I just wanted to holla at y'all young playas and make sure you
got the *real* campus tour. Feel me?"

I was feelin' Fats. It was refreshing to hear some of that left
coast slanguage again. We followed him all around the campus,
stopping every few steps for him to pull up his baggy Dickies.
It seemed like he had a story to tell about each building we
passed. When we passed Woodruff Library he told us about
how hard it was for him to study the one time he'd gone in there
to get some work done.

"Everybody calls the library Club Woody because everybody gets geared up to go in there at night, just like a club," he
said. "If you're trying to come up on a dime who can probably
help you with your homework, the library is the place to be."

As he took puffs of his Black & Mild cigar, he told us all
kinds of stories about everything from the run-down corner
store across the street from the library called the Shack to all
of the different ways he'd managed to fail the classes he'd
taken. First, he told us about the morning he fell asleep on his
Spanish final in Douglass Hall. He told us about the time he
got caught cheating on an algebra test in Carmichael Hall. He
said that he had the answers to the test programmed in his two-
way pager. Halfway through the test, he got a text message from
the teacher that said: Cheaters Never Win, Turn in Your Paper
Now! He couldn't stop laughing when he told us about the
infested couch in Turner Hall.

"Some breezy in Turner Hall had caught crabs and sat
down on the main couch in the waiting area wearing some
booty shorts. I guess the critters crawled out of her crevice
and marinated in the couch because every dude who sat on

that couch came out with the itch. Gotta watch them girls in Turner, cuz. If they don't turn on you, they just might burn on you! I ain't Usher. Ain't no way I'm figna let it burn, cuz. I don't know about y'all, but Fats just ain't going out like that."

By the time we made it back to the Student Center it was almost time for our mandatory meeting with our resident assistants in Marshall Hall. We had about ten minutes to spare. Fats wrapped up his tour with a few closing comments.

"I got the hookup on a little bit of everything, cuz. If I ain't got it, I can get it. If I can't, I know somebody who can. Get at me if you need anything. I got pull like tug-of-war around here."

Just as I was about to merge back across the street toward Marshall Hall, I felt a tug on the sleeve of my white Lacoste polo. It was Fats. He was standing next to some cat who'd come on the tour of the campus with us. It was hard not to notice him. Dude was wearing a black Dobb hat with a burgundy feather on the side of it. Even with his hat on, you could see he had more waves than a tsunami. He was rocking a burgundy short-sleeved dress shirt, black linen pants and a fly pair of black-and-gray Steve Maddens. A toothpick rolled back and forth across his bottom lip as he talked on his cell phone. I was just waiting for him to pull a pimp cup from his back pocket.

"Say, pimp skillet," Fats said. "Ain't too many player-type individuals on campus. Most of these clowns are about as square as a box of Apple Jacks, ya dig?"

"Game recognize game," I said.

"Well, it would be very valuable for you to link up with pimperoni to my left," he said, motioning toward the pimp-in-training. "I met him earlier today, cuz. He's cool people. We linked up like a booger and a nose and we've been kickin' it all day, so I know y'all can do it big in Marshall Hall like I used to."

"Fa sheezy," I said. "What's your name, family?"

"I'm gonna call you back, baby," he said, holding up a finger as if to ask me to give him a second. "I'm serious, boo. As soon as I get done handling this business, I promise I'm gonna call you back…for real… I love you too, Chantel."

"Damn, cuz," Fats said. "You be dripping like a faucet on that phone. I just knew you were going to be blowing kisses through the phone any second."

"That was wifey, folk," the guy said. "You know how that be."

"Nah, cuz," Fats said. "I know how daytime minutes be. Anybody calling me before nine p.m. better have a real emergency to talk to me about."

"She's paying my cell phone bill, so I ain't really tripping on that."

"Say that, then, pimpin'," Fats said. "That's exactly what I'm talking about. That's why y'all two need to link up. You're cut from the same cloth, cuz."

"What's your name, blood?" I asked.

"My government name is Lamont, but my pimp friends call me Fresh," he said, removing his hat just long enough to pull a brush from his back pocket and quickly touch up his Caesar.

"Why they call you that?"

"I got my first pair of gators when I was in sixth grade and I wore them on the first day of school. I got to school late, so when I came into class everybody saw my shoes. The teacher said, 'You must think you're fresh with those fancy shoes on.' I told her, 'I'm fresh without them.' Ever since, everybody in that class started calling me Fresh, and it just stuck."

"I can dig it with a shovel, family."

"But come to think of it, I didn't start going by Fresh until my uncle, Bishop Don Magic Juan, told me that I should use it as my pimp name."

"Hold up, blood. Are you talking about Bishop Don Juan that be with Snoop Dogg all the time?"

"That's my uncle, folk."

"I smell that, playboy," I said.

"What's your name, pimpin'?" he asked.

"James. But everybody calls me J.D."

"What floor you stay on, joe?"

"Who's Joe?" I asked.

He laughed.

"It ain't no thing," he said. "That's just our way of saying homie."

"Where you from, blood?"

"Chi-town."

"I'm staying on the first floor," I said. "What floor are you on?"

"The third."

Fats interjected, "We used to get blowed on that third floor, cuz. If you want to blaze that chronic, all you've got to do is slip a wet towel under your door and you're good to go. Y'all don't know nothing about that chronic in the Chi, though."

"I done been on that chronic before. One of my cousins is from Long Beach. But y'all don't know nothing about that dro. Y'all ain't never smoked none of Chi-town's sticky, icky ooh-wee!"

Just as our conversation on illegal substances was about to intensify, I glanced at the sky-blue face on my watch. The long hand showed two minutes after the hour.

"Damn, we ain't gonna make it to that mandatory R.A. meeting on time, blood," I said.

"You ain't lying, joe. Let's get there."

Both of us dapped Fats up and jogged across the street to our dorm. We were late.

CHAPTER 6

DISCERNMENT & DISCIPLINE

When we made it to the staircase leading to my dorm it looked like a ghost town. Nobody was outside. The stoop next to the steps leading to Marshall Hall was vacant except for a couple of crows pecking on leftover chicken bones. I assumed everyone was already in their dorm meetings, but I didn't think we would be the last two to make it to ours.

I was right and wrong. Everyone else was in their dorm meetings and we were the last two to stroll into ours. The room was slightly musty, filled with about three hundred guys, most wearing cutoff T-shirts and flip-flops. The fact that there was only one way in and one way out made sneaking in impossible. As I got closer, I overheard Varnelius talking about curfews. He was wearing a purple T-shirt with a red V in the middle, mirroring the Superman logo. It had the word "Man" written underneath in gold. As we neared the entrance, Fresh and I looked at each other. Without speaking, we decided to split up. I veered to the right side of the room, while Fresh tried to blend in with the left side of the crowd. The damn feather in his Dobb hat blew our cover. Varnelius stopped in midsentence, cleared his throat and rubbed his hands together like he was about to dig into a bowl of gumbo. He had a devilish smirk on his face.

"You with the pimp hat and your boy," he said. "Y'all grab a seat in the front. There's plenty of room."

I knew that was falsified. It had to be a trick. There were no seats in the front. Instead of walking to the front, I tried to play dumb. I looked around like he wasn't talking to me. But everyone else in the room had turned their mugs to look at me. My roommate was standing right next to me staring in my direction. *Sellout,* I thought.

"Yeah, you," Varnelius said in an uppity tone, pointing me out. "Cool Cali. Come on up to the front."

I took sluggish steps, shuffling around guys seated on the floor. Fresh and I reached the front at the same time. There were four guys who looked like upperclassmen sitting on a desk just behind the head honcho. I figured they were either late like us, or the floor R.A.s. I looked around for a vacant seat. Just as I thought—not one. I looked for a spot on the dirty gray tiled floor, but the only spaces to sit down were so close, looking up at him talking would have been like sitting in the front row at a movie theater. Instead, we just stood there, looking like fish out of water.

"Y'all fellas know this meeting was scheduled to start at eight o'clock sharp, right?"

I knew he had an ulterior motive. Fresh and I shook our heads in unison.

"I see y'all wearing some pretty stylish watches. Young playas in the game. I like that. What's that you got there, a Fakeob?" he asked Fresh, referring to his cubic-zirconia-riddled knockoff Jacob watch with the multicolored face.

"Nah, this is a real Jacob," Fresh said. "Maybe it's just your first time seeing one."

Varnelius switched to a more serious tone. He was noticeably perturbed about being challenged. "Maybe you're right. Maybe there's so much bling-bling in it, *you* couldn't tell the time. But if you haven't noticed by now, you and your buddy here are late. We started this meeting five minutes ago. If I recall correctly, the agenda said, in bold words, that this meeting was to start promptly at eight. Obviously, y'all have a hard time comprehending the rules. But the rules are all we have to go by in Marshall Hall. And breaking them isn't something that V-Man or any one of the floor R.A.s sitting on the desk behind me will tolerate. *Capeshe?*"

Anybody who refers to himself in the third person is obviously feeling himself way too tough. We just shook our heads, hoping to spare ourselves from further lecturing. We started to sit down.

"Wait," he said. "You didn't have a problem interrupting the meeting, so don't be so courteous all of a sudden. Fellas," he continued, talking to the crowd. "We want to have a lot of fun with you all this year, but we've got to stick to the rules. There aren't that many of them. No loud music after ten. Clean up behind yourself. Don't pull the fire alarm unless you see smoke. And visitation hours are over at eleven o'clock. Not eleven-oh-one. Not eleven-oh-two. Eleven o'clock p.m. But since your new friends from California and...where are you from, sir?"

"Chicago," Fresh said.

"Since your friends from *Cali* and *Chi-town* can't seem to tell time, we're going to have to postpone visitation until they grasp the concept. You have them to thank for restricting your hormones. In other words, no females are to be inside Marshall Hall until further notice."

The crowd groaned and looked at us like we were the cochairs of the Klu Klux Klan. V-Man told everyone in the meeting to report to our respective floors to meet with our floor R.A.s in a private cluster setting. The crowd grumbled and murmured their way out of the room. V-Man was making it really tough for us to make friends, so for the most part Fresh and I stuck together. I gave him a pound before he cut the corner to go upstairs to his floor meeting. Just as I was about to shake the spot and get to mine, I noticed my roommate coming from our room, holding his inhaler in one hand and the orientation booklet in the other. He was wearing a T-shirt that drooped to his knees with a Teenage Mutant Ninja Turtle on the front and some dingy, white K-Swiss classics. Timothy was about five-nine, and couldn't have weighed more than a hundred and thirty-five pounds soaking wet with bricks in his pockets. He was all skin and bones. His pajama nighty made me laugh.

"Where you headed, blood?" I asked him, with a smile.

"Outside," he responded.

"I thought we were supposed to be meeting with the R.A.?"

"He told us to meet him outside on the stoop. Weren't you listening?"

I disregarded his last comment. I'd already been ridiculed enough. I didn't have the patience to answer to Revenge of the Nerds without disrespecting him. "Why are you taking the orientation booklet with you?"

"I just want to brush up on some of the course descriptions for my classes. From what I understand, Dr. Johnson's First Year Seminar class is extremely challenging."

"I'm taking his class too. What time are you taking it?"

"I believe, nine a.m."

"We're in the same class, then," I said.

I followed Timothy outside, giggling at the illustration of Master Splinter on the back of his nightshirt. I hadn't seen that cartoon since I was a little kid. I didn't know they still made those T-shirts. And I damn sure didn't know anyone my age who owned one. I hoped this was an isolated incident.

When we got outside, there were about fifty guys crowded around the stoop. The stoop was a short set of steps attached to Tubman Hall, our sister dorm, which was conveniently located right next to ours. Timothy walked to the far side of the stoop. I heard some of the foul comments about his nighties from a distance, but Lawry's was the loudest.

"Oh, hell to tha naw, shawty!" he shouted.

I posted up at the top of the steps. I didn't want anyone to know I was affiliated with Timothy just yet. Just as I was about to check the time on my watch, a slender light-skinned dude with wavy hair stood up on the cement bench about three feet from the center of the stoop.

"What's up, fellas?" he said in a tender voice. "My name is Lester Santiago and I'm going to be the first-floor R.A. this year. I know all of you want to get back to your rooms and finish unpacking, so I'm going to make this short and sweet. I'm from Detroit. And anybody who knows about D-town knows we love to kick it. I look forward to making this the best year possible for y'all. If you want to smoke weed, don't let me smell it. If you want to drink, pour me a glass, but don't get behind the wheel. Other than that, I really couldn't care less what y'all do. I'm not here to be your mama or yo' daddy. I just want y'all to have a good time. As long as you respect each other and keep the first floor clean, y'all can do pretty much whatever you want. As long as y'all don't get caught by V-Man, y'all straight with me. But if he gets you, he's got you. Any questions?"

"When do we get our visitation back, yo?" Dub-B asked.

"Like I said, that was V-Man's call. It's really on him to decide."

A thunderous storm of complaints torpedoed Lester's way. He defensively put his hands on his hips and shifted his body weight from his right to his left side. As far as I could tell, Lester was hella cool. But his body language was a little on the feminine side.

"Look," he said as his eyes widened. He spoke in a whispered tone with one hand still on his right hip and the other pointing from side to side. "If you guys want to sneak somebody in here on the late night, that's on you. I'm not saying it's okay to do it. All I'm saying is if V-Man catches you, you will have to deal with the consequences. And you can't get into Marshall Hall without passing his room. It's right there." He pointed to the window to the immediate left of the front door of Marshall Hall.

"Questions?" he asked, looking around with his lips half-way poked out.

"When is the first dance gonna be, shawty?" Lawry asked. "If we can't get no cut in the room, at least I can get crunk."

"I'm surprised you guys haven't heard about it by now. The Olive Branch is going down tomorrow night. That's got to be one of the best parties I've been to since I've been in college."

"Where's it gon' be at, shawty?" Lawry asked, with excitement in his voice.

"It's on the football field. I'm telling you. It goes down. All of the freshmen from Lighthouse, Elman, Dorris Brown and U of A will be there. All on one football field at the same time."

"All twelve Dorris Brown students are going to be there or just the three freshmen?" someone asked jokingly.

Everyone laughed except me. I didn't think Dorris Brown losing its accreditation was funny. Especially since the school had to basically close because none of its students could receive financial aid from the government. The registration packet said that Dorris Brown was the only school in the Atlanta University Center founded by a black person. I didn't see how these fools could laugh about something so serious.

"On the real, though, B, how much is that ticket running?" Dub-B asked, while trying to bring his laughter to a halt. "You know a playa's money is funny. Gotta save something to cop them books, son."

A few of the guys who were standing around me looked around at each other in amazement. They couldn't believe how hard Dub-B was trying to act black. I gotta admit, he had the voice down.

"That's the best part about it. It's free! All you have to do is wear the Olive Branch T-shirt you got in your registration packet and you're in there."

The way the fellas began grinning and rubbing their hands together, you would've thought Lester had just told everyone they'd won an all-expense-paid trip to the Bahamas with Beyoncé.

"Any more questions?" Lester asked.

I wanted to ask him why, out of all the schools in the AUC,

he mentioned Lighthouse first, but I didn't. Timothy tilted his head back, pumped his inhaler and took in a deep breath of his prescribed air. When no one responded, Lester unofficially adjourned the meeting by jumping off the cement bench. Everyone began to walk back into the building. Before I joined them, I heard Lester's soft voice.

"Hey, Cali," he said.

"My name is J.D.," I responded.

"My bad, playa. J.D. it is. What part of California you from?"

"Oakland."

"Them Oakland 49ers ain't gonna be about nothing this year. They need a new coach."

"The 49ers play in San Francisco, blood. And I got the Oakland Raiders to win the Super Bowl."

"Oh yeah, them Raiders are going to be serious this year. Anyway, I stopped you to tell you not to worry about that little performance V-Man put on in there earlier. That's just how he is. He's always power-tripping. He was the same way when I was a freshman staying in Marshall three years ago and he was my floor R.A. But anyway, anytime you need anything, just holla at me," he said, extending his hand toward mine.

I shook his hand. The nails on his long fingers were perfectly manicured and gleamed as if they had just been coated with clear polish. His palms were sweaty and his hands were unusually soft. I figured he had probably played high school basketball in Detroit or something since he was about as tall as me. Either that or he had never had a job working with his hands in his life. I shrugged it off, wiped my damp hands on my denim shorts and went inside.

As I turned the corner to walk down my hallway, looking down at my cell phone to check my missed calls, I felt someone brush up against the side of me, damn near knocking me off balance. Normally, I'd get mad at anybody crazy enough to run up on me like that, without at least saying "Excuse me," but when I peeped the situation, I couldn't do anything but laugh.

Fresh was sneaking a girl, disguised in baggy sweatpants and a hooded sweatshirt, up to his room. We hadn't even been to our first class yet, and Fresh was already breaking the rules.

"Pardon my pimpin'," he said, as he looked back, wearing a sly grin.

"Are you sure we aren't going to get caught?" she asked, speed-walking with her head down.

"Just be cool, baby girl," he said. "I live right up these stairs. We're straight."

Although I didn't get a good look at her face, even through her sweats I could tell she had a fatty. I just shook my head and smiled as I opened my door. By the time I made it inside my room, my roommate was already knocked out, snoring obnoxiously loud. Aside from that, going from my queen-size bed back at home, to this twin-size cot wasn't an easy adjustment to make. I had a hard time falling asleep.

CHAPTER 7

OLIVE BRANCH

No pep talk or warning could have prepared me for what I saw. When we walked into the Panther Stadium my eyes damn near popped out of their sockets. There were thousands of people—mostly females—bumping and grinding in the end zone on the far end of the field. Everyone was told to walk along the track that circled the football field to get to the other side, but I felt like breaking into an all-out sprint down the sideline. To describe the way I felt at that moment as culture shock would be an understatement. I was overwhelmed.

When we made it to the end zone, I felt like doing a touch-down celebration dance. I'd been to clubs, house parties and school dances in Oakland before, but I'd never in my life seen that many black people in the same place at the same time without fighting. I was in awe.

"Close your mouth, shawty," Lawry said. "Welcome to the A! This is how we get down!"

I tried to keep my composure, but I was on the verge of losing it. Every time I took a step, I was surrounded by ten different females, and their differences were as beautiful as Oprah Winfrey's bank statement. Their skin tones ranged from piano-key ebony to that of a sandy beach. Some of the girls had their hair styled short like Halle Berry, while some rocked braids, and others' fell past their shoulders. The facial ratings scaled from "She must look like her dad"—threes—to "What part of heaven are you from?"—tens. I was paralyzed. I could see that Fresh and Lawry had fallen under the same hypnotic spell. None of us could move. A girl walked by us wearing some see-through nylon shorts that looked like panties. She had her T-shirt tied up in a knot on her side, and was wearing some red six-inch heels. All of our heads turned simultaneously, like she had an invisible string tied from her ass to all of our necks. My mouth watered.

"Damn, blood, she got a watermelon booty," I said.

"Right, joe," Fresh said in approval. "Big and juicy. Just right for a playa like me."

Lawry made a bold move. He reached out to grab her hand and caught her wrist. She turned around and looked at him like he had run over her foot with his car, until he let go. It didn't take long.

"Damn, shawty, these girls bourgeois as hell," Lawry said, looking like he got caught digging in his nose. I could tell he was embarrassed. But I'm sure he didn't care. There were so many dimes in this party, a nigga could strike out ten times in a row and still be in the game.

The DJ played East Coast rap for at least a half hour straight. I wasn't really feeling that theme, so I walked around peeping the scenery. When I tried to call Todd on his cell phone to let him know what he was missing, he answered but said he couldn't hear me because the music was too loud. All I could do was shake my head as I looked around. There were so many different people from so many places, doing so many dances I'd never seen in my life. I saw a few girls doing the Harlem Shake to one of P. Diddy's songs. I saw Dub-B grinding on a petite light-skinned girl with her long hair braided like Alicia Keys. Although he looked like he was concentrating, he was surprisingly on beat. I thought the white dude would have two left feet, but he didn't miss a step as the two grooved to a G-Unit cut.

Just when I thought the party couldn't get any better, the DJ took it to the next level, when he switched to a dirty South vibe and played "Yeah" by Usher, Lil Jon and Ludacris. Fresh and Lawry trailed me until their songs came on.

When the DJ flipped the script to Chi-town flavor and played R. Kelly's "Step in the Name of Love," I noticed a large crowd form a circle around two people. In the O, whenever people were crowded in a circle like that, two people were in the middle fighting. I pushed and shoved my way to the inner ring of the circle and couldn't believe what I saw. It was Mr. I'm-so-pretty-I-carry-a-brush-in-my-back-pocket—Fresh, doing a dance everyone called "Steppin'." I'd seen it on the videos, but never before in person. His feet moved in perfect sequence with the girl he was dancing with. And she was a shapely, chocolate stallion, with wavy hair that bounced off her shoulders every time she turned her head. When R. Kelly said spin, Fresh held her by her hand, spun her around, then spun himself, still shuffling his feet fluidly. It looked like they had practiced this routine before or something. I overheard a girl who must've been from Chicago talking to her friend. She said, "Ooh, he's juking, girl. That's how we do it in the Chi!"

At that point, I realized why he'd earned the nickname Fresh.

I stepped away from the chaos to grab some H2O from the student government–run concession stand on the sideline. I'd just paid for my Dasani when I saw her. My heart skipped a beat or three. It was the badass O.G. who'd given me my registration packet. Her face looked like Vivica Fox. Her eyes were as seductive as Lisa Raye's. She had a small waist, but the junk in her trunk looked soft enough to use as a pillow. I'd seen some superbad breezies in the Bay, but this was the most beautiful female I'd ever seen in my life. I had to find out her name. I knew I had to make my move, but I was having a hard time thinking of the right thing to say. Usually my game was tight, but for some reason this breezy had my head gone. All I could do was stare.

"She does the same thing to me too, cuz," I heard someone say.

I turned to my left. It was Fats.

"What up, family?" I said, dapping him up.

He was wearing a navy-blue L.A. Dodgers T-shirt, some blue Dickies that looked like the same ones he'd just worn the other day and a pair of navy-blue Converse sneakers.

"I thought this was for freshmen," I said. "How did you get up in here, blood?"

"You know the University of Atlanta motto, right?"

"Nah, blood. What's that?"

"Find a way or make one."

"I can dig it."

I turned my head back toward my future wife, but she had disappeared. I cursed under my breath. Just as I contemplated hunting her down, she reappeared. She was standing with the orientation guides. A couple of them were wearing their O.G. T-shirts. But a couple of the cuter ones wore pink and green Alpha Pi Alpha sorority jackets. She was one of them. Her jacket had her line name, *Overdose,* written on the back. At that moment, I was feigning for a hit. I saw her look in my direction. I gave my lips an LL Cool J lick for sex appeal. Just when I thought I'd caught her eye, her head started turning slowly in the other direction. She was looking at someone. I surveyed the crowd and noticed all of the fine girls doing the same thing. Did they know something, or someone, I didn't? I saw her whisper in her soror's ear, then point in the direction everyone else was looking. I spotted the figure everyone was looking at, but couldn't make out who it was because of the large crowd around him.

"What's everybody looking at, blood?" I asked.

Before Fats could open his mouth, I saw for myself. Some cat wearing a U of A football jersey with Number One on the front perched himself on top of a statue of a panther, which was just past the goalposts. I could see his diamond-cut earrings and platinum-coated pendant hanging from the chain around his neck, gleaming, from where I stood. And I was at least forty yards away.

"That's Downtown-D, our star quarterback," Fats said. "His real name is Deiondre Harris."

"I know he ain't a freshman," I said. "What's he doing up in here, blood?"

"He does what he wants to do, cuz."

"I saw the football team's record from last year in the registration packet. They only won seven games. What's all the commotion about?"

"We lost our first five games in a row because D was academically ineligible. Once he stepped in, we were undefeated for the rest of the season, cuz. He's that real. I've seen him throw a football from where he's sitting, damn near through the goalposts."

"That fool is only sitting ten yards away from the goalposts," I said, with a tinge of Haterade in my voice. "I could do that."

"Nah, homie. I wasn't talking about the goalposts he's sitting in front of. I'm talking about the one on the other end of the football field. No joke, cuz. They did a special on that nigga on ESPN last week. He's supposed to be the first player to ever come out of an HBCU and be one of the top ten picks in the NFL draft."

"Like that?" I asked. "I know he's probably got all the breezies on lockdown, then, huh?"

"Look at 'em," he said, pointing to the flock of females hovering around the hulking, dark-skinned figure. "Got 'em lined up like little kids at the mall waiting to take a picture with Santa Claus on Christmas Eve."

Normally, I wouldn't care about Downtown-D and his corny little fan club. But when I saw the girl I'd been eyeing all night intentionally walk toward the herd of groupies, I was hurt. I didn't even know this girl's name, but I felt some kind of connection to her. I wanted to say, "Where the hell you think you're going?" but I would have been out of pocket. But the second I heard Tupac's "I Get Around" blast through the huge speakers, I flipped my switch back to player mode. I popped my collar, and hit the end zone determined to dance with the first Coke bottle-shaped stallion that caught my eye.

CHAPTER 8

THE CLASSROOM

If I had gotten up the first time the buzzer on my alarm clock sounded off, I would've been on time. But, as always, I sleepily reached my arm from my bed to my desk and felt around for the snooze button, without looking at the time. I needed at least five more minutes of sleep. I dozed off again. My slumber was interrupted by an eerie feeling that my little five-minute catnap had turned into a deep hibernation. I wiped the drool from the side of my mouth, smeared the sleep from the corner of my eyes with my knuckles and looked at the clock. My eyes widened. According to my clock, I'd been knocked out for a cool hour, and my class was starting in eight minutes. I hopped out of my bed so fast you would've thought my sheets were on fire. I grabbed my clock to investigate why the buzzer hadn't gone off a second time. For a second, I thought that my brand-new alarm clock might be bootleg. But apparently, I'd inadvertently swiped the alarm switch to the off position while fumbling for the snooze button.

I cursed under my breath, while looking through my closet for something to wear. Timothy's bed was neatly made and his backpack was gone.

"Timothy knows he could've woken me up," I mumbled. "Now he got a nigga late to class."

My hands moved frantically about my closet. I knew that I had to hurry, but picking an outfit to wear on the first day of class was no rush job. I didn't want to wear something that looked like I had just popped the tag, but I knew I had to come with something tight. I decided on my black, short-sleeved Lacoste polo, a pair of denim shorts, and my black patent leather Jordans. I laid the fit on my bed and headed for the bathroom. I saw Lawry coming from the showers as I closed my door.

"Say, shawty, you figna be late to our first class on the first day, ain't ya?" he asked.

"My alarm clock was tripping, family," I said. "I see you ain't too far ahead of me, though. Save me a seat."

Just as I stepped foot inside the bathroom, I heard Lawry's Deep South accent again.

"You got some scissors I can borrow? I'm trying to squeeze the last drop of toothpaste out of this tube, but it looks like I'm gonna have to cut it open to get some out."

I knew that he would need every drop of Colgate in that tube, so I ran to my room and grabbed a pair of scissors from Timothy's desk. I gave Lawry the scissors and told him he could just give them back to me in class.

"Good lookin' out, shawty," he said. "I appreciate ya. Hurry yo ass up! Class starts in five minutes."

I searched frantically for an open shower stall. There was a vacancy in the stall on the end. I hopped in the shower, lathered my possibles—armpits, feet, private parts—and rinsed off quickly.

When I made it back to my room, the numbers 9:01 were scrawled across my alarm clock in red. Either my clock was a little fast or I was officially tardy. I threw on my outfit, brushed my waves, sprayed myself with some Aqua di Gio cologne and hit the door. Four more minutes had expired from the clock before I finally left for class.

I searched my bag for my class schedule as I walked down the hallway. I found it squished in between two spiral notebooks. First Year Seminar was probably the easiest class on my schedule aside from Music Appreciation, English, African-American History and algebra. I figured if I really gave my all, I could make at least a B in most of those. The only class I was really worried about was biology, because science was so boring to me I usually couldn't help falling asleep in class.

But at the time, I was more concerned about trying to find my First Year Seminar class, especially since I didn't remember seeing Washington Hall on the campus tour. I started to take out the map of the campus they'd given us in our registration packets, but I didn't want to look like a lost freshman, so I acted like I knew where I was going. I saw an older woman with short hair and thick glasses walking near the stoop outside my dorm, so I asked her for directions.

"It's right over there, baby," she said, pointing to the white brick building just on the other side of the basketball court.

I thanked her and hustled toward my classroom. My schedule said the class was in room 328. I hustled up two flights of stairs and opened the door leading to the classrooms on the third floor.

"Why am I always late for everything?" I muttered to myself under my breath as I turned the knob to walk inside.

The classroom was kind of small. There was a medium-size wooden desk in the front. A chalkboard hung on the wall just behind the desk with the name Dr. Oliver Johnson scribbled across it. The fact that there were no windows made it seem a little stuffy. I noticed a black clock just above the chalkboard. I was thirteen minutes late.

There were about thirty-five wooden desk chairs in the room. I spotted one open seat in the back row. The professor was pacing up and down the rows passing out some paperwork. He was standing near the empty seat when the door loudly slammed shut behind me. I shrugged my shoulders, put on a face that said, "Oops, my bad," and walked to my seat like I was five minutes early. I was trying to slip into my seat without making eye contact with the teacher. But I knew I'd blown my cover when the door slammed. He'd stopped passing out the papers to look at me. When I made it to my seat, he was standing right next to it. I had to look him in the eye.

Dr. Johnson was a hulking figure. He was a caramel-complexioned brotha who had to be at least six foot four and weigh in around two hundred-plus. His guns were tremendous. The veins on his forearms popped as if he'd just finished lifting weights. His neatly manicured dreads were pulled back into a ponytail, draping over the back of his beige button-down polo. His shirt was neatly tucked into a pair of stonewashed jeans, which were cuffed over a fresh pair of butter-colored Timberlands. He even had a Sidekick clipped to his waistband.

"And you are?" he asked in a serious tone.

"James," I said.

"James who?"

"James Dawson."

"Nah, you're James who was late to my class," he said, with a laugh.

Everybody else in the class laughed too.

"Where are you from, Mr. Dawson?" he asked.

Here we go again, I thought.

"Oakland."

"Well, you're not on West Coast time anymore, Mr. Dawson. Let's try to make it to class on time. Ya feel me?"

"I feel ya."

I was relieved by the fact that he didn't make too big of a deal about my tardiness. I was pleasantly surprised by the male-to-female ratio in the classroom. Of the thirty-five freshmen in the class, twenty-eight of them had to be females. Make that twenty-nine, because some female with short hair, thick thighs and a nice backyard walked in just after I did. There were no more seats, so she had to borrow one from the class next door.

The professor sat on the edge of his desk, his arms folded, watching as the girl struggled to maneuver the desk through the small doorway. When she finally got it in, she placed it on the side of the wall and sat down, looking embarrassed.

"A real gentleman would've offered his seat to that young lady," the professor said, looking directly at the girl who'd just walked in. "But now that I see we don't have any of those in this class, and everyone is here, I guess we can get started."

The girl smiled bashfully as he passed her a packet from the thin stack of leftovers on his desk.

"My name is Dr. Oliver Johnson, but y'all can call me Dr. J. As long as your name is on the roll sheet that I'll have by next week, I will be your professor for First Year Seminar. If not, you're in the wrong class, and you might as well drop out of school now since I won't be your teacher.

"Just kidding," he said, laughing. "But on the real side, the packet I have passed out is what we call a syllabus. That is your table of contents, North Star system, compass or whatever other guidance mechanism you can think of for this class. The syllabus will provide you with your homework assignments, their due dates, quiz and test schedules. You will find the class rules and regulations there as well. You've got two options. Either stick to the script and get an easy A, or you can try it your way, ad-lib, and flunk. The decision is yours. What you put into this class is inevitably what you will get out of it. Grades are a reflection of a student's effort, not his or her capability. All of you are capable of getting As in here, but how many of you will live up to your potential is questionable. Hopefully all of you, but only time will tell."

I could tell that Dr. J was one of those cool teachers who didn't take no shit. The syllabus was no joke. When I looked at the course description in the registration packet, First Year Seminar seemed like one of those easy A classes. But Dr. J was trying to make this class harder than it really had to be. It was supposed to be a class where students learned about the history of the institution. But Dr. J had turned it into HBCU History 101. He told us to find out who our dorm was named after and write a two-page, double-spaced paper on that person. Although I didn't like the idea of getting a homework assignment on the first day of class, or the second or third for that matter, I figured since I only had this class once a week, I had time to get it done. But I was tripping when he told us we were going to start next week's class with a quiz on the lyrics of the school's anthem. He was clearly taking this First Year Seminar gig a bit too far.

Just as I thought about switching out of his class to a teacher who didn't try to make it so difficult, she walked through the door. Once again, my heartbeat became irregular, and I was short on oxygen. It had to be...yep, it was her all right. It was the APA I'd met during orientation, who was looking like a million bucks at the Olive Branch. She was wearing a tight, charcoal-colored BeBe T-shirt and a black wraparound skirt with shingles on the bottom that fit her like O.J.'s glove. She was rocking a sexy pair of pumps that wrapped around her ankles. From head to toe, she was a purebred stallion. Her long, curly hair was pinned up in a bun. And her body was outlining the rest of the girls in chalk.

Dr. J continued talking about the quiz, but nobody listened. All eyes were on her. Even the girls were peeping. She was that bad. When Dr. J saw that the class's attention was elsewhere, he paused to introduce the vixen.

"It's about time you got here," he said, spinning around in his desk chair to look at her with a smile. "I was starting to get worried. Before you sit down, let me introduce you to the class. This is Katrina Turner. Katrina is an ATL native, and a junior, majoring in criminal justice."

"I'm actually from Athens," she said, interrupting him.

"Next time, correct me outside," Dr. J said with a laugh. "At any rate, she was a standout in my First Year Seminar class two years ago, and will be my assistant this semester. As a matter of fact, is there any advice you'd like to give the students?"

"Wow! You're really putting me on the spot here. Well, first of all, I would say that paying attention to the study guides is most important, because Dr. J pretty much puts everything that will be on the test on the study guides that he hands out. Oh yeah, and don't come late. Believe me, you don't want to get on his bad side. On a more serious note, though, I would like to invite all of you to stop by our Alpha Pi Alpha sorority incorporated booth outside the Student Center to pick up free goody bags and safe sex pamphlets that we will be giving out this afternoon, in accordance with our safe sex week that we're sponsoring."

"Well, that was a mouthful," Dr. J said. "I'm sure Katrina will be available if any of you have questions about the class, so feel free to ask."

Every playa in the class was thinking the same thing. I couldn't see Fresh's face. But I saw him whip out his brush and start manicuring his waves. Dub-B was easy to spot. He was the only white guy in the class. He was sitting near my roommate in the front of the class, hunched in his seat, slowly stroking his red goatee. I peeped Lawry sitting across the room licking his lips, rubbing his hands together as if he were sitting down in front of a hot slice of apple pie and vanilla ice cream. I knew he'd have questions for her. But so would I. All of a sudden, spending two hours in this class one day a week didn't seem so bad after all.

CHAPTER 9

THE CAF

When I caught up with Fresh, he was cutting across the basketball court talking on his cell phone, headed toward Marshall.

"What up, pimp?" he asked, turning around to dap me up, before redirecting his attention toward his conversation.

"Look, baby, I told you I'm not trying to avoid you. It's just that since I've been out here, I've been trying to get on my feet so I haven't had as much time to talk to you lately. You know I love you, though... C'mon now, boo, you know it ain't even like that. I'm not even thinking about these bust-downs out here. Why would I, when I have a queen like you at the crib? Now, I'm gonna call you back in a few so I can holla at my boy... All right, boo. I love you too. Bye."

After closing his flip phone, Fresh took a deep breath, looking exhausted. "Boy, I'm telling you. This female is driving me insane. I mean, don't get me wrong, joe. I love her and all that. But damn! Ever since I left the crib it's like she calls every ten minutes, asking where I'm at, what time I got there and who I'm with. All that's doing is driving me away, joe."

"Who you telling, blood? If there's one thing I can't stand, it's an insecure breezy."

"I know, right," he said. "Anyway, where you headed? You look like you've been knocked out."

"I was. I just got out of biology class. I can't stay awake in there for nothing. I was in the back row getting my snooze on. I'm about as hungry as the werewolf of London, though. I need to grab something to eat on."

"Right, joe. I was just thinking the same thing. Let me run upstairs and drop off my book bag in my room, so we can shoot over to the Caf. I hope the dinner is as good as breakfast was this morning."

"I might as well throw my bag inside my room too," I said. "Just meet me outside on top of the steps."

"Bet," he said as he lifted his ID card to the electronic sensor pad to open the door. "I'll be right back." He flung the door open.

I followed him inside. I was so hungry I damn near made it back to the front door before it closed behind me. Fresh had changed into a black short-sleeved polo and a pair of black Steve Maddens.

"You getting kinda clean just to hit the Cafeteria, ain't you?" I asked.

"You know a pimp like Fresh gotta stay as sharp as a barber's clippers," he said, carefully brushing his waves. "Plus, it's six o'clock. I don't know if you're hip, but that's prime time for some right now pimpin' in the Caf."

Fresh kind of reminded me of Todd. He was as slick as black ice, but hella laid-back. I'm not the type to kick it with just anybody, but Fresh was cool like that. He had one of those rare, one-of-a-kind personalities you never forget. I followed him.

When I opened the double doors leading to the foyer area outside the Cafeteria, I saw that Fresh was absolutely right. The Caf was crackin'! The area outside of the Caf was set up like the inside of a fast food joint. They called it the Den. Most of the people sitting down at the tables in the Den were upper-classmen and most of them were females. I could feel most of their eyes on me. I exchanged eye contact with a bad dime at the table closest to the door, just before she dipped her chicken strip in her barbecue sauce. Our eyes followed each other's until we were out of one another's peripheral vision. I made a mental note to crack my whip the next time I saw her.

Our pimp struts came to a halt when we jumped in the back of the lengthy line, which snaked all the way from the cashier's desk in the Caf to the staircase next to the men's bathroom. While waiting in line behind Fresh, I peered through the clear Plexiglas window separating the Caf from the Den. The Caf had more dimes than a piggy bank. Just as I began scanning my pockets in search of my ID card, I felt a wave of people behind me push the line, thrusting me forward. I didn't turn around until I felt someone step on the heel of my Js. I turned around with my fists balled up ready to cut somebody's grass. But I unballed my fists when I saw who it was. Downtown-D and about four three-hundred-pound offensive linemen had shoved their way to the front of the line. I lifted my ankle and looked back over my shoulder to check my Js for a scuff, and then I looked at Downtown-D like he'd lost his mind.

"Hold up with all the hostile looks, man," he said with a Southern drawl. "I ain't mean to get ya."

Some short girl standing in line with her hair pulled back in two French braids smacked her lips, put her hands on her hips and let him have a piece of her mind.

"I don't care who you are!" she shouted. "Downtown, uptown, or whoever you wanna call yourself. You gotta stand in line like everyone else!"

Instead of responding to the girl standing in line, Downtown-D turned to the dark-skinned lady wearing a hairnet sitting at the cash register and posed a question.

"Does it look like I'm wearing an apron and got a menu in my back pocket to you?" he asked.

"Nah, baby," she said with a deep Southern accent.

The star quarterback turned around to the line, looking directly at the girl who'd made the smart comment.

"Exactly," he said emphatically. "Because I'm not a waiter. And I ain't about to wait in this line. Somebody better tell her who I am."

The offensive linemen slid their ID cards to the cashier one at a time. Downtown-D didn't even take out his ID card. He just nodded at the cashier and followed them inside. When Downtown-D made his entrance, at least half of the girls in the Caf stopped eating long enough to glue their eyes to his body. I figured it must be nice to have that kind of attention. The last time I had a bad breezy checking me out like that, it was because I had a piece of toilet tissue stuck to the bottom of my shoe.

By the time she swiped my card, Fresh had disappeared around the corner leading to the buffet line, and Downtown-D was halfway there. I should've been walking behind him carrying neck braces for the ladies. I tried to stagger my strut to maximize my attention. But Downtown-D was clearly the man of the hour. I was just the guy walking behind him.

The walk from the cashier's desk to the buffet area was like walking down the catwalk in a Sean John fashion show. Every step and exchange of eye contact had to be carefully calculated. Everybody was rocking the tightest gear—from the hottest urban fashion lines to the newest Gucci purses. The lunchroom looked like a nightclub. I caught a few eyes, but most of the bad breezies were focused on Downtown-D.

I thought the Cafeteria food was going to taste like that slop they serve in the county jail, but I was wrong. There was a tall dark-skinned guy wearing a chef's hat, standing over a pizza bar scattering pepperoni over hand-tossed dough and sprinkled mozzarella. There was a breakfast cereal bar with all of my favorites—Lucky Charms, Frosted Flakes and Waffle Crisps. That was right next to the waffle batter, syrup and waffle maker. But the aroma that smelled the best was coming from the steam rising off the collard greens, macaroni and cheese, candied yams and fried chicken. Judging by the length of the line, everybody else obviously felt the same way. I scooped up a red tray, some silverware and a bowl of fresh salad before jumping in the line. On my way to the end of the line, I saw Fresh headed toward the lunchroom area, struggling to balance his cell phone between his ear and his shoulder and to hold up his overloaded tray at the same time.

"Hey, baby, I'm trying to find a seat in the lunchroom right now," he said, looking annoyed. "We were just talking less than five minutes ago. Let me call you back when I get to my dorm. Yes, I'm gonna call you back this time. Last time, I had fallen asleep. I know I always say that, but I'm for real this time. I know I said that last time, but look, I've gotta go. All right, I love you too. 'Bye."

He paused for a second before looking at me. "You got a girlfriend, joe?"

"I had one back at the crib, but we broke up right before I came out here."

"You're a lucky man, folk. I'm telling you, my girl is getting on my last nerve. With her calling every five minutes, I've barely had time to bust down the new bust-downs I've come up on since I've been here."

"You better keep your game tight," I said.

"That goes without saying," he said. "Anyway, I'ma go hold a table down for us."

I nodded my head and walked over toward the lunch line. Luckily for me, this line was moving faster than the one during registration. I grabbed my plate, set it on my tray and headed to find Fresh.

Trying to look cool while balancing a plateful of soul food and a cup of sweet tea on a tray was harder than honors calculus. One slip or mistimed step could ruin your whole reputation. And since I was a freshman without a car, my rep was just about all I had, so I took my time.

I saw my roommate sitting at a table by himself with his napkin tucked into the collar of his shirt, eating soup and crackers near the emergency exit door.

"Hey, James!" he yelled out, waving excitedly, like he'd known me for years.

I started to act like I hadn't heard him at all, but he kept waving. It was still a little premature for me to be publicly associated with ol' Timmy, but in order to avoid further embarrassment, I walked over to his table.

"What's crackin', Timothy?" I asked, looking down at his table cluttered with textbooks. "What you studying?"

"I'm just doing a little research on Thurgood Marshall for our First Year Seminar paper," he said. "I figured now would be the best time for me to formulate an outline."

"We just got that assignment today!" I said, laughing. "You're getting started already?"

"I figured it would be to my advantage to get it out of the way."

"More power to you," I said.

"You might want to get started on yours too, James. It couldn't hurt. I wouldn't mind sharing my notes with you."

"Man, we've got a whole week to finish that assignment! I ain't even thinking 'bout that right now. And from now on, it's cool for you to call me J.D.—especially in public."

"Well, aren't you going to sit down and eat?"

"Nah, I'll let you get your study on," I said as I spotted Fresh waving me toward his table near the back of the Caf. "I'll holla at you back in the room, though."

By the time I made it to the table, Fresh had almost finished his food. He was sitting at a table with Lawry and Dub-B, just across from a tableful of other cats I'd seen in Marshall Hall.

"Yo, this yam pie is off the hook, son," Dub-B said, forking a large bite of dessert into his mouth.

Everybody at the table started cracking up. I laughed so hard I almost cried.

"Yam pie?" I asked, wiping a tear from the corner of my eyelid.

"What the hell is you talkin' about, Wonder Bread?" Lawry asked in his thick Southern accent. "That's called sweet potato pie, shawty."

"Wonder Bread," Fresh said, pointing toward Dub-B. "I like that name for you, joe. From now on, that's what we're calling you—Wonder Bread."

"All of my homies call me Dub-B," he said. "That's what I go by."

"Exactly," Fresh said with a laugh. "Dub-B stands for Wonder Bread."

The veins near Dub-B's temples pulsated and his face turned red, as he angrily shoved the last piece of sweet potato pie from his plate into his mouth. For the first time since I'd met him in the registration line, Dub-B was losing his cool. I had to cut the tension.

"Speaking of a sweet potato," I said, nudging Fresh with my elbow, "whatever happened between you and ol' baby you were stepping with at the Olive Branch? She was the truth!"

"Who you talking 'bout, Alexis?" Fresh asked.

"The one you were dancing with when R. Kelly's song came on," I said.

"The one whose ass was about as thick as the Yellow Pages, shawty," Lawry added.

"Oh yeah," Fresh said. "I don't know what the hell that has to do with a sweet potato, but that's her. She goes to Elman."

"So what ever happened with that?" Dub-B asked.

"Nothing," Lawry interjected. "He just said she goes to Elman. You know those girls be acting like they're too cute to poot—unless you're a Lighthouse man."

"Oh, c'mon, now," Fresh said casually. "You know I hit that."

"No bullshit?" Lawry asked.

"It's a small thing to a giant," Fresh said. "You've seen me with her before, J.D."

"When?" I asked.

"That's the same girl you seen me sneaking into Marshall the night V-Man called us out about coming to our meeting late."

"Well, say that, then!" I said.

"Ooh!" Lawry screamed as he got up from the table. "I know she had some wet-wet."

"Yeah, she's a real freak," Fresh said. "Where you headed?"

"Back for seconds," Lawry said as he walked back toward the kitchen. "I'll be right back."

"I like how Fresh is trying to act all cool and player about Alexis now," Dub-B said. "But that night, it looked like y'all were falling in love on the dance floor, B."

"I know you ain't talking, joe," Fresh said. "You were hugged up with that one girl all night."

"What girl?" I asked.

"The light-skinned chick with the long braids."

"It ain't nothin'," Dub-B said.

"It had to be something," Fresh said. "I saw you holding on tighter than a hubcap in the fast lane."

"She was tight, though, huh?" Dub-B asked.

"Oh, she was bad as hell," Fresh said. "She kinda reminds me of Alicia Keys. Where's she from?"

"Maryland," Dub-B said.

"I've met a lot of cute girls from Maryland since I've been here," I said. "What's her name?"

"I think she said her name is Jasmine. I've got so many phone numbers the last couple of days, sometimes I get them confused. But I'm almost positive her name is Jasmine."

I knew that there were lots of fine girls who went to the University of Atlanta. But I was hoping there were two light-skinned girls from the D.C. area with braids named Jasmine who looked like Alicia Keys. If not, I knew Lawry was going to be heartbroken. Just as I thought about the repercussions, I saw him out of the corner of my eye, making his way back to the table. I decided to abruptly switch the subject again.

"Anybody else taking Professor Obugata for biology?" I asked.

"Hell nah, shawty," Lawry said, laughing. "You talking about that dude from Africa, with the thick accent?"

"Hell yeah, blood."

"I could've told you not to take his class," Lawry said.

"I wish you would have."

"I barely passed it when I took it in summer school, and I'm a *biology* major."

"Man, I can't stand science as it is," I said. "But I couldn't understand what he was saying, even if I knew what he was talking about. The only part I understood was when he said we've got homework tonight, and our first quiz next week."

"Good luck," Fresh said.

"You're gonna need more than luck to pass that class, shawty," Lawry said.

CHAPTER 10

BACK TO CLASS

On Sunday night, I asked Dub-B to come by my room the next morning at seven-thirty. Monday morning, I heard what sounded like the Atlanta police chief knocking at my door bright and early. I wiped the sleep from my eyes and looked at my alarm clock. It read 7:29 a.m. Although Dub-B talked, dressed and played basketball like he was black, after this timely effort, there was no questioning the fact that he was still as white as snow.

"Who actually wakes somebody up on time?" I mumbled as I rolled out of my bed and stumbled to the door. Dub-B was standing on the other side wearing a blue Yankee hat tipped over his eyes, a navy-blue New York Yankees T-shirt with a picture of Jackie Robinson painted on it and a fresh pair of navy-blue Timbs. He looked like he was headed to a Dipset video shoot.

"What up, kid?" he asked in a hyper voice.

"Not me, I was knocked out," I said, crashing back onto my bed.

"Get up, J.!" he said. "You told me to wake you up at seven-thirty."

"I know what I said 'cause I said it. I forgot you don't operate on BPT."

"What's BPT?"

"Black people time! I wouldn't expect you to know nothing about that, Wonder Bread."

"Whatever," he said. "I know one thing. If you don't hurry up and get dressed we gon' miss out on breakfast."

I threw on a pair of royal-blue basketball shorts, a fresh white tee and a pair of tennis shoes, and headed for the bathroom to brush my teeth. My roommate was already gone to the Caf. As usual, his bed was perfectly made. When I made it back to my room, Dub-B was sitting on the edge of my bed watching "*SportsCenter.*"

"You just missed the interview with Deiondre Harris," he said.

"On ESPN?"

"Yeah, son. I couldn't believe it either! Dude is mad athletic. His arm is crazy! They said he's supposed to be the first quarterback from a black college to get picked in the top ten of the NFL draft next year."

"Is that right?"

"Word is bond. They were comparing his rushing yards to Walter Payton's because he got drafted out of a black college too. I didn't even know that. I can't wait to see what Downtown-D is going to do in the homecoming game."

After catching a few more highlights, we headed to the Caf. It didn't take long for me to find out that breakfast was the best meal of the day in the Caf. Just as Dub-B polished off the last of his bacon, cheese eggs and grits, he asked the one question I didn't want to hear.

"Did you finish up that paper on Thurgood Marshall?"

"What paper on Thurgood Marshall?"

"The one that's due in…" He paused to check his Movado. "Twenty-five minutes."

"Oh, shit," I said. "I had forgotten all about that. Did you finish yours?"

"I'm almost done."

"Let me hold that real quick, blood."

"Mine ain't even all the way complete yet," he said. "I still have to type it out and put on the finishing touches, but I'll tell you what Web site I got all of my information from."

I could tell he was lying. For one, he was looking everywhere except my eyes. And if he was, in fact, still working on it, he would've just said that. But any time someone offers you an alternative that involves actually doing the research yourself, they don't want you to copy theirs. His final copy was probably sitting right in the notebook in his book bag. He didn't look like he was in a rush. I started to con him out of the paper, but I decided to just throw something together real quick—cut-and-paste style. I got the Web address and headed straight for the Marshall Hall computer lab.

When I made it to the dorm computer lab, Varnelius was the only person inside. He was wearing a purple Omega Beta Phi T-shirt, pajama pants and some corduroy slippers. We exchanged glares. But I didn't have time to play games with V-Man. I had to find an open computer. My frantic search for one was brought to a halt by V-Man's annoying voice.

"Did you sign in?" he asked.

I tried to act like I didn't hear him. Then he repeated himself.

"I didn't see a sheet," I said, with an attitude. "But I ain't really had the time to look."

V-Man motioned toward a piece of paper on the desk at the front door. I knew he was just asking me to sign in to aggravate me, but I did it anyway. I had him all figured out. As long as he knew he was getting under my skin, he'd keep pouring it on. But the more I acted like he was irrelevant, the less he got on my nerves.

I quickly logged on to a computer and found the Web site Dub-B told me about. He was right. All of the information I needed to do it was there. The only problem was that I had less than ten minutes to complete the assignment. Luckily, I knew that this job would only require two items from the toolbar—the cut-and-paste tools. I hurriedly slapped a two-pager together that sounded way better than anything I could ever have written myself. I misspelled a few of the words on purpose, just so it resembled my work, and hustled back to my room. After throwing on some sweats, I knocked out a quick fifty push-ups to pump up my chest, because I knew Katrina would be in attendance with her fine self.

As soon as I made it to the door of my First Year Seminar class, Dr. J was closing it shut. He gave me an ice-cold stare, then a fake smile as he reopened the door for me.

"Still on West Coast time, I see," he whispered under his breath.

I could feel Dr. J's eyes following me as I searched for an open seat. Once again, the class was as overcrowded as a slave ship. I must've been the last person to make it to the class, because everyone, including Dr. J's exquisite assistant, Katrina, was already seated. Just as I was about to sit down at an empty desk, I heard Dr. J clear his throat.

"Not so fast, sir," he said.

Without making eye contact with him, I sat down next to a thick redbone and unzipped my backpack, as if I hadn't heard him talking to me. Once I looked up, I saw Dr. J looking right at me.

"You weren't in that big of a rush to get here, so don't be in such a hurry to sit down," he said. "Come on up here and rap with me a taste."

I swiftly turned my head to look at the people sitting around me, as if his comments were directed toward one of them, but all of them were looking back at me with that "He's talking to you" face. Somewhere between checking out the tiles on the ceiling and looking on the floor for loose change, I exchanged glances with Dr. J.

"You talking to me?" I asked in a surprised tone.

"Yeah, you," he said. "Cool Cali."

Just as I was slowly rising from my seat, Dr. J caught me off guard.

"Oh, and bring your assignment with you," he said.

After fumbling through my backpack for my paper, I made my way to the front of the class.

"Let me borrow that assignment so I can copy it real quick, shawty," Lawry whispered as I walked by.

By the time I made it to the front of the class, I could sense Dr. J was up to something foul.

"Well, I see we've got one scholar in the class," he said, while looking at my paper. "I've got to admit, I think I may have underestimated you, Jamie. This looks very professional, or as you would say, off the heezy. I'm proud of you. I hope the rest of your fellow scholars were as studious as you were."

"The name is James," I said with a laugh. "And that's off the hizzle. But now, I can dig the compliments."

As much as I appreciated his kind words, something told me this was some sort of good news, bad news speech. And I was running out of good news.

"So, tell me, which dorm do you stay in?" he asked.

"Marshall Hall," I said.

"How 'bout you tell the class three facts that you included in your paper about the history of Marshall Hall that they may not be aware of?"

Uh-huh. Just as I suspected. I stumbled to come up with a clever, roundabout answer. I counted to three in my head as I recited my three facts aloud.

"Marshall Hall was founded by a man named Thurgood Marshall," I said.

Fact number one.

"Marshall Hall is the only male dorm on campus."

Fact number two.

"And when I moved into Marshall Hall two weeks ago there was a huge roach on my floor when I opened the door. But from what I hear, roaches have been around Marshall Hall for a long time."

My third fact drew thunderous roars of laughter from my

classmates. Everyone was cracking up, but Fresh laughed the loudest. They knew I was bullshitting. But unfortunately, so did Dr. J. At first, he chuckled. Then his face turned to stone. Dr. J was visibly upset by my reply. But the way the class responded seemed to add to his frustration. Something told me that Dr. J was having a bad day, and my impromptu BS might have added fuel to the fire.

"Thank you for that little bit of insignificant information, James," he said. "Go ahead and have a seat. You're a pretty funny guy. I wonder if you'll be laughing when you see your final grade."

I heard Timothy snicker as I walked sluggishly back to my desk with my head down. I pulled my sagging sweatpants back up to my waist before slouching into my seat. Silence followed me to my desk. When Dr. J finally broke the serenity, I could tell he was steaming.

"Everybody in this class starts out on the same page, with an A-plus," he said. "It's up to you to lower your own grade by coming to class late and blowing off homework assignments. When preparation meets opportunity, the end result is success. In my class, you will be afforded plenty of opportunities. Whether or not you're prepared when they arise is up to you."

Although Dr. J was looking at everyone around the room, I felt like he was subliminally talking to me. It kind of reminded me of when my mom used to drag me to church on Sunday mornings, and the preacher's sermon was about fornication. I hadn't been prosecuted, but I felt guilty.

"I see some of us have already begun to take initiative, making a few moves," he said. "Too bad some of us are moving in the wrong direction. Everybody please pass your papers to the front of your row."

Dr. J lifted his arms in the air, using hand signals like a traffic controller directing the onslaught of papers to the front. Then he pointed toward what had to be the most beautiful teaching assistant in University of Atlanta history.

"Katrina, if you would be so kind as to pick up these A-plus papers from my scholars I'd appreciate it," he said.

When Katrina stood up I saw mountains move. I felt like maybe I should have knocked out an extra fifty push-ups before thinking of stepping to a woman of this caliber. She was wearing a white blouse that exposed just enough flawless cleavage to make me wonder what else she was hiding under there.

I was intrigued.

How much of her white lace bra you could see depended on how low she'd bend down to pick the papers up from the desk. But you could see her cute belly ring clinging to her tight abs from any angle.

I was impressed.

Her firm breasts were held in place by toothpick-thin brown strings that held her blouse together. I licked my lips uncontrollably. You would've thought I was LL Cool J. She wore some fly-ass blue jeans that clung to her hips. And from what I could tell, there was definitely no more room in those jeans. You could set a cup on her booty and it wouldn't fall off.

I was aroused.

Just as all of the blood in my body rushed to my groin area and my anatomy began to protrude through my sweats, I was turned off by the sound of Dr. J's voice.

"What I'm about to say may be music to your ears, so enjoy it, because you won't hear it often. I've got to catch a flight to Washington, D.C., to sit on a hip-hop summit panel at Boward University with Russell Simmons. Unfortunately, my flight leaves in an hour and a half, so I'm going to cut class short today."

I had already started packing up my things before he finished his sentence. Just as I had zipped up the last open compartment of my book bag and began to stand up, my bad class experience turned worse when Dr. J spoke again.

"So you're all welcome to…"

He paused, and mostly everyone followed my lead, grabbed their bags and stood up. Then he continued.

"You're all welcome to clear your desks and get out a pencil or pen to take a quiz on the school anthem."

The classroom responded with an overwhelming "Aaaaaahhhhh!"

"C'mon with that, shawty," I heard Lawry yell from across the room.

"That's bogus," Fresh said. "He's tweaking, joe."

Dr. J laughed. "Hey, I didn't tell y'all class was dismissed. Now this is just a standard, one-page, fill-in-the-blank quiz. I'm taking it easy on y'all."

One of the females in the class let out a high-pitched whimper that sounded like someone had stepped on a puppy's paw. The girl next to me whispered to her friend, "What is this, *Lean on Me?*"

Her big-boned friend responded in a heavy East Coast, Rosie Perez-ish accent, "I know, yo. Who he think he is, Mr. U of A?"

I giggled.

Apparently, Dr. J overheard the joke. All of a sudden, he became stoic. "Hey, this is college. Deal with it. If you study, you'll get an A. If not, you won't. It's as simple as that. For those of you who refuse to study, just keep in mind, this class will be offered again next semester. God bless us all. Now that we've got that nonsense out of the way the desks should be cleared, pencils should be out and we should be just about ready to get this show on the road. I've got a plane to catch. When you finish the quiz, you can leave."

Just as my heartbeat started racing, I felt someone tap me on my right shoulder. When I turned to see who it was, I saw Lawry sitting a couple of rows back with his hand in the air trying to get my attention.

"You got a pencil or a pen I can borrow?" he asked.

My hand shook uncontrollably as I reached in my bag for an extra pen. The shaking stopped momentarily when I turned around to pass the pen back to the girl who tapped me on my shoulder, so she could pass it to Lawry. Then the slight shaking resumed. For the first time since I got to college, I was hella nervous. I unconsciously resorted to one of my worst habits. I slumped in my chair and began biting my fingernails in a daze. By the time the quiz was passed back to me, I had nibbled on just about every one of my fingernails on my right hand. The only thing that stopped me from devouring my entire hand was the sight of Katrina distributing the tests. I couldn't let her see a grown-ass man with his thumb in his mouth. I removed my finger from my mouth to grab my quiz.

The quiz might as well have been written in Japanese because I didn't understand a word. I guess studying would have made it easier. But for now, cheating was my only option. I kept my head down, but my eyes scanned all of the desks around me. Usually, I could get over, but this quiz was one of those "either you know it or you don't" types of tests. And I didn't know a thing. It was hard to make out what my classmates were writing, because I wasn't familiar enough with the material to make an educated guess. The fact that everyone around me seemed to be breezing through the quiz made me even more frustrated.

Three minutes into the quiz, Dr. J interrupted to make a quick announcement. A few of my classmates pouted in disgust, as if they were on a roll. But I wasn't bothered. In fact, I hadn't written a thing.

"The hip-hop summit will be aired live on BET at noon on Saturday," he said. "So, if you would like ten points added on to your quiz grade, it would behoove you to tune in and write a one-page essay on what you learned. This extra-credit assignment will be due when we meet again next Monday. I won't be accepting papers that aren't typed, double-spaced or don't have a cover page. So ain't no half-steppin'."

Less than one minute after Dr. J's little announcement, half of the class had finished the test. Unfortunately, all of the students sitting around me were included in that number. Timothy was my last hope. He was sitting in the very front row, but I could vaguely make out the answers on his test when he held his paper up to double-check them. Apparently the prescription for his glasses wasn't strong enough, because he held his paper up in the light like he was investigating a counterfeit twenty-dollar bill to check his answers. I tried to capitalize on the situation, but reading his answers from where I sat was like reading the bottom row of letters at the optometrist's office. I tried to squint hard enough to make out an answer, but it was no use. Besides, the last time I tried to make out the words on Timothy's paper, I saw Dr. J looking at me out of the corner of his eye, and I had to fake like I was trying to blink an eyelash out of my eye to create a diversion. At that point, I chalked it up. It was officially a wrap for this quiz. Besides, after Timothy left, I was the last student left in the class. I tried to drop my answerless quiz on Dr. J's desk upside down, and hurry to the door before he found out I had left the blanks the way they were when the quiz was given out. But he was on to me. Just as my sweaty palm grasped the doorknob, I heard his voice.

"Not so fast, Mr. Dawson," he said. "I don't think you read the directions."

"I read them," I said, staring at the clock on the wall to avoid making eye contact with him.

"Well, it looks like you had a problem following them. There's nothing on this paper except for your name and the date. As far as I'm concerned, you can take this with you."

I grabbed the quiz from his desk, stuffed it in my pocket and headed for the door. I had walked out of the door and was headed down the hallway when I heard his aggravating voice again.

"Hold up, James," he said in an authoritative tone as he walked toward me clutching his leather Gucci briefcase under his armpit. "I ain't gonna let you off the hook that easy."

I rolled my eyes, took a deep breath and turned around to see how Dr. J would put the finishing touches on the torture.

"Man, don't give me an attitude, because I'm only trying to help you out," he said. "What's your major?"

"Business."

"After you get your degree, what do you plan on doing with it?"

"I know I want to be an entrepreneur. I know I don't want to work for a company my whole life. I don't know exactly what I want to do yet, though. I guess that's why I came to college. Ya know? To figure it out."

"Hey, there's nothing wrong with that. You've got plenty of time. Honestly, I used to be just like you. When I left L.A. for Lighthouse College, I felt like I was leaving my homeboys behind. Most of them were still on the block, gangbangin' and smoking weed. For some reason, I felt like I owed them something. I felt like I had to represent by sagging my pants and actin' a fool on campus. By the time four years rolled by, all of my *real friends* who came into college with me were ordering caps and gowns for graduation. I had to stick around for an extra year to get my diploma. I was full of potential without a hint of responsibility or motivation."

He put his hands on my shoulders and looked me square in the eye. "You're not in high school anymore, brotha. This university couldn't care less whether you come to class on time, or at all for that matter. Nobody is going to call home and leave a message on your mama's answering machine telling her you haven't been in class. There aren't any parent-teacher conferences. Once the school gets your money, the responsibility is placed squarely on your shoulders, man. And right now I'm concerned that you're not taking that responsibility seriously. You follow me?"

"I got you," I said.

"I see you waltz into class late as if it's fashionable. I mean, you're already on academic probation. You don't have much room for error. If you don't get a 2.5, you're going home, and you won't even be able to apply to any school in the Atlanta University Center again. This is a one-shot deal for you, bruh. Don't blow it. I've seen it happen to too many young guys just like you. Hell, it almost happened to me. You go away to college hoping for a change of pace, and end up hanging with the same crowd and doing the same things you were doing back home. Don't let that happen to you, my man. You feel me?"

"I hear you," I said.

"Look, I'm not trying to tell you how to live or how to choose your friends, but I've been in your shoes before. And if you haven't heard anything I've said to you today, hear me when I say this—don't make friends based on where you are in life. Make them based on where you're going. Don't let the people around you dictate your future."

"I can dig it," I said.

"Why did you choose to come to this university anyway?" he asked.

"I just needed a change of environment. I needed to get out of the hood and make something of myself."

"Well, by coming to class late and neglecting to study for your tests, you're only making a fool out of yourself and whoever's paying your tuition. You're on the right train, but you're on the wrong track. And I can help you get back on course if you let me. Can you get down with that?"

"Fa sho."

"A wise man once told me '*All progress requires change, but not all change is progress.*' So, are you content with change or are you looking for progress?"

"Progress."

"In that case, I've got an ultimatum for you. But you've got to keep it on the low, because I don't do this very often."

"Cool."

"You can either bite the bullet and take a zero for this assignment or head next door to DuBois Hall and sign up for a tutor. I know it's only the first week of school, but I figure we can nip this problem in the bud before it starts to affect your grade. If you bring me a blue slip from the dean of student affairs saying that you've signed up for a tutor, I will think about dropping this grade. The choice is yours."

At that point, I had a newfound respect for Dr. J. I had never heard a man break down the science of my actions like that in my life. Other than my mom and my sister, I didn't think anybody really gave a shit. But Dr. J was the first person to get at me with a genuine concern for my success, and I respected him for that. I could only think of one question to ask him.

"Which way is DuBois Hall?"

"It's just a few buildings down," he said, smiling as he patted me on the back. "As a matter of fact, I'm headed in that direction, so I can show you."

"Good lookin' out," I said.

"Hey, that's what I'm here for," Dr. J said. "And remember, this is only your first test. Believe me, there will be plenty more where this one came from. So hopefully, you'll have all of this out of your system by the next one. Get yourself signed up to a good tutor, and you'll be just fine."

"You think so?"

"Hey, man, the only time you can't afford to fail is the last time you try."

CHAPTER 11

THE STOOP

It seemed a little awkward. I'd never signed up for a tutor before. I'd always been too proud to ask for help. But this time, I knew I needed it. Plus, I really wanted to live up to the promises that I'd made to T-Spoon and my mom. As it turned out, signing up was easier than I thought. At first, I was a little embarrassed. I tripped and damn near fell down the steps in DuBois Hall as I headed for the Tutorial Center, because I kept looking behind my back to see if anyone was following me. Ironically, I ended up being embarrassed anyway because the secretary sitting at the desk saw me stumble, and she was fine as hell. She had to be in her late thirties, but she had a young, sexy aura about her. She tried to muffle her laugh, but she didn't do a very good job of it.

"I didn't even see that," she said, raising her coffee mug to her mouth to hide her laughter.

"Keep that on the low," I said, trying to laugh it off.

After that brief exchange, the rest was easy. All I had to do was write down my name and phone number, along with the best days and times I would be available. I stopped writing for a second to watch my back and make sure nobody was spying on me signing up. Once I was sure the coast was clear, I signed and dated the sign-in sheet and handed it to Stella, the secretary.

"See, it wasn't that bad was it?" she asked, hinting at my apprehension. "We'll give you a call in the next few days to confirm which days and times a tutor will be able to meet up with you."

"Good lookin'," I said as I headed for the door.

As I approached my dorm I was surprised to see everyone who stayed in the dorm, including all of the R.A.s, standing outside near the stoop. It looked like the building had been evacuated or something. I walked a little faster when I heard a fire engine siren and saw the reflection from its lights. Just as I made it to the staircase, four firemen rushed past me, headed for the entrance to my dorm. Since following them inside didn't seem like a viable option at the time, I headed to the top of the staircase to investigate the scene. As I scaled the stairs, I noticed three fire engines lined up back-to-back along the curb in front of my dorm. I saw Lawry chilling on the stoop smoking a Black & Mild. He was sitting next to Dub-B and Fresh. Dub-B was sitting in between some girl's legs holding a handful of black rubber bands, getting his hair braided.

"What's crackin' wit' y'all pimps?" I asked, dapping each of them up with my closed fist. "Why y'all out here looking like y'all at a middle school fire drill?"

Dub-B was the first to speak out. "It's hot as hell out here, kid," he said, tugging at his Marcus Garvey T-shirt for ventilation. "You know we ain't out here for our health, yo. See, what happened...your boy Lawry was trying to cop this female's number. But he started talking too fast, and the heat from his breath got too close to his collar and started scorching! It just spread like a wildfire, kid. It was bananas!"

Everyone laughed except Lawry. He took a long drag of his Black & Mild, stared Dub-B down and exhaled two clouds of smoke through his nostrils before opening his mouth to speak.

"I know you ain't trying to jone on me, Wonder Bread," he

said, with a hint of intensity in his voice. He was clearly offended. "No, the hell you ain't tryin' to get crunk. Why don't you tell them what really happened, shawty? Tell 'em about that care package you got."

"What care package?" Dub-B asked.

"C'mon, Wonder Bread. The one your mama sent you with Usher's hit single wrapped in her draws. Tell 'em about how when you opened the package the entire thang burst out in flames."

Everyone sat still-faced, waiting on the punch line.

"'Cause she had to *let it burn*," Lawry sang, using his best Usher impersonation.

Nobody laughed except Lawry. For one, Lawry's comeback wasn't that funny. For two, it was a low blow. I personally would've tried to knock that nigga's head off his shoulders if he would've said something like that about my mom. But Dub-B played it cool.

"I told her not to let you go down on her with your hot-ass breath, but I guess that's what she gets for not listening," Dub-B said. "Play with fire, you get burned."

Once again, everybody except Lawry started cracking up. He looked hella embarrassed. Dub-B wasn't done yet.

"I don't got a problem with you talking about my mom," he said. "But my name is Dub-B. That's what I go by, and that's what I prefer to be called."

Lawry looked like a school bus had run over his big toe. Our laughter undoubtedly made the situation worse.

"I'll call you whatever I want to call you, *Wonder Bread*," he said as he put his Black & Mild out on the railing aligning the stoop. "Who the hell started calling you Dub-B in the first place? Just because you walk around here wearing baggy jeans and black power T-shirts don't give you no ghetto pass. Not round here, shawty. Next, you're gonna think it's cool to start saying nigga, and we gonna really have problems."

"Whateva, yo," Dub-B said. "You're taking it mad overboard."

"Nah, shawty!" Lawry said in a fed-up tone. "You think just

'cause you got a little ball game and talk all that New York slang, it's cool for you to act black. But somebody's got to pull your card, shawty! This is an H-*B*-C-U—Historically *Black* College—and I ain't figna let all that *acting* you doing ride."

An uncomfortable silence followed. But Dub-B didn't wait long to respond.

"So y'all think I'm acting, B? Because if y'all think I'm acting, then y'all must've been acting too—pretending to be my friends."

"Hey, I ain't said shit, joe," Fresh said with a grin on his face, as he pulled a brush out of his pocket and began to tighten up his waves.

"You cool with me, blood," I said, cosigning.

"I'm too old for this shit, B," Dub-B said, looking right into Lawry's eyes. "Ever since I was a kid, people have been trying to figure out why I act the way I act. I'm to the point where people can either accept me for who I am or just go on about their business, yo. It's not my fault that mostly everybody else who looks like me grew up listening to the Vanilla Ice, and I liked MC Hammer. This is who I am, kid. I dress the way I dress because I prefer looking fly. I rock Marcus Garvey tees because I like what he stood for—self-pride. I'm comfortable with who I am. But don't let my security make you feel insecure, B. I can't explain the reason I talk the way I talk, but can you explain why you call everybody shawty?"

"Nah, shawty," Lawry said, seemingly lost for words.

"It is what it is, B," Dub-B said. "My parents don't understand it either. I'm a white kid who thinks Eminem is overrated, keeps a fresh pair of Air Force Ones and has a subscription to *Vibe* Magazine. But this is who I am. This is me, every day. If you got a problem with that, then you do you, and I'll do me."

"Just know, I ain't the nigga you wanna test, shawty," Lawry said as he turned and walked away.

Dub-B turned to us with a look of disarray. "He be bugging out, kid."

I wondered if I'd missed something. I thought maybe the big

secret about Dub-B trying to get with Lawry's crush Jasmine had been leaked before I walked up. Once again, it was up for me to try to ease the tension.

"You're hilarious," I said. "What was that all about?"

"I can't even call it," Dub-B said. "I mean, it's like lately, Lawry can't take a joke. I was just fucking with him about his breath."

"I wouldn't even trip off of him if I were you," I said.

"Yeah," Fresh said. "You was jappin' on that boy. He's on some ol' bogus shit."

"But now, what's up with the dorm, blood?" I asked.

"About twenty minutes ago the fire alarm went off and your boy V-Man came around to everybody's room telling us to evacuate the building," Fresh said.

"I think somebody just pulled the fire alarm, playing around," Dub-B added.

The girl braiding Dub-B's hair began pulling his stringy hair harder and braiding tighter in frustration because he kept moving his head around.

"Sit still," she said with an attitude. "I ain't got all day to be sitting here braiding your hair for free when I could be getting paid for braiding somebody else's. It's hard enough gripping your thin-ass hair as it is. Now pass me the gel."

Dub-B didn't respond. His mouth was wide open and his head was slowly following something. Fresh had the same dumbfounded look on his face. Apparently he and Dub-B had spotted the same thing, and I was missing out.

"What y'all staring at?" I asked.

Dub-B broke the silence without taking his eyes off the prize.

"I think that's her," he said.

"It ain't but one body on this campus that grown and sexy," Fresh said. "That's gotta be her."

"Who?" I asked in a high-pitched voice, as I tried to follow their heads to the dime piece in question.

"With a walk that mean and a shoe game that ill, I don't see how you could even ask that question," Dub-B said.

When I finally spotted the treasure that Fresh's radar had already picked up on, no further explanation was needed. It was good ol' Katrina—Dr. J's voluptuous assistant. She sashayed toward the stoop at a quick pace in her jean skirt, pink pumps and matching pink and green tank top. There were other females outside, but she stood out like a sore thumb. I knew what I had to do. She was walking swiftly, like a last-minute Christmas shopper in a mall on Christmas Eve, five minutes before closing time. Just as she was about to walk past the stoop, I made my move.

"Excuse me, gorgeous," I said, walking directly in front of her to impede her progress. Surprisingly, it worked. "I think we've met, but I don't think we've been formally introduced. My name is J.D. I don't usually go out of my way to meet a female, but something tells me that you're worth it. What's your name?" I asked as if I didn't already know.

"Katrina," she said. "But everybody calls me Kat."

I tried to capture her eye contact, but she was clearly more interested in the melee behind me.

"What's really good with this dorm over here?" she asked. "Why is everybody standing outside?"

"I think somebody pulled the fire alarm or something."

"Why am I not surprised?" she said as she laughed and shook her head. "Freshmen are so immature."

With that statement, she'd indirectly shot me down before I even had a chance to crack my whip. But I was determined to at least let her know that I was interested in her, especially since she had no problem keeping conversation going. She looked me up and down and kept talking in between laughs.

"Hey, don't I know you from somewhere?" she asked.

"Well, I think I've seen you around a few times," I said, trying to avoid the whole tissue-stuck-to-the-bottom-of-my-shoe memory.

"Aren't you in Dr. Johnson's class on Mondays?"

"Yeah."

"I know I've seen you there," she said, momentarily giving me hope, "but I think I remember you from somewhere else too."

"Girl, you shouldn't be having those kinds of dreams about people without at least getting to know them first."

"Boy, please!" she said, laughing. "I know where I remember you from—orientation. You were the one with that toilet tissue stuck to the bottom of your foot, right?"

"Are you sure that was me?" I asked, smiling.

"Yeah, that was you!" she said, laughing.

I figured laughter was a good thing.

"You're the guy who Dr. J picks on in class all the time."

"You noticed that too, huh?"

"He played the hell out of you earlier today. That was funny," she said, still looking at the firemen standing behind me talking to V-Man on the top steps. "I see these dorms are still as ghetto as they were when I stayed in 'em."

"Safe to say. But I ain't even trippin'. At least I know the fire alarm works, in case there's ever a real one."

"Oh, you stay here?" she asked, looking surprised.

I could tell that was a setup, but it was too late to lie. Maybe I had said too much. Maybe I should've gotten straight to the point and asked for her number, instead of letting her know I stayed in a freshmen dorm. But then again, maybe she didn't care.

"Unfortunately," I said.

Before the word got completely out of my mouth, she was checking the time on her platinum-looking Tiffany watch. Maybe she did care.

"Look, D.J., I'm late for a meeting and I've really gotta go. But I'll see ya around."

Her mouth was saying one thing, but her body language said another. She said that she had to go, but hadn't stepped away from my personal space, so I kept the conversation crackin'.

"At first, I wasn't even going to ask you for your locker combination, but I can see we need to exchange digits so that we can get better acquainted. And the name is *J.D.*, baby."

"Locker combination?" she said, with a look of confusion. "What's that, my phone number?"

"You know it," I said, flipping my phone open in preparation.

"That's a new one. It's actually kinda cute. But I've really got to go."

By this time, I figured I had her on my line. I couldn't let her get away without at least trying to reel her in. "Well, before you leave, what's up with an e-mail address or something? I just want to get to know you."

"You're a cutie. But I don't think that would be a very good idea."

"Why's that?"

"I admire your persistence," she said, looking me in the eye for the first time. "What's your classification?"

"What you mean? I'm straight. I ain't with that funny shit."

She laughed again. "I mean, what year are you?"

"I'm twenty," I said, tacking on a few extra years, just in case.

"No, I mean what *grade* are you in?"

"Oh. I'll be a sophomore next year," I said, trying hard to avoid saying the word "freshman." "But what does that have to do with me giving you a call?"

"I don't give my number to freshmen," she said as she began walking away. She looked over her shoulder and smiled. "But I've really got to be somewhere, so I'll holla."

I think my uncle Leroy said it best—I hated to see her go but loved watching her walk away. As much as I would've loved to have her number, at least she knew my name now. I stood there in a sort of daze, just admiring her ass twitch. I had my back turned to Fresh and Dub-B, but I knew they were watching me in my moment of despair. I tried not to wear my emotions on my face, but I guess I didn't try hard enough. I turned around when I felt someone's hand on my shoulder. It was Fresh.

"You need some help picking up the pieces, joe?" he asked.

"What pieces?"

"The pieces of your face that just fell on the ground," he said, laughing. "She ain't even have to play my boy out like that. I didn't appreciate that, fam-o. That wasn't even kosher."

"She just ain't never seen a real pretty thug in the flesh before," I said as Fresh spun me around by my shoulder, and I followed him back to the stoop.

"You think he's hittin' that?" Fresh asked.

"Who?"

"Who you think? Dr. J, fool."

"Oh, boy," I said, accidentally visualizing Dr. J pulling Kat's tank top over her head, then unzipping her skirt. "Ain't no telling, blood."

"Dr. J as smooth as they come, though, kid," Dub-B added. "You know he be bumpin' mad honeys, yo. He's probably splitting that ripe banana. I know I would."

The girl braiding his hair was about two rows away from being finished. But she was still frustrated.

"I wish you would quit moving so I can get done," she said.

Just as the girl put on the finishing touches, V-Man stood on one of the cement benches and announced that the firemen were fed up with people crying wolf, and threatened to take away our visitation rights for the rest of the semester if they had to respond to one more false alarm.

But V-man's threats paled in comparison to the feeling of rejection I suppose Fresh could still see written all over my face.

"Ain't no slackin' in your mackin', pimp," he said. "Hey, my uncle Bishop Don Magic Juan always says you miss one hundred percent of the shots you don't take. And I ain't ever seen a man catch a fish without casting his pole in the water. I saw you get shot down. But I also saw half the females out here all in your mix when you were choppin' it up with ol' baby. Just know that for every 'no' you get, two 'yeses' are on the way."

"Fa sho," I said, confirming Fresh's philosophy. I'd probably never tell him, but although I already knew that, I needed to hear it—for my swagger's sake.

"So, what you about to get into, joe?" he asked. "I'm

probably 'bout to go back up to my room and get on the sticks for a minute."

"You got that new *Madden* on *PlayStation?*"

"You already know. Why? You trying to come get whooped up?"

"I really got some homework I need to be knocking out. But I guess I can come mop you up real quick."

"Okay, now," he said. "Don't let your mouth write a check that your ass can't cash!"

"Who you running with?"

"Don't be a fool. You know I'm coming with my Chicago Bears. Their defense is nasty."

"You're gonna have to score some points to beat me, though. Since you're staying with your hometown squad, I guess I'm gonna have to massacre you with the Raiders."

"Well, I'm figna set up the game. You know where I'll be when you're ready for that ass-whippin'!"

After Fresh bounced, the crowd slowly disappeared as guys began making their way back into the dorm one by one. On the way inside, I noticed Timothy sitting on one of the cement benches with his legs crossed and his head in a book. He was wearing the free T-shirt that we were given in our registration packets, a pair of what looked like his little brother's khaki shorts and some Birkenstock sandals. I had a good mind to walk right by him, but something told me to stop and say what's up.

"What up, blood?" I asked, extending my balled-up fist for him to dap me up.

He looked up and slapped my fist with an open hand, as if he was trying to shake my hand. Poor Timothy was as confused as they came. Maybe he didn't know any better. I just shook my head in disgust.

"What you reading, square?" I asked.

"What?" he said, frowning his face up as if I were a disturbance.

"I said, what are you reading there?"

"The New Testament," he said before unzipping the pouch he had strapped to his waist and pulling out a yellow highlighter.

"Man, you be on them scriptures real tough, blood," I said. "You're really into that Bible, huh?"

"I don't see how you can function without it," he said.

"You must've grown up in the church," I said.

"I did," he said. "But I know lots of people who didn't who still believe in the Bible."

"It's not that I don't believe in the Bible," I said. "I mean, I went to church when I was growing up too—mostly on Easter Sunday and Christmas—but I went."

"If that's the case, you should be a believer."

"I am. I mean, I think I am. I guess. I don't know. I believe in Jesus and all that, but I just have my questions about it all, you know? I mean, the Bible was written like ten thousand years ago. I just don't see how I can apply a lot of the stuff in there to real-life situations that are going on in the world today."

"Are you kidding me?" he asked. "The Word is directly applicable to everything going on in the world today. Everything you've gone through, everything you're going through, and everything you can possibly go through is already written somewhere in that Bible. You just have to be diligent enough to seek that knowledge. In fact, I never study anything without it right by my side."

"Really? Why not?"

"It's just kind of reassuring, I suppose. It reminds me that all things are possible through Christ who strengthens me."

"Oh, boy!" I said. "Whoa! That was deep. But you know the Bible was written by *man,* right?"

"Yeah, and so is *King* magazine, but you read that all the time. And you believe everything they write about the rappers in *The Source* too, don't you?"

"You've got a point there, blood," I said.

"Speaking of a point, I'm about to go to the library to work on a PowerPoint presentation for my Comparative Religion class."

"I almost signed up for that class. How is it?"

"It's relatively interesting," he said. "The professor primarily discusses the origin and philosophies of a variation of religions, in addition to the societal contributions of various denominations."

"So basically, y'all be talking about church up in there?"

"One could say that. Hey, while I'm at the library, I'm going to study for our first biology quiz too. I generally prefer to read the Word before I study. It helps me focus. Would you like to join me?"

Even though I knew I could use the study session, playing *Madden* with Fresh just sounded like a better way to pass the time than reviewing biology notes with Timothy.

"I would, but I just told Fresh I was going to meet him in his room to beat him in this video game," I said.

"Are you sure?" Timothy asked. "You know we only have three quizzes in his class before the final, and they make up thirty percent of your grade. It was written in the syllabus that he gave out the first day of class."

"You read that?"

"Sure I did. It was only seven pages."

"Man, you be all over it, blood. I bet you had straight A's in high school, huh?"

"I actually got two B's, one in my gym class my freshman year, and one in driver's ed my senior year," he said, with a frown. "Those doggone grades actually brought my GPA down to a 3.987. But I was still valedictorian of my class."

"That's what's up."

"So, what do ya say the two of us head down to the library and review some of my biology notes?"

"I'm going to study on my own a little later on," I said, turning to walk away. "Maybe next time."

CHAPTER 12

CLUB WOODY

My Mom called me every single day for the first couple of weeks I was at school. But I guess since I'd been away for a month, she figured I'd adjusted, so she didn't need to call every five minutes. Now, when she called, it seemed like we always had more to talk about. She'd tell me how pumped Robyn was to be the only sophomore who made the varsity cheerleading squad and how much she couldn't stand her new boss at her job. But what I loved to hear most was my mom's hood update.

"And your friends ain't doing nothin'," she'd say. "I see 'em hanging out right there on 106th and Foothill on my way to work every day doing the same thing they were doing before you left. They just stand out there in the cold on that same corner, smoking the same weed and slangin' the same drugs to the same fiends, like don't nobody know what they're doing. I thank God every day you got out of here, J.D."

"So do I, Mom," I said. "So do I. I just wish some of my boys could be out here with me—especially Todd."

"Now that's my boy, right there. I hope the two of you stay close, even though you're at two different schools. When is the last time you talked to him?"

"We're down for life. I just talked to him earlier today."

"How's he doing up there at Crampton?"

"He said he loves it up there. Todd fits in everywhere, though. He said he's still trying to adjust to balancing football practice with studying, but other than that, he's cool. He didn't say it, but he sounded a little homesick to me."

"What about you? You miss home yet?"

"Nah. Not really. I mean, I miss you, Robyn, Grandma and a few of the homies, but I don't really miss Oakland like that. Not yet, at least. I do miss Keisha, though."

I guess my mom could tell I had a heavy heart about Keisha, because she kept trying to give me advice about the situation.

"Breaking up with Keisha may have been a good idea after all, J.D.," she said. "I've got love for that girl, but I think she's being a little selfish. At your age, you don't need to be serious with no female anyway. When I got serious with your father in my freshman year, I wound up getting pregnant with you and dropping out of school. I don't regret any of the decisions I've made, but I see more in you. You don't have time to worry about no girls back home when you're in Atlanta with all them girls anyway."

"How you know about the females out here, Mom?"

"For one, let's not forget who dropped you off at school. I saw all them fast-ass girls eyeballing you. Plus, the night before I left I went to this club on Peachtree Street. It was off the hook! Jamie Foxx was in there with his big, fine, sexy self."

"All right, I ain't tryin' to hear all that."

"Okay, well, let's change the subject, then."

"Sounds like a plan."

"How did you do on your first biology quiz?"

"So you said Jamie Foxx was up in the club, huh?" I asked, trying to switch the subject back.

There was no way I could tell her that I'd completely forgotten to set my alarm clock, and slept in so late that by the time

I made it to the class Professor Obugata wouldn't let me take my first exam.

"Who else was up in there?" I asked.

"Oh, I thought we were done talking about the club. I know I am. So, what's up with the quiz score, bruh?"

An incoming call from that sexy secretary in the Tutorial Center office shortened our conversation and temporarily saved my life.

"Mom, this is the lady in the tutorial office on the other line calling in. Let me call you back."

"Yeah, right," she said. "Give me a break, J.D. I just got off the plane, not the boat. Keep it real, playa. The *tutorial office?*"

"I'm serious, Mom," I said. "Let me catch this lady before she hangs up. Gotta go. Love you. 'Bye."

"Love you too," she said, just before I clicked over.

The secretary was calling to remind me that my first session with my tutor, Ms. Turner, would be starting in thirty minutes in the library. I was relieved that my tutor was a female, and hoped she'd be cute. With a few sprays of cologne, I was headed down the strip, toward the library. I had never even been inside the library before. I remembered what Fats had said about Woodruff Library being called "Club Woody" because it was the social melting pot for students in the AUC. As I walked to where I was supposed to meet my tutor, all I could think was Fats was definitely a man of his word. The library was crawling with females. Everybody was sitting in front of their open textbooks, but few were actually studying them.

Some of my apprehension was relieved when I saw other guys from Marshall Hall being tutored. To my surprise, I saw Lawry sitting at one of the tables in the far corner with seven other guys, most of whom I didn't recognize. As I approached their table, none of the guys even looked up. They seemed to be the only group of guys in the library actually studying their notes. When I got close enough to tap Lawry on the back of his head, the guy sitting across from him looked up hurriedly and covered his notes, as if I was coming over to secretly copy off him. All of the other guys, strangely, followed suit. At second glance, I realized the guy who sparked the group's paranoia was Timothy.

"I should've known," I said jokingly. "Ain't nobody trying to copy off of your paper, blood."

"Oh, what up, J.D?" Timothy said, sticking out a balled-up fist to dap me up.

"What up, huh?" I said, extending my fist to give him a pound with a confused look on my face.

"I mean, what's good? What you up to?" he said in a hurried tone, seemingly annoyed by my presence.

I noticed that all of the guys sitting at the table were wearing khakis, black dress shirts and penny loafers. And oddly, none of them had returned their attention toward their studies. All of them were kind of just looking around in a daze.

"Oh, boy!" I said. "You're dapping people up now? Saying 'what's good?' What y'all studying, ebonics?"

All of the guys laughed halfheartedly.

"Something like that," Lawry said. "This class we taking ain't no joke. The professor got us in study groups already. We got a big test coming up."

"Your professor makes y'all dress alike too?" I asked nosily.

"Nah, shawty," Lawry said. "See, we're supposed to be in a corporation so…it's like we're running a business so…"

Timothy finished his sentence. "So we have to look professional."

"Well, remind me not to sign up for that class next semester," I said with a laugh. "I'll let y'all get back to it. I got some studying to do myself."

I thought a few of the guys sitting at the table looked a little old to be taking a freshman course. But I shrugged it off as I made my way to an empty seat, nodding my head at a few people I recognized from my classes on my way.

I began nibbling on my fingernails nervously as I looked around in search of my academic savior. I'd been sitting all of sixty seconds when I felt someone tap me on my left shoulder and faintly whisper, "Are you James Dawson?"

When I turned to look over my left shoulder to see who it was, nobody was there. When I looked to my right, the one person on campus I would personally have selected to be sitting in the chair next to me was sitting there. It was Katrina.

"So you need a little assistance in First Year Seminar, huh?" she asked.

I was so happy and didn't know what to say. I couldn't believe Ms. Turner was really fine-ass Kat. The irony of the situation made me take a look around and smile. I saw the envious eyes of guys looking up from their textbooks to glare in my direction. Of all the possible tutors on campus, something told me I got the pick of the litter.

"A little help in First Year Seminar wouldn't hurt," I said. "But then again, chemistry is always important."

"You signed up for help in Dr. J's class, and that's what I'm here to assist you with, so let's get to it," she said as she removed her pink and green line jacket and slipped it over the back of her chair.

"This isn't a sprint, it's a marathon," I said, with a hint of seduction in my voice. "Take your time, sweetheart. This tutorial could take all night."

"I don't have that long."

"I'll be here as long as it takes."

"What's up with you?" she asked. "Are we still talking about this tutorial session or what?"

"I was," I said, sounding surprised. "I don't know what you're thinking about. Get your mind out of the gutter."

"That's you!" she said.

"Didn't say that it wasn't. But I'm a Scorpio. I can't help it. What's your excuse?"

"I don't need one."

"Good. Excuses expose your weaknesses."

"Where do you get this stuff? Are you sure you're a freshman? You would think you were older than twenty."

"Don't trip, baby, my age is catching up to me," I said as I dug my First Year Seminar book out of my backpack.

"Can't say that I've heard that one before," she said, giggling. "You're something else with these one-liners!"

"Judging by your line name, obviously somebody must think the same thing about you, Miss Overdose."

"Yep, you're right," she said. "I'm too much for you. Now, let's get down to business."

Kat whipped out her class schedule and asked for mine so she could set up study session hours that worked for both of us. I'm glad she did, because if she hadn't, I might have gone all semester without ever knowing we were in the same biology class. There had to be at least one hundred students in that class. She told me that she'd waited three years to take biology because she didn't like science, but she needed to take the class to meet her graduation requirements. I tried to act like I was interested, but realistically, I couldn't care less. I knew I could kill three birds with one stone if I played my cards right. I could ace First Year Seminar and biology and come away with the queen of the deck. My mojo was definitely working, because her conversation went from "What could a freshman ever do for me?" to "You are kinda cute for a freshman," by the end of the study session. It was definitely time for me to take a second stab at asking for her number.

"So, what you got up for tonight?" I asked.

"I'm probably going to study for our next biology quiz. You know we only have two more before the midterm. That first one was kind of rough. How did you do?"

"I don't even want to say," I said.

"C'mon, just tell me. I don't think anybody did that well. At least, I didn't."

"What did you get?"

"A dang eighty-four."

"Since when has an eighty-four been a bad grade?"

"Since third grade, when I got in trouble for bringing home

a B on my report card," she said. "Haven't had one since. I was traumatized when I saw that grade last week."

"I need to be studying with you more often," I said.

"Why, what did you get?"

"Man, I messed around and slept right through that quiz," I said. "Well, actually, I woke up right before class was just about over, but the teacher wouldn't let me in."

"Oh, that was you arguing with Professor Obugata at the door?"

"Yeah."

"I was wondering who that was," she said, laughing.

"He could've let me take that test. He was hating. What's so funny?"

"I'm just laughing at the way he came back from the door mumbling to himself. You know it's hard to understand what he's talking about anyway, but when he gets frustrated, it's even funnier. I wish you could've seen it. You really ruffled his feathers."

Just then my cell phone rang. I tried to search for it and silence the Tupac "I Get Around" ring tone that was blasting from my pocket. When I finally got to it, I was happy to see who was calling.

"Robyn!" I said aloud, completely inconsiderate of others studying nearby. Kat nudged me as a reminder. I continued in a softer tone. "What's crackin'? I haven't heard from you in a minute. What you been up to?"

"I've got good news," she said. "You won't believe it!"

"What?"

"I passed my test today!"

"What test?"

"At the DMV, silly. I got my driver's license today!"

"You did? Good for you! Did they give you an address that I can send my license to? If you're going to be on the road, I need to surrender my driver's license right away. I hope they've got some good deals on bus passes."

"Whatever!" she said. "Don't hate."

"I ain't hating. I guess I know who will be picking me up from the airport now. You just make sure the seat belts are working in whatever car you pick me up in."

"Anyways. I don't know what you're talking about. I got a ninety on the test. The only thing I need to work on is my parallel parking."

"Yeah, I know. Mom told me about what happened last time. Hey, Rob, I'm gonna call you back a little later. I'm in the library studying right now."

"In the *library? Studying?* Are you okay? You're not running a temperature, are you?"

"Anyways! I'm gonna call you back later."

"Sounds good. Love ya!"

"I love you too," I said as I hung up.

"Wow!" Katrina said. "Playa, playa! Booty calls coming in before ten p.m., huh? That's a new one for me."

"*Booty call?* Girl, please. That was my little sister, Robyn. She was calling to tell me that she got her license."

"Aw, how cute. How old is she?"

"She's sixteen."

"Man, I sure miss those days. High school was so much fun. College was too, the first couple of years. But now that I've started to take courses pertaining to my major, it's no joke."

"I see that. It looks like you've got every book in the library except for the Bible stuffed into your backpack."

"I know, right. All this studying is kicking my butt."

"So, what's on your agenda after you finish studying?"

"I need to go to my room and do a little more studying for a microeconomics exam I have coming up in a few weeks. I swear that class is my Achilles' heel. A few of my line sisters are trying to convince me to hit up Club One Tweezy with them, though," she said. "Who knows? I might get out and have a few drinks with them or something. By then it should be just about your bedtime, huh?"

"Not unless you plan on tucking me in."

I'll never forget the next three words that came out of her mouth. It beat "I love you" by a long shot.

"I just might," she said.

"If I had your phone number I could reach out and touch bases with you," I said. "Who knows when I'll need a little extra help on an assignment?"

"That would be nice, huh?" she asked.

"Fa sho."

"I just don't think that's the proper way to go about this. Since I'm the tutor and you're my pupil, why don't you give me your number? Then I can call you when the time is right."

"Hey, I know that one," I said. "The girl asks the guy for his number, and then she never calls. Spare me the embarrassment. There's no use in me giving you my number if you're just going to play games."

"If there's one thing I don't do, it's play games," she said in a serious tone as she reached into her purse and grabbed her cell. "Now, are you going to give me your *locker combination* or what?"

I fought off excitement. It was almost too good to be true. But I just played it cool, grabbed her cell and punched in my name and phone number, hoping she'd call.

After she reversed the game, and got my digits, we studied for nearly an hour. Studying with Kat definitely had its pros and its cons. Her patience made her the perfect tutor for me, especially since my attention span was about as short as Mini-Me's arms. But she couldn't help it that her one fault was the thing that attracted me to her the most—her sexiness. Every time she flipped the page in my First Year Seminar book with her French-manicured nails, licked her lips before speaking or looked me in the eye, I was thrown totally off track. By the time we were midway through our first study session, I already had a PHD—pretty hard dick, that is. Before long, miscellaneous dialogue found its way into our conversation.

"'Sup with the decorations?" I asked, tugging at a red ribbon she had pinned to her shirt. "Is it Christmastime already?"

"Observant, aren't we?"

"Inquisitve."

"I see," she said. "And no, this is not a Christmas decoration, silly. It's an AIDS awareness ribbon. This week my sorority is conducting safe sex seminars on campus and offering free HIV testing for students."

"That's what's up. You seem really excited about it."

"I am."

"Well, have you been tested yet?" I asked.

"Of course I have. Please, I don't play around with that."

"Me neither," I said. "I heard the number of people with the package on campus is crazy. I don't want no parts of that."

"Well, you'd better wrap it up. Half of all new HIV infections occur in people under twenty-five. People don't understand the seriousness of this epidemic, mainly because there are so many myths and misconceptions out there. It's one of the top ten leading causes of deaths for blacks."

"I'm not surprised," I said. "I know just how that shit happens too."

"Is that right?"

"Yeah," I said. "Half the dudes on this campus are as sweet as a box of Cinnamon Toast Crunch, and probably going bareback on each other. But a lot of females down here like a sensitive man—one they can go shopping with, and talk to about their problems. So the females go shopping with the soft guys and they do each other's hair. Then the girl ends up testing her *little friend* to see if he's really gay. Then the two of them wind up having unprotected sex. It's all one big nasty circle."

"It's funny that you've only been here one semester, and you think you've got it down to a science like that," she said, laughing. "And I bet some of what you just said is right. But truthfully, it's more than just a gay thing now. Most females become HIV-positive through heterosexual sex. But the worst part about it is that one out of every three people infected with HIV doesn't even know his or her status. Most people are scared to go get tested. So they just keep passing it around."

"You're kind of sharp on these statistics," I said. "I mean, you've got the facts memorized. Are you trying to tell me something?"

"No, silly!" she said, playfully slapping me on the shoulder. "One of my mom's brothers passed away about a year ago because he had AIDS."

"Oh. I'm sorry to hear about that."

"Thanks," she said. "But everybody knew it was only a matter of time with him because he was out there pretty bad."

"What you mean?"

"He was gay. I mean, he was all the way out of the closet. But it's funny because he was my favorite uncle. Actually, for a minute, he was like my best friend."

"Your uncle was your best friend?"

"Yeah. I know it sounds crazy, but when I think about it, for a while he probably was. That's probably because he loved to go shoe shopping with me at the mall. Shoot, we even used to get our nails done together and he loved to help me talk about my boy problems too."

"It sounds like you two were really close."

"We were. See, my mom is the oldest of seven, and he was her youngest brother, so we were almost the same age. He moved out here from San Francisco when I was a freshman in high school, and he was a junior. So let me see… Yep, Uncle Kahlil was only two years older than me. I remember because his birthday was two days before mine."

"That's cool," I said. "I don't have a problem with those types of homosexuals. I mean, if you're gonna be gay, then do you. But I can't stand the dudes who try to switch-hit on the low. You know, the kind who want to have a girlfriend one week and a boyfriend the next."

"That's exactly why I decided to have my sorority sponsor

the safe sex week. I've seen the effects AIDS can have on a family. We watched my uncle die and there was nothing we could do about it," she said, tearing up. "I refuse to be a statistic. That's why I get tested on a regular basis. I don't know what I'd do if I ever got AIDS. Shoot, my mom would probably kill me before I died from it."

"*Your* mom? My mom left me an economy-size box of condoms when she helped me move in. She told me that she didn't want me to come back home with anything other than good grades."

"Your mama gave you some condoms? You're a little freaky thing, ain't you?"

"Hey, it's better to have 'em and not need 'em than need 'em and not have 'em. Wouldn't you agree?"

"I guess so," she said. "But wait a minute...how did we even start talking about all this anyway? I'm supposed to be helping you study."

"Hey, there's nothing wrong with us getting to know each other in the meantime," I said, gently running the tip of my finger across her ribbon, in a slightly seductive, stroking motion. "Besides, we probably won't be having our midterm in Dr. J's class for a little while anyway."

"Bite your fingernails, huh?" she asked, abruptly changing the subject while peering at my fingers with a look of disgust.

"Observant, aren't we?"

"Inquisitive."

"It's an ugly habit."

"I see."

"Hey, at least I don't smoke cigarettes."

"Stressed out?"

"I'm a black man living in America. That's life."

"I may have something that'll calm your nerves," she said as she slipped her jacket back over her shoulders and got up from the table. "I'll talk to you later, J.D." She smiled as she walked away.

I gave her a stone-faced look and nodded my head so she wouldn't think I was overexcited. As soon as she walked out of the door, a Kool-Aid smile perforated my face.

Who said you never get a second chance to make a first impression?

CHAPTER 13

THE HALLWAY

By October, dorm life was finally starting to grow on me. I'd gotten used to sleeping on a twin-size bed, scrounging up quarters to wash my clothes and Timothy's annoying complaints about me cleaning up my side of the room. The Cafeteria food had grown on me, I'd learned to tune out the loud music being played in the wee hours and I was used to Lawry knocking on my door every morning asking to borrow my iron and ironing board. I had even learned to cope with the fact that we could only have female visitors from 6:00 to 11:00 p.m. But I still had an issue with the roaches.

It had gotten so bad, I had to buy a small can of Raid for my key chain, just to be on the safe side. Just last night, I came into my room after eating dinner in the Caf and saw a roach scatter across Timothy's desk onto his senior pictures, which were propped up in that pleather display case they give you to put your photos in. I swear, the roach posted up on this man's photo album, posing like it was his prom date or some shit. It went from picture to picture standing on one side of Timothy, then electric sliding to his other side, vogueing like a supermodel. I laughed for a second. But ain't nothin' cool about insects, so I whipped out my economy-size can of Raid and sprayed him down. I picked up the lifeless pest with a ball of paper towel and hurried to the door holding it as far away from my body as possible. At that point, I was so disgusted I couldn't even stand the thought of a roach corpse marinating in my trash can. Just as I was about to reach for the doorknob the door swung open and Lawry stepped inside, coming face-to-face with the dead roach, which couldn't have been more than five inches away from his lips. If he had puckered up, he would have been kissing an antenna.

"Aaagghhh!" he screamed as he jumped back. "Shawty, what the hell is wrong with you?"

"That's what you get for busting in my room without knocking like that," I said, laughing as I walked briskly to the bathroom to dump the roach in the toilet.

"I ain't neva scurred," he said as I walked away. "But that ain't cool, shawty."

When I came out of the bathroom, Lawry was posted up outside my door talking to Fresh, who was standing on the wall across from him. I dapped Fresh up and stood beside him.

"I'm telling you, it's nothing, shawty," Lawry said, crossing his arms defensively.

"It looks like more than nothing to me," Fresh said, taking a closer peek at Lawry's left eye.

"What's wrong with him?" I asked.

"You don't see his eye, joe?" Fresh asked. "Look how swollen that joint is."

"Now that I really look at it, your shit is on sweezy, blood," I said. "What happened?"

"I've been trying to tell this nigga I was playing basketball the other day up at the gym and got hacked all across my face," Lawry said. "I almost had to get into it with one of them boys."

"You should have," Fresh said. "That looks like a technical foul to me. I hope you at least got to shoot some free throws."

"That's real talk," I said, in between laughs. "What y'all got up for tonight, though?"

"On some real shit, I need to be studying for that big midterm in Dr. J's class tomorrow, joe," Fresh said.

"That test is tomorrow, ain't it?" Lawry asked. "I had forgotten all about that."

"Now that I think about it, I'm gonna just read over my notes in the morning," Fresh said as he bent down to tie up his Timbs. "I ain't even gonna try to cram all that in tonight, folk."

I had been studying for the midterm with Kat for the past two weeks, so I wasn't trippin'. Ever since she helped me make a seventy-eight on my first test in Dr. J's class, and an eighty-four on my second, I figured the midterm in his class would be a breeze. It was the biology midterm I was worried about. Since Professor Obugata announced last week that the grades were so bad on the first quiz he was willing to drop each student's lowest quiz score for the semester, I hadn't been so concerned about getting a zero on the first one because I'd missed it. I knew I didn't have any room to slip up on any of the others, so I'd been studying with Kat just about every other day. With her help, and the assistance of the girl sitting in front of me who had no idea I was looking over her shoulder at her Scantron, I scored a seventy-four on the second quiz and got a sixty-nine on the third. Normally, I would've been cool with those grades, because I only needed a D in biology to pass the class, since it wasn't a part of my major. But since I was on academic probation, I needed to keep a 2.5 just to stay in school, and that meant I couldn't afford any D's. I had planned on linking up with Kat later tonight to study, but I didn't want to let the fellas know that I was being tutored. My pride wouldn't let me.

"Y'all heard about that midterm party going down tonight at Club 580?" Lawry asked.

"A *midterm* party?" I asked. "Damn, they throw a party for everything down here, blood."

"I heard some females in class talking 'bout going to it. They said there's gonna be some shuttles leaving from the Elman parking lot going to the party."

"Why you worried about getting on a shuttle?" Fresh asked. "You're about the only one in this dorm with a car."

"My car is so fucked up right now, I'd rather walk or catch the shuttle," Lawry said. "It only starts when it wants to. I'm down like four flats on a dump truck. When my car does start up, it sounds like a lawn mower. I'm about to take my rims off of it and sell them. They're worth more than my car anyway."

"I wish I had my whip out here," Fresh said. "I probably still wouldn't be able to afford gas money, let alone have some bread to go to a party. I'm broke as hell. My mom was supposed to wire me some money, but she hasn't gotten around to it yet. We might not be able to get in, but we can still do some parking lot pimpin'."

"If both of y'all put up three bucks, I can holla at my boy Stretch upstairs and see if he'll let us slide with a ten-dollar bottle of Grand Marnier for nine bucks."

My eyes widened. I hadn't drunk any Grand Marnier since prom night. I knew I should probably be studying with Kat, but I had been so stressed out writing papers for my other classes and studying for tests, I figured a swig or two could do me some justice, especially since I didn't know anybody out here other than Fats who was old enough to buy a bottle for me.

"Stretch who?" I asked.

"You ain't met Stretch, fam-o?" Fresh asked. "You've seen him before. He's gotta be the tallest cat who stays here, other than Dub-B. I say he's at least six foot seven."

"Oh, you're talking 'bout that lanky dude from Houston who stays on the third floor? The one who is always carrying that black water bottle around with liquor in it?"

"Yep," Fresh said. "I think he's a borderline alcoholic. That nigga comes to our First Year Seminar class, drinking early in the morning. As a matter of fact, he's always getting drunk in the other class I have with him. That dude is wild, joe. He's cool, though. He stays right across the hall from me."

"He got drink for sale like that, blood?" I asked.

"Man, shawty got everything you can think of up there," Lawry said.

"Now that I think about it, my money is kinda funny right now too," I said. "I think I can scrounge up three to drop on it, though. Let me go to my room and see what I can come up with."

As I walked into my room I overheard Lawry ask Fresh, "Got a dollar I can borrow, shawty?"

"Damn!" Fresh screamed.

I laughed as I dug in Timothy's laundry change box to *borrow* a dollar. I had good intentions of returning it, so I refused to let guilt set in. When we made it to Stretch's door, I could hear Martin Lawrence's first stand-up comedy show, *You So Crazy,* playing on the inside. Fresh ran across the hall to his room to get an extra dollar to cover Lawry. Fresh told us to wait on him to knock on Stretch's door, but as soon as he left, Lawry banged his fist on the door anyway. The second he knocked on Stretch's door, the TV was muted, and the room fell silent. Lawry banged on his door a few more times as Fresh came running back toward us from his room.

"I know he's up in here," Lawry whispered as he continued to beat on Stretch's door.

"I told you to wait for me to knock on the door," Fresh said. "You can't just knock on that man's door like that, folk. He ain't never gonna answer. Watch out." He playfully shoved Lawry aside.

It's hard to explain the secret knock that Fresh used to get Stretch to open the door. But it went something like the baseline on the old-school Zapp & Roger classic, "Computer Love." It sounded like "boom…chick…boom, chick, chick, chick… boom, boom, boom…chick…boom!"

On the last boom, the door swung open on cue, and Stretch ducked his head under his doorway, suspiciously sticking his long neck out to see who his visitors were. All three of us looked up at him at the same time.

"Oh…Fresh," he said with a big grin, and an even bigger Houston accent, as he looked down on us. "What it do?"

"Just tryin' to see what you was working with up here," Fresh said, exchanging a handshake with Stretch.

"Already. Say no more," he said, motioning for us to come inside.

When I walked into his room, the first thing I noticed was an autographed high school basketball jersey hanging on his wall, and all of the basketball trophies aligned along the top of his bookshelf. Then I noticed that he had combined two beds, putting the head of one bed at the foot of another. That was hella smart, considering he would have had to sleep like an embryo if he didn't want half of his body to be hanging off the bed.

"What's up, ATL?" he asked, looking at Lawry. "What happened to your eye, my nigga?"

"Hoopin'," Lawry said. "With some fools from Texas as a matter of fact. You know y'all can't play no D."

"Is that the word on the streets?" Stretch asked sarcastically, before turning to dap me up. "What up, Cali? What's going down tonight?"

"We were talking about going to the club, but money is funny right about now," I said. "I'll be straight when my refund check posts in my account. But until then I'm lying low, blood. We're probably just figna sip on something."

"Already," Stretch said as he got down on his knees and reached under his bed to reveal an enormous suitcase. "I'm waiting on my refund check too. I got what ya need, though."

"Good," Fresh said. "Since we can't go to the club, the least we can do is get slammed."

"I feel ya," Stretch said as he fiddled with what looked like a complicated combination lock on the suitcase. "I thought y'all were them law boys at first. You know they kicked my door in a couple of weeks ago. Somebody was snitching, so I gotta be extra cautious these days."

"I feel ya, shawty," Lawry said. "What you planned on getting into tonight?"

"Man...I was talking to my T-Lady when y'all knocked on my doe. But I need to start studying for this First Year Seminar test tomorrow."

I was thrown off by a word he used. Confusion must've been written all over my face.

"What's wrong, man?" Stretch asked. "You must've ate that spaghetti in the Caf."

"Nah, blood," I said. "I was just wondering what 'T-Lady' means."

"Oh," he said, laughing. "My T-Lady. That's my mama. You ain't neva heard that before?"

"That's a new one for me, family," I said.

"I ain't never heard that one either, joe," Fresh said.

"Must be an H-town thing, because I'm from the South and I ain't neva heard of that," Lawry added.

After entering a combination fit for a bank storage vault, Stretch finally cracked the suitcase open. My eyes lit up like a Christmas tree. This cat had more merchandise than a real liquor store. He had the bottles stacked on top of one another in Alpha Mu Alphabetical order, with the amaretto on top of the Armadale vodka.

"Oh, that's that shit right there, joe," Fresh said, picking up the bottle of Armadale.

"You already know I got that throwed inventory for y'all boys," Stretch said, rubbing his chin. "I got them bootleg CDs going for five bucks, and the DVDs for ten. I even got that blue diamond in stock for y'all boys."

"Blue diamond? What's that?"

"That's that Viagra. It'll have you going all night."

"I'm cool, blood," I said.

Who needed Viagra with all the liquor he had in stock? He had everything from two-dollar shots of Seagram's gin to a fifteen-hundred-dollar bottle of Rémy Martin Louis XIII. It didn't take long before we found what we'd come in search of. The Grand Marnier was right next to the Hennessey and Hypnotiq. After bargaining with Stretch to let us slide with a twelve-dollar pint for nine bucks, we came to an agreement. He said he would let us slide with it, as long as he could drink with us. Fresh told Stretch that we would be getting slizzered in his room. Just before we walked out, I asked Stretch what baller he had autograph the high school jersey hanging up on his wall.

"That's my boy Deiondre Harris's jersey," he said. "We balled on the same high school squad in Houston."

"Damn, Downtown-D can hoop too?" Fresh asked.

"He's just an all-around athlete. He is the only person in history to be named Mr. Basketball and Mr. Football in Texas in the same year. He was on the first-team All-American hoop squad as a sophomore. To this day, D is the only nigga I've ever seen take one step and do a three-sixty. We won three state championships at Hill Ridge High School."

"That's crazy," Fresh said. "Y'all must've had a squad. What's good with that bottle, though?"

"I'ma bring it over there to y'all boys in about five minutes. I gotta call my T-Lady back and give her my account number so she can wire me some dough… Oh yeah, before y'all leave, anybody need any textbooks? I got those for the low too."

"What you got?" Fresh asked.

"Everything," Stretch said, reaching under his bed and pulling out another suitcase. When he opened it, I couldn't believe my eyes. He literally had photocopied versions of just about every textbook in the bookstore. "I'm all out of biology and Spanish books. But if you need books for any other class, I got you."

"How much is this precalculus book going for?" Fresh asked.

"Man, I've been letting those go for thirty-five," Stretch said. "But I'll let you slide with one for about twenty-five. Just make sure you send me some clientele."

"I got you," Fresh said. "Just set that book to the side for me. I should have the money by this time tomorrow. I *really* need that book, though."

"If you need it like that, just take it," Stretch said. "You live right across the way. Just bring me the bread for it when you get it."

"I save more money fucking with you than switching to Geico," Fresh said as he picked up the textbook off the bed. "Man, you must've saved me about seventy bucks! There was no way I was paying ninety-five bucks for that book in the bookstore. I was just going to have to share with somebody else for the rest of the semester, but I was getting tired of that. Good looking out."

"Speaking of looking out, any of you guys taking Professor Obugata for biology?"

"I am," I said. "Why?"

"Y'all got quiz number two coming up, right?"

"Yep."

"I got the answers to that on sale too."

"You've got the answers to the quiz?"

"Got 'em."

"You've gotta hook me up with those, blood!"

"For the low price of $21.65, you can hook yourself up. As a matter of fact, for you…no tax. We can make it an even dub."

"That's nothing," I said, reaching in my pocket for my wallet. "Are you sure these are the right answers?"

"C'mon, playa. I wouldn't even do it like that, baby! This one is a money-back guarantee. However, it comes with one warning."

"What's that?"

"If you haven't been getting a hundred percent on the rest of your tests and quizzes, I suggest you mark a couple answers wrong intentionally, just so you don't look too suspect."

"Good lookin'," I said as he passed me a palm-size cheat sheet.

"Already," Stretch said. "I'll be over there to holla at y'all boys in a minute."

When we walked into Fresh's room, a viciously funky odor

lurked. It was thick, humid, sticky and reminiscent of Lawry's morning breath. I tried to hold my own breath and make sure I didn't open my mouth. Lawry broke the uncomfortable silence.

"Damn, shawty," he said, plugging his nose. "Why the hell does it smell like old bus seats in here?"

"That's my roommate, folk," he said. "He weighs about two hundred pounds, but he's barely five feet tall."

"If that was my roommate, I would make homeboy wash his ass," Lawry said.

"It's not that he ain't clean," he said, reaching in his drawer for some Glade to spray. "He takes showers. He's just got a lil' odor to him. I don't think he can help it."

The Glade did the trick temporarily, but Fresh's spot was clearly not the room to get drunk in. You didn't need a drink to get nauseous up in that piece.

"Your boy Stretch is the man, though," I said. "He's got the hookup on a little bit of everything, huh?"

"Yes, sir," Fresh said. "He'd probably be able to stack some serious bread if he didn't have to support his habit."

"I never would've thought he was a smoker, with him being a hooper and all," I said.

"Oh, I don't know if he smokes weed or not. But he drinks like a fish. I don't even know how he keeps his stash stocked. Ever since I've known him, he's had a drink in his hand—even in class."

As if on cue, Stretch stepped through the door.

"Y'all boys ready to do this?" he asked as he hoisted the pint of Grand Marnier high in the air.

"Fa sho," I said. "But let's shoot back down to the first floor. Y'all are hot as fish grease up here. Plus, the R.A. on my floor is cool."

After sitting around the washer and dryer drinking, shooting craps and talking shit for about an hour or so, I'd learned a lot of things I didn't know about my new friends. All of us had stories to tell about the cities we were from, and how we ended up at U of A.

"I would have went to a D1 school to play ball, but my grades were fucked up," Fresh started. "In high school, instead of going to class, me and my niggas would roll up a fat sack, get blowed and go to Frenchy's to eat fried chicken before practice. My grades were always just good enough to play, but that shit came back to haunt me when I started looking for a college to go to. I just transferred from Houston Community College. I'm supposed to be a sophomore but some of my credits didn't transfer, so I'm a freshman credit-wise."

As Lawry crouched to shake the dice up in his hand to roll them, I noticed the R.I.P. tattoo with T-Love written in cursive underneath it on his right shoulder again. He was wearing a wife beater, which left it exposed and easy to read. Normally, I wouldn't have asked him about his tat in front of other people, but the Grand Marnier had my mouthpiece going.

"That tattoo is tight, family," I said. "Who is T-Love?"

Lawry looked hesitant to comment, shifting his body uncomfortably. His hand stopped shaking and he swallowed a big gulp of Grand Marnier.

"That's family business," he said, looking me in my eye. "But since we gonna be going to school with each other for the next four years, and y'all my patnas, I consider y'all my extended family."

Lawry had never looked or sounded this serious since I'd met him.

"I ain't even supposed to be here right now, shawty," he said. "Three years ago, me and my cousin Tyrone—we call him T-Love—we was moving work out of this trap in Decatur. We had ounces of that hard white pumping every hour on the hour. The money was coming so fast I thought about dropping out of school to hustle full-time. Everybody in the hood knew we were in the game coming up. Two years ago, on Halloween, three niggas kicked our door in wearing those white ghost masks."

He stopped to take another swig of the Grand Marnier. Usually, when somebody takes a gulp as big as he did, their facial expression would frown up a little bit. But he didn't twitch.

"When my cousin saw that all of them were strapped, he punched the window out with his bare hand and shoved me out. That's when them pussy-ass boys started firing. They only hit me once, in my stomach," he said, pulling up his wife beater to show us the quarter-size bullet entry wound just under his right rib, then turning to show us the exit wound in his back.

"Luckily, the paramedics found me before they did, and that bullet went in and out," he said.

He finished his cup of Grand Marnier and his eyes became slightly teary. "They got my cousin, though. When they took him out, they got a piece of my heart, shawty. It was rough. But like I said, at the time I wasn't even planning on going to college. It just so happened that my pops and Dr. Broadlax were line brothers when they were in undergrad at Boward, so he pulled some strings and got me in."

"I didn't know your pops is Greek," Fresh said. "What frat is he in?"

"He's a Q-dog."

"I can't picture Dr. Broadlax pledging Omega Beta Phi," Fresh said.

"Whoever Dr. Broadlax is, if he got Lawry into school after all he went through, he must have pull around here," I said. "Who is he?"

"He's the school president," Lawry said. "I know you haven't had a chance to read the whole First Year Seminar book yet, but damn! I'm gonna need for you to know who the school president is."

"I haven't had a chance to look through it yet," I said.

"You couldn't have," Stretch said, laughing. "His face is on the very first page."

Stretch kept the stories going, as he schooled me on the ingredients of sizzurp—the purple drink that Houston rappers boast about in their songs. Until our conversation, I had no idea that "lean," "bar," or "drank," as he called it, was actually liquid codeine mixed with Sprite.

"I'm trying to tell y'all, man," Stretch said. "We be going hard in the H, fool! You think you getting fucked up on this Grand Marnier. Boy, you wouldn't know what to do if you were on that lean. I'ma put y'all boys on, one of these days. As a matter of fact, if y'all come down to the Bayou Classic with me for Thanksgiving break, I'll have some down there."

"You know somebody down there who sells it or something?" I asked.

"My cousin does," Stretch said. "He's supposed to meet me down there and ride back to the A with me to get off a couple of pints down here. So you know we gonna be pouring up some drank on the road."

"You talking about the Bayou Classic in New Orleans, right?"

"Already."

"How you getting down there?"

"They got a party bus going for like two hundred and fifty bucks. It covers everything from your hotel room to tickets to the game and all that. I'm gonna ride back with my cousin, though."

"Man, I wish I had the bread to get down there with you," I said. "I'm probably gonna be right here in the A, eating over at my uncle Leroy's crib."

"Not me!" Fresh said. "I'm headed back to the Chi for Thanksgiving. I need me some home cooking."

Fresh told us about where he and his homies kicked it on the West Side of Chicago. He talked about how he inherited his pimpin' persona by watching the real pimps on Kedzie Street, bragged about how many people show up at the Taste of Chicago, and told us about how much he missed getting the wings with mild sauce at Harold's Chicken and coming up on females at the Regall Theatre.

"Let me ask you something, blood," I said. "If you so in love with your girl back home, why are you always talking about coming up on other breezies all the time? I mean, if your girl didn't call you every ten minutes, I wouldn't even know you had one."

"Man, it's like this, joe," he said. "I love my girl to death. I mean, she's been down since day one. But I look at my girl like chicken."

"What you mean, blood?" I said, laughing.

"It must be finger-licking good," Stretch said, cracking up.

"Stay with me, y'all," Fresh said. "Don't get it twisted. Chicken is my favorite dish, but there's only so many ways to cook it. I mean, after you've had fried chicken, baked chicken, barbecue chicken, chicken strips, chicken noodle soup, lemon pepper chicken, buffalo wings, chicken nuggets, chicken fettuccini, jerk chicken—"

"Damn, Bubba Gump!" Lawry said, interrupting him. "What is you trying to say, shawty?"

"Every once in a while, a nigga wants a piece of steak, or a pork chop, or a fillet of salmon!" Fresh said. "Every now and then, a nigga just wants something different. Not to say that I don't appreciate my lady, because I do. As a matter of fact, she's coming down for homecoming next week."

"Coming down for *homecoming?*" Stretch asked. "You bringing sand to the beach, ain't you?"

"Nah, joe," Fresh said. "If anything, she's a beach ball."

"So you're gonna order chicken strips at the all-you-can-eat buffet, huh?" Stretch said, laughing.

"That's why I'm glad I can order off of any menu I want," I said. "There just isn't as much to choose from in the Town as there is out here."

"What y'all do for fun out there in the Bay?" Fresh asked.

"In the Town, everybody gets hyphee at the sideshows on the weekends," I said, reminiscing as if everyone else knew exactly what I was talking about.

"What the hell is hyphee?" Lawry asked.

"Getting 'hyphee,' 'going dumb,' 'getting stupid,'" I said. "I guess it's the same thing you guys call getting 'crunk.' Basically, getting hyped. You know?"

"I got you, shawty," he said. "That's a new one for me. Never heard it before."

"Anyway, like I was saying, the sideshows are off the chizzle! We be riding mustard and mayonnaise scrapers, going stupid, doing figure eights in Mustang 5.0s and Camaro Z28s at the Pac 'N' Save on 106th. We don't do sideshows as much as we used to because the rollers be booking niggas for smoking up the block. But when we do, it's always crackin'!"

Just as my words trailed off, and my daydream about my city faded out, Dub-B's neck swung around the corner. He gripped the wall, hiding the rest of his body behind the corner, and spoke in a whispered tone.

"Yo, any of you guys seen V-Man?" he asked in such a low voice it was hard to hear him over the rumbling of the dryer. His face was a pinkish-red, his fingers trembled along the wall and he looked like he'd seen a ghost.

"Nah, joe," Fresh said. "Why?"

Instead of answering, Dub-B instantly disappeared back around the corner, before reappearing with Jasmine. Like most girls who snuck into the dorm, she was disguised in baggy clothing. But even with a hooded U of A sweatshirt on, there was no hiding those Alicia Keys look-alike braids coming from under her ball cap. We all laughed as she came running around the corner. Well, everybody except for Lawry. The sight of Dub-B ushering the girl he called his "wifey-to-be" to the door turned his face to stone.

"Hurry up, ma," Dub-B whispered as their speedwalk transcended into a slow jog.

"Nah, slow down, shawty," Lawry said, hopping down off the dryer, clasping her wrist as she attempted to whisk by. "Don't you think you've got some explaining to do?"

"Explaining?" she asked, rolling her eyes, before looking down at her wrist in his hand, and looking back at him like he was crazy. "Explain what? If anything you need to explain why you're grabbing me by my wrist."

"Yeah, I think you need to take it easy," Dub-B said.

"I've already told you to stay in your place, Wonder Bread," Lawry said as he pointed a finger in Dub-B's face with one hand and released Jasmine's wrist from the other. "This ain't got shit to do with you. This is between me and my girl."

"*Your* girl?" Dub-B asked, looking dumbfounded at Jasmine.

"*Your* girl?" Jasmine asked, looking at Lawry with the same expression on her face. "I see you've been drinking, but you must be drunk if you think I'm your girl. It's not even like that between us. I don't even look at you like that. We're just friends."

I knew that one hurt. If there's one thing that can hurt a man's pride more than anything, it's a woman he wants to be with telling him they're "just friends." In all honesty, there's nothing too friendly about that gesture. That comment alone probably hurt more than the fact that his "wifey-to-be" was getting her walls painted white.

"Just friends, huh?" Lawry asked, in a solemn tone.

"Yes, just friends!"

Damn, she did it again, I thought.

"Now, if you'll excuse me, I've got to go," she said.

"Oh, so it's like that, shawty?" Lawry asked.

"Yeah, it's like that," Dub-B said as he looked down on Lawry, grabbed Jasmine by the waist and bent the corner.

Once again, it was up to me to change the subject. I wish I would've thought of a smoother transition.

"Damn, I knew she was cute, but I had no idea she had an onion booty!" I said as her rear end jiggled down the hallway.

"You ain't lying!" Fresh said. "What the hell is an onion booty anyway?"

"That's an ass so fat it could make a grown man cry."

Everyone except for Lawry chuckled. Stretch shook his head back and forth in amazement.

"That boy Dub-B is all right with me," Fresh said. "That boy cold for pulling ol' baby."

"I ain't really feelin' your boy Wonder Bread," Lawry said, with a tinge of hatred in his voice. "Ol' pussy-ass, Jon B. wannabe, *Cry Me a River*-ass boy. He's gonna get his. Mark my words, shawty. I got something for ya boy!"

All of us fell out laughing. Stretch laughed so hard, Grand Marnier came running out of his nose.

"You still mad at Dub-B for jappin' on you that day when we were all outside on the stoop?" Fresh asked.

"Ain't nobody even thinking 'bout that, shawty."

"I know you ain't mad at Dub-B for coming up on Jasmine. If you wanted that, you should've had your game tight."

"It really ain't got nothing to do with her," Lawry said, lying through his teeth. "Girls like her come a dime a dozen. There's just something about that Wonder Bread I really don't like. It's like he's tryin' to be something he ain't. But since the white boy wants to be brown, I'ma help him with that."

"How you plan on doing that?" Stretch asked.

"You'll see," Lawry said.

Our conversation was broken up by the sound of a group of guys who sounded like the Harlem Boys Choir, chanting "We are the Men of Marshall Hall…M-O-M-H" over and over again. That was followed by a series of synchronized stomps and hand claps. Fresh checked his watch for the time.

"It's damn near two o'clock in the morning, joe," he said. "Who's making all that noise?"

"The Marshall Hall step team must have just made it back from practicing over there in the parking deck," Stretch said.

"How you know we got a step team, blood?" I asked.

"My roommate is on it. I'm surprised you haven't heard them practicing every night for the past week. They're actually back pretty early tonight."

"What are they practicing for?" Fresh asked.

"The freshman dorm step show is next week during home-coming."

"I heard that shit be crunk too," Lawry said.

"I heard homecoming is going to be off the chain this year," Stretch said. "Everybody's been talking about it on the yard. I know y'all boys going to that coronation, right?"

"What's that?" I asked.

"That's the formal homecoming ball," Stretch said. "This lil' broad I'm talking to was telling me about it. She said everybody be dressed up, but it goes down. She said that's the best part of homecoming besides the concert."

"You bought your ticket yet?" Fresh asked.

"Already. It's free, though. All you gotta do is show your ID card to the lady at the homecoming booth in the Student Center."

"Say that then," I said.

"I'm all over that tomorrow," Lawry said.

"Me too," Fresh added. "I got a suit that's figna kill 'em."

I didn't doubt it.

Just as we were about to head back to our rooms, I peeped Lester walking down the hall toward us. When I spun around to tell Lawry to hide the bottle, I accidentally bumped his elbow, knocking the bottle of Grand Marnier out of his hands. It shattered all over the floor.

"Damn," I said, spinning back around to see if Lester saw what had just happened.

Surprisingly, he looked just as embarrassed as I did. He was standing side by side with a short, dark-skinned guy wearing pink Fendi shades and a matching purse.

"Just go on to my room, Norm," Lester said, giving his little friend a slight nudge. "I'll be there in a sec so we can finish working on the routine for the step show."

As his friend proceeded to walk away, switching harder than any of the girls on campus, Lester turned his attention toward us.

"What you boys still doing up?" he asked.

"That's what we need to be asking you, shawty," Lawry said, with a snicker.

"I see y'all been drinking without me," Lester said, avoiding Lawry's subliminal joke. "Don't worry, as long as you clean up this broken glass, I haven't seen anything. And neither have y'all. Cool?"

"Sure," I said jokingly. "We'll keep it on the *down low,* brotha."

"Speaking of down low," Fresh said, looking toward me. "What's up with your roommate? I never see him around anymore. I mean, he's always been a little off, but I ain't seen him at all the last couple of weeks."

"Me neither," I said. "But I'm not complaining."

At that moment, Timothy came walking out of the room, as if on cue. He was wearing a freshly starched dress shirt, khakis and some penny loafers. He hurriedly locked the door behind him and turned to walk away, stepping over the spilled alcohol and glass, without ever acknowledging us.

"Speak of the devil," Fresh mumbled.

"What's crackin', fam?" I asked.

He turned around as if he'd heard a ghost. That's when I noticed he was wearing sunglasses.

"Oh, hey, J.D.," he said nervously. "What's up, fellas?"

"I'm out, y'all," Lawry said as he dapped everyone up and headed toward his room. "I'm figna throw on some clothes so I can go over to Winfrey Hall and borrow this study sheet from shawty round the way."

"I need to be doing the same thing," I said. "Where you headed, Timothy?"

"I've got a study session I'm headed to," he said.

"At this hour?" Stretch asked.

"Honors courses can be quite difficult," he said. "Courses such as First Year Seminar and Comparative Religion are a breeze, but I find microeconomics to be rather challenging. I need all the studying I can get."

"Where you studying, Jamaica?" Stretch asked, laughing.

"Yeah, what's up with the shades, blood?" I asked.

"I visited the optometrist earlier, and he dilated my pupils, so he recommended I wear these protective glasses today," Timothy said hurriedly. "I'd love to stick around and chat, but I've gotta run, guys."

"You going to a study session without your Bible?" I asked.

"I don't need it for this one," he said, "but thanks for your concern."

Just as he turned to walk away, Lawry's door swung open, and he came out dressed in attire similar to Timothy's, except his shirt was wrinkled. Like Timothy, Lawry hurried toward the front door.

"Hot study, buddy?" Fresh asked as Lawry stormed down the hallway.

"Something like that," Lawry responded.

Stretch looked at me. I looked at Fresh. Fresh looked at Stretch. Then all of us shrugged our shoulders.

"I know I've had a few," Stretch said. "But is it just me, or was there something wrong with that picture?"

"I'm telling you, blood," I said, "Lawry and my roommate have been acting really funny lately. Both of 'em have been going to late-night study sessions for some class they're taking. And it's not like Timothy to go anywhere without his Bible—especially a study session."

"What's the big deal about him studying without a Bible?" Stretch asked.

"I'm telling you, that dude never makes a move without his Bible, blood. I think he takes it with him when he goes to shower. It just ain't like him to leave the dorm without the Good Book. But then again, it ain't like him to fall asleep in class either, but just the other day I saw him nodding in biology."

"As much as you be knocked out in class, I don't know how you saw anybody else fall asleep," Fresh said.

"Yeah," Stretch said. "You were probably dreaming that. I

got three classes with your roommate and I ain't never seen him fall asleep."

"I'm telling you, that fool was knocked out, family. Snoring like he hadn't slept in days. Well, actually, he always snores like that. But I'm telling you, he was sitting in the front row looking bad."

As we were sitting around trying to get to the bottom of things like some off-duty private eye detectives, I felt my phone vibrate. When I checked it, I saw that I'd missed a call from Kat, but she'd left a message.

"Aaah, shit!" I said.

"What it do?" Stretch asked.

"A nigga got a call from Kat about fifteen minutes ago. She left a message too."

"Who?" Fresh asked.

"Katrina, nigga!"

"You talking 'bout fine-ass Katrina from Dr. J's class?" Stretch asked.

"Yes, sir!"

"If she's calling at this hour, you already know what it is, joe," Fresh said. "You better call her back."

"Let me check this message first and see what she's talking about," I said, pressing the speakerphone button on my cell, as the fellas huddled around listening to the message.

"Hello, James. This is Katrina. I was just giving you a call to see if you still wanted to get together to study. You know that research paper is due for Dr. J's class next week, and we have another quiz coming up in biology... Well, I know it's kinda late, so if it's not past your bedtime, give me a call back. 'Bye."

"Past your *bedtime?*" Stretch asked, nudging Fresh, as the two burst out in laughter.

"Ha, ha, ha!" I said sarcastically. "Laugh now. That was an inside joke. Y'all wouldn't know nothing about that. On some real shit, though, what y'all think I should do?"

Without looking at one another, Fresh and Stretch, sounding like K-Ci and JoJo, sounded off in union.

"Call her!" they said.

After giving it a little thought, catching Kat on the rebound in her moment of vulnerability didn't sound like a bad idea. Besides, I figured, I had some studying to catch up on anyway.

"How much did you say you were letting that blue diamond go for?" I asked Stretch.

"For *that* mission," he said, "you can *have* one."

CHAPTER 14

UPPERCLASSMEN DORMS

Kat met me outside of Heritage Hall, the upperclassmen dorm she stayed in. She was wearing a U of A halter top exposing her toned abs, some sweatpants and had her hair pulled back in a ponytail. Still, everything about her was sexy—from her fragrant Victoria's Secret perfume to her Coke-bottle shape. When the elevator stopped on her floor and the door opened, my heart skipped a beat. She could've taken me right then and there. My mandingo was on full throttle. When I stepped out of the elevator, I peered out of the window to my right to get my bearings. We were right down the street from the Shack. I could vaguely see the smoke rising from the chimney at Marshall Hall on the other end of the campus. I surveyed the area, making sure there weren't any R.A.s in the vicinity. Then I remembered I was in an upperclassmen dorm. They didn't have to abide by visitation hours like we did.

"C'mon," she said, tugging me by my arm. "You can sightsee when we get to my room."

"That's just what I was thinking," I mumbled under my breath. I didn't think she heard me, but apparently she did.

"You are such a little freak."

"Hey, I told you I was a Scorpio."

"How could I forget?"

Kat stayed in room 312 at the end of the hall. When she opened the door I immediately became envious of how she was living. She had a nice-size living room area with an entertainment system, a TV that couldn't have been any smaller than forty inches, a small kitchen and a refrigerator. The room really wasn't that large and the accommodations weren't five-star, but her place seemed like a luxury suite compared to the shoe box I was living in.

"Damn," I said, looking around. "This is all you?"

"Nah, I've got three roommates."

Her living quarters shrank all of a sudden.

"But this is all me," she said, opening the door to her bedroom. It was about the size of my half of the room in Marshall Hall. But after sitting down on the edge of her bed and looking around the room, I had to admit it was comfy. But more importantly, her room was bombarded by sensual undertones. From the pink and green candles surrounding the pictures on her nightstand to the soothing echo of the water from her plug-in waterfall fixture splashing against the rocks at its base. Not to mention the pink satin pillows at the head of her bed, and her alarm clock radio tuned in to the slow jams station.

"Is it hot in here, or is it just me?" she asked.

Where I'm from, that line is a trick question. If it were as cold as the North Pole, I would've told her it was burning up, if it meant clothes coming off.

"Yeah," I said. "Y'all got the heat blasting in here."

"Well, I'm going to slip into something a little more comfortable, and we can get started studying."

"What could be more comfortable than a halter top?" I mumbled to myself after she'd left the room.

The minute she left the room, I got up to take a closer look at the four pictures on her nightstand. The framed five-by-seven photo of her hugged up with Downtown-D at the coronation didn't surprise me. Neither did the picture of her with her parents at her high school graduation. For the record, her mama was fine too. She could've easily passed for an older sister. The third picture was an eight-by-ten of her standing with the other members of the University of Atlanta royal court. She was standing right next to Miss U of A, wearing a pink gown and a white sash that read Miss Junior. On the edge of Kat's desk, next to a basketball trophy, was a picture of her with some of her line sisters in a pink and green frame.

I wasn't trying to be nosy, but she'd left her top drawer open, so I closed it for her, because I felt like that was the right thing to do. But before I closed it I took a peek inside. There had to be at least fifty pairs of sexy underwear in that drawer. No grandma big bloomer panties, either. I'm talking about lace thongs and silk jump-offs—all of the essential get-it-crackin' garments. When I stuck my hand inside the drawer to move aside a pair of panties that were prohibiting me from closing it, my fingers ran across a hard, steel item that couldn't have been lingerie. At first, I thought it might have been something freaky, like a whip or a dildo. After checking behind me to make sure she wasn't coming, I pulled the drawer open a little wider to find out just how freaky Kat was living. What I saw stunned me. Kat was packing not only the entire Victoria's Secret fall line, but a chrome-plated 9mm revolver with an onyx handle. I quickly shut the drawer and jumped back on the bed. With that type of artillery, I certainly wasn't going to be pulling any fast moves on Kat tonight, or any time soon for that matter.

When she returned, she was rocking some sexy U of A shorts that stopped inches from where her thighs began.

"I love what you've done with the place," I said sarcastically, as if I'd been there before.

At that point, I was desperate to try anything to keep my eyes from focusing directly on her dreamy, exposed legs, which she had obviously just taken the time to lotion up.

"I know my room is small," she said. "You don't have to rub it in."

"On some real shit. You got it hooked up in here with the little pink and green theme going."

"If you think this is something, check this out," she said, clapping her hands twice. On the second clap, the bright light on the ceiling dimmed and changed color to lime-green.

"Oh, boy!"

"You like that?"

"Fashigity."

"I thought you would," she said, sitting down on her bed right next to me. "Hey, I just noticed something."

"What's that?"

"You kinda look like Larenz Tate," she said, smiling from ear to ear. "Has anyone ever told you that?"

"All the time."

"Yeah, I bet. You probably get over on all the little freshmen girls with that look, huh?"

"Sophomores, juniors, seniors, recent college graduates..."

"Oh, you got it like that, huh?"

"I don't know. I guess that depends on whether or not you like Larenz Tate?"

"*Like?* Have you seen *Love Jones?* Boy, Larenz Tate is sexy as hell."

"So I guess that means..."

"That means it's still a little hot in here," she said, fanning herself. "I could use a drink. How 'bout you?"

"I've already had one or two," I said. "But what you sippin' on?"

"I would make some pink panties but I don't think we have all of the ingredients. I think there's a bottle of white Zinfandel left in there."

"Hook it up," I said.

She came back from the kitchen with two wineglasses and the entire bottle of white Zinfandel. She had trouble opening the bottle with the corkscrew, so I gave her a hand. I stood close behind her, leaning in just enough for her to feel the bulge in my pants graze her apple bottom. I know she felt me. But she wasn't trippin'. An uncomfortable female would have scooted to the side, but she stood firm. I gently placed my left hand on her hip and covered her right hand with mine. I tightened my grip on her hand, twisted the corkscrew and popped the cork. There was something unusually erotic about the sound of the cork popping and the light mist that arose from the bottle.

Somewhere between talking about atoms and neutrons, and downing our first glass of bubbly, Kat and I began to discuss life. She told me about her favorite seafood restaurant in Atlanta and I told her that I preferred chicken and waffles. We talked about our biology professor's African accent and terrible toupee. I told her that I was majoring in business management because I hadn't figured out exactly what career I wanted to pursue. She told me that the only reason she chose criminal justice as her major was because her mom wanted her to be a lawyer. She said that if she had her choice, she would have majored in fashion design and try to land a job as a stylist to the stars, because she loved to shop.

"You seem kind of high-maintenance," I said.

"Let's see, I get a manicure, pedicure and my hair done once a week. But I don't know if I would call myself high-maintenance. I just like to look nice."

Two glasses of Zinfandel later, Kat began to open up. I don't know how we got on the subject, but she started telling me about her ideal man. The more she talked, the more it sounded like she was describing Downtown-D.

"I don't usually date guys who don't have a car," she said.

"So you don't think your future husband could have a bus pass in his wallet right now?"

"I doubt it. That sounds like the kind of guy who asks me to go to the movies, and then asks me to cover him because he *forgot* his wallet. My future husband is probably driving a

Benz right now. Don't get me wrong, it's not that I'm superficial. I just know that I'm a good catch. I'm the president of our APA chapter, I have my own car and I have good grades. I just want my man to be equally yoked. I don't think that's too much to ask."

Half a bottle of Zinfandel later, I became liberal with my questions. "What's up with you and Downtown-D? Is that your guy?"

"He *was* my boyfriend, but he didn't know how to act, so it's over between us. I mean, don't get me wrong, I loved that boy with all of my heart. I guess that's always been my problem. When I fall in love, I fall hard."

"That's not always a bad thing."

"When you're blinded by love, it can be. True love can make you naive, to a fault. I would've done anything for Deiondre. But this time, he just pushed me over the edge. A woman can only take so much. You know that saying, 'You never know what you've got until it's gone'?"

"What about it?"

"Deiondre is about to find out what that really means."

"So, was he the only guy you were talking to?"

"That all depends on what you mean by talking to. Yes, Deiondre was the only person I was having sex with at the time. But I have male friends."

"Damn, how many guys have you had sex with?"

She hesitated. "Only four."

I remembered what this pimp who used to work over by my high school told me about how to figure out how many guys a girl *really* slept with. He said that however many guys a female tells you she's slept with, multiply it by two to get the real number. Considering my past, eight wasn't so bad.

"You always use protection?" I asked.

"I used to until I started dating Deiondre exclusively. He's the only person I've ever had sex with without a condom. But he was my boyfriend, and we were monogamous for three years. I wasn't worried about getting pregnant because I was on birth control the whole time. Lord knows, I've got way too much going for me in my life for me to have a baby now. Come to think of it, even though he was my boyfriend, I shouldn't have even had unprotected sex with him. You've got to be careful who you sleep with down here."

"Who are you telling? I definitely ain't trying to have no kids no time soon."

"*Kids?* Shoot, if my parents even *thought* I was having sex with anybody, both of them would be on *America's Most Wanted.*"

"Your parents are on you like that?"

"Are they? My parents are overprotective times a hundred. I couldn't even go on a date until I was a senior in high school."

"That could be a good thing. If you weren't having sex, at least you didn't have to worry about catching something."

"*Catching* something? Please. I don't know what I'd do if somebody gave me an STD. I'd probably have to kill 'em."

"Oh," I said, rubbing my chin. "So that's what that strap in the drawer is for, huh?"

"How do you know there's a gun in my drawer?"

"I saw it when I was looking at the pictures on your desk."

"Oh."

"You got beef like that?"

"My daddy is the captain of the Athens Police Department."

"So he gave it to you?"

"He taught me how to shoot if I have to," she said, laughing. "But that gun ain't even mine. Deiondre left that over here last week. He needs to come pick it up before I wind up shooting his ass with it."

"Speaking of shooting, I see you got a basketball trophy over there. You don't look like the hooper type."

"I get that a lot."

"So, what's your favorite position?"

"I played the two, but my favorite position is probably point guard."

I took another sip of my wine and went for the kill.

"I wasn't talking about basketball," I said, looking deep into her eyes.

I was attracted to her like a moth to a flame. Apparently, the feeling was mutual, because before I knew it, her lips were touching mine. After one kiss, I was convinced there was passion in her lips. While I was placing my wineglass on her desk, my tongue found its way to hers, engaging in a playful game of Twister. I took the glass from her hand, placed it on the desk next to mine and placed my hand behind her head. I ran my hand through her hair as we continued our lustful lip-lock. Our chemistry was perfect. First, she took control, slowly sucking my tongue with hers and nibbling my bottom lip. Then I took over. I kissed her softly on her neck, tenderly sucking ever so often, catering to her moans. Her familiar fragrance entranced me. She was wearing Pink—the same perfume I'd bought from Victoria's Secret for Keisha last Christmas. The scent alone made me horny. I slid my hands under Kat's shirt and ran my fingers up her spine until they found her bra strap. In one smooth motion, I'd unfastened her bra and pulled her shirt over her head. Just as I slithered my tongue from her neck to her nipple, R. Kelly's classic jam "It Seems Like You're Ready" began playing on the radio. Perfect timing, I thought. Kat was moaning every time my tongue touched her body. She was as wet as Niagara Falls, and my dick was hard enough to cut diamonds. I'd never seen breasts as beautiful as Kat's in my life. They were plump, firm and soft at the same time. They were just the perfect size—not too small and not too big. I'm generally an ass and thigh guy. I figure, once you've seen one pair of tits, you've seen them all. But I'd never seen a girl with invisible nipples like Kat's. She looked like a centerfold. I took my time, and she enjoyed every minute of it. By the end of the song, both of us were completely naked.

This was the moment of truth. In the fifteen seconds it would take for me to corral a condom from the pocket of my jeans, Kat would have time to think, which for me meant one of two things. She could become increasingly horny and begin playing with herself, as she moaned lustfully, begging me to hurry back to the bed. Or she could overthink the situation, come to her senses and realize that she still had feelings for Downtown-D, and was seconds away from giving it up too soon to a transportationless freshman who she really didn't know all too well.

I tried to kill two birds with one stone, by kissing her neck and rubbing her shoulder with one hand while slinging my other hand off the side of the bed to grab my jeans. After nearly two minutes of fumbling around with my jeans, turning my pockets virtually inside out in search of contraception, I realized I didn't have any. In my haste to get with Katrina, I'd completely forgotten to grab a couple of rubbers from my stash. This was the worst-case scenario.

"Everything okay, baby?" Kat murmured as she gently French-kissed my neck, pulling my body closer to hers.

Once again, I was faced with two options. I could ask Kat if she had any condoms and run the risk of her getting out of giving it up by shooting me the oldest line in the book—"Maybe this just wasn't meant to be." Or I could run the risk of having baby mama drama for the next eighteen years, or worse, contracting an STD, and go skinny-dipping. The choice was mine. As I pondered the repercussions, I knew the logical choice would leave me with a bad case of blue balls, and no story to tell my boys in the morning. And with Kat being the biggest safe sex advocate on campus, and arguably the best looking, option two didn't sound so bad.

"What are you doing?" she asked as she licked the back of my earlobe and cuffed my butt cheeks in her hands. "I want to feel you inside me."

With that, I decided to take my chances. My heart beating like a snare drum at a rock concert, I wiggled in between Kat's moist thighs and went to work, as Tyrese's "Signs of Love Making" played softly on her stereo. The sequence of events that followed ended as quickly as they started. There were a total of ten pumps in all. The first five thrusts were the best. My pelvis stroked her clitoris with every fluctuation. Her pussy felt like a heated glove, giving my shaft a warm squeeze every time I entered her. I was definitely in rhythm. I knew that Downtown-D would be a hard act to follow, but judging by her consecutive moans and increasing moisture, I was meeting the quota. Her sexual energy fed my ego. The second five pumps were the most intense. They were also my last five. All of a sudden, the sex began feeling too good. The glove was fastened too tight. The heat was too warm. And I was too excited. I knew that things were getting out of hand, but slowing down would have been harder than stopping an oncoming train with my bare hands. I thought about everything that I could to keep my mind off the enjoyable sensation. I imagined Michael Jordan's NBA Championship game-winning shot over Bryon Russell, the Soul Glo commercial in *Coming to America,* and that white guy wrestling crocodiles on the Discovery Channel. I even tried reciting my ABCs in my head. Nothing worked. By the tenth stroke I knew that there was no stopping the inevitable—Kat was going, and I was coming. I tried to wallow in between Kat's thighs and pretend I hadn't climaxed, but it was no use. I was as soft as sushi. She looked up at me and whimpered, looking disappointed. I couldn't blame her. Tyrese hadn't even started singing the chorus yet.

I was past embarrassed. I felt humiliated. I felt like my basketball team was down by one point with two seconds left in the fourth quarter, and I had air-balled a wide-open layup. I'd been called many things in my life, but a minute man had never been one of them. I didn't know what to say, but I knew I had to say something.

"What's wrong, sweetie?" she asked, with a slight smirk on her face.

I was hoping the question was rhetorical. But the uncomfortable silence that followed assured me she was actually awaiting an answer.

"What can I say, baby?" I said as I pulled out. "I mean, you've got that Aquafina flow. I wish you would've warned me."

"J.D.," she said, looking underneath the sheets. "*Please* tell me you were wearing a condom."

"I thought you knew I wasn't wearing one. I mean, you didn't see me put one on, did you?"

"I thought that's what you were doing all of that fumbling around for," she said, covering her face with her hands. "Oh, my goodness! You came inside me too, didn't you?"

"I didn't mean to," I said. "I was just caught up in the moment."

"*Caught up?* Look, you're doing way too much right now. I can't believe you just did that! That's not cool. That can't ever happen again."

For a second I just lay there, uncomfortable, not knowing what to say. "You're on the pill, right?"

"Yes, I'm on the pill. Thank God! But that doesn't mean… Ugh… Okay," she said, shaking like she got a chill. "Thinking about what just happened makes me nervous, so I'm going to let it go because it's just going to keep messing with my head. All I know is you better not have anything."

"I was just thinking the same thing," I mumbled under my breath.

"What did you say?"

"I said you don't have to worry about me having anything," I said.

"Well, I hope not… I don't know… Maybe all of this just happened too fast."

"Maybe you're right," I said.

"But I guess what's done is done," she said, matter-of-factly. "So, is that it? Are you finished?"

"Please, baby," I said. "That was just warm-ups. All I need is five minutes, some Kool-Aid and I'm straight. We ain't even got to the game yet."

"I can give you a few minutes. I just hope you've got more stamina come game time," she said. "If not, I might have a spot for you on the bench."

"I'm a starter, baby."

"A finisher too, I see."

"Oh, I see somebody's got jokes," I said. "We'll see who has the last laugh."

CHAPTER 15

KING OF THE CAF

My tutorial sessions with Kat had finally paid off. For one, I'd stunned her with my performance in round two. By the morning, my magic stick had her digging her nails into my back, curling her toes, screaming out loud and calling me daddy. I couldn't help smiling every time I thought about it. But more importantly, I'd scored an eighty-seven on my First Year Seminar midterm.

At first, I couldn't believe it. I hadn't seen an eighty-seven on a piece of paper with my name on it since finding out what my jersey number was going to be in Little League football, when I played wide receiver. I was so excited I folded the test in half and placed it in my back pocket, just in case I had to whip it out on somebody. Dr. J didn't say much about my test score. As a matter of fact, he didn't say anything. He just dapped me up on the way out, and nodded his head, giving me an "I knew you could do it" look. His assuredness made me think that just maybe my score wasn't a fluke after all. I couldn't help but walk out of class with my chest poked out and a million-dollar smile on my face. I bumped into Timothy on the way down the steps.

"So, how did you do on the test?" I asked.

Before he could answer, I contemplated what I'd just said. It had been so long since I'd fixed my lips to ask that question, it almost seemed surreal. The only students who ever asked that question were the ones who always made good grades. I was never one of them. I was usually the one crumbling up my test and tossing it in my backpack before anyone else could see my score.

"I'd rather not discuss it," he said.

"C'mon, man, what did you get?" I asked. "You couldn't have done worse than me."

Yet another line from the "I-did-better-than-you-and-I-know-it" smarty-pants booklet. I thought to myself, *Where is this stuff coming from?*

"If you wouldn't mind, I really would prefer not to disclose my test results with you or anyone else," he said.

"You did that bad, huh?"

"You just won't leave it alone, will you?"

"C'mon, man, I'm your roommate. You can tell me."

"I got a freakin' seventy-two!" he said, flailing his arms.

"A seventy-two?"

"Yes, seven-two! A seventy-two! For the first time in my life, I got a C on a test. Are you happy now? I mean, hell! Can you give it a rest already?"

"Easy on the curse words, man," I said with a giggle. "My bad. I didn't know you were taking it so seriously."

"I take every test seriously. I know I could've done better. It's just that I haven't had time to do anything lately. I haven't had time to eat. I haven't had time to sleep. I haven't even had time to study."

"What have you been doing?"

"You wouldn't understand, man. You just wouldn't."

"You still reading the Bible on the regular?"

"What makes you ask that?"

"I don't know. I guess because I'm so used to seeing you carrying it around everywhere. And lately, you just haven't seemed like yourself."

"Well, it's funny you should mention it, because I've been doing some thinking lately. And the more I analyze the situation, the more I think, you may have been right about what you said that day about the Bible."

"*I* was right?" I asked in disbelief.

"I think that you proposed a valid point. I've been doing a lot of research on different religions in my Comparative Religion class. And I've come to the conclusion that I should be more open-minded about different types of religious beliefs and faiths. Until now, I'd never really paid any attention to Buddhist or Muslim faiths."

"Hold up, blood," I said. "You telling me you figna be out there in the middle of the street wearing a bow tie selling the *Final Call* and bean pies?"

"I haven't exactly decided to take it that far just yet. All I know is that I feel like I've been living my entire life in a box—going to Sunday school, going to church, going to Bible study—and I'm just tired of doing the religious thing. I'd rather do it because that's what I want to do, not because it's what I'm trained to do."

"So, what you trying to say?"

"I'm just confused right now. And until I clear things up, I've decided to go easy on the Bible for now."

"You sure about that?" I asked.

"To be honest, I'm not sure about too much of anything these days," he said as he cut across the grass toward the dorm. "I'll see you around."

"Hey, before you go…" I said, scurrying over toward him. "Dr. J told me something not too long ago that really made me put my life in perspective. I was thinking it might help you too."

"What did he say?"

"He said that all progress requires change, but not all change is progress."

"Philosophically speaking, that's one of the deepest things I've heard in a long time. But what does it mean?"

"Hey, that's for you to figure out, blood," I said as I turned to walk away.

"Thanks for listening, J.D. Thanks a lot."

"It's nothing," I said as I headed toward the Caf.

Not even Timothy's midsemester crisis could rain on my parade. That day, I strutted into the Caf with the wind at my back and confidence written all over my face. I had good reason to hold my head high. The combination of my midterm results and my night with Kat made me feel like I was the man on campus, if only for that day—and nobody was going to ruin it. I'd come to terms with the possibility that I may be as close to walking in Downtown-D's shoes as I'd ever be, so I embraced it. I could feel the females watching as I glided toward the table where all of my boys were sitting. I felt like I was walking on a cloud.

"That's my guy," Stretch said with a large grin as he dapped me up.

"You a fool, blood," I said.

"On the real, though, I'm proud of you, G. You know how many guys would kill to be in your shoes right now? Didn't you see the way she was looking at you in class?"

"I already know who you guys are talking about," Dub-B said.

"You don't know shit," Fresh said.

"I'm not blind. Katrina was looking mad nice in class today. I seen her giving J.D. the eye."

"Y'all boys are wild," I said nonchalantly. "I don't know what y'all talkin' 'bout."

"I ain't gon' lie," Stretch said. "She look like she got that touch-and-bust, man. For real! I hope you took some Viagra before you hit that."

"You know a playa ain't never needed all that to keep thangs crackin'," I said, getting up from the table to go get my lunch. "I've been putting my hound hand down ever since I was ankle-high to a pigeon's thigh."

"So you hit that, son?" Dub-B said excitedly.

I didn't answer.

"You da man, kid!" he continued. "I ain't even gonna lie. I didn't know you had it in you. Your game gotta be mad tight to crack a top-notch shorty like that."

"It's about time," Fresh said. "It's damn near Thanksgiving break and J.D. is just now getting his first piece."

"Hey, I'm into quality, not quantity."

"Oh, don't get it twisted," Fresh said. "Katrina is fine as hell. She kinda looks like something I'd have on my team. I'm not hating. I'm congratulating. Shit...she got any friends? Put your boy on!"

"You're the last nigga I need to be putting on," I said. "Ain't your girl coming down from the Chi for homecoming?"

"You know it."

"You need to be worried about how you're gonna shake all the other breezies you got thinking they're wifey."

"All my hoes know their place," he said cockily. "Believe that. I only got room for one wifey, and that's Chantel. All of them know about her. That's what makes me so cool. I keep it real with them, so they can't ever say I'm leading them on. They already know what's up."

"So you're telling me Alexis knows about your girl back home?" Dub-B asked.

"C'mon now, I'm more player than that," Fresh said. "You know me. I don't chase 'em, I replace 'em."

"So she does know about your girl back home?"

"Nah, but that's only because I ain't told her yet," Fresh said. "Besides, she stays in the dorms over at Elman, so even when my girl comes down to visit, she will never find out."

"Doesn't she kick it with a few girls who go here though?" I asked.

"Yeah," Fresh said. "She has a cousin who stays right next to our dorm in Turner Hall, but I'm telling you, she will never know a thing."

"Hold up," Dub-B said. "What happened to *'I tell all my hoes up front'*?"

"Like I said, I just ain't got around to it yet."

"All that time y'all be spending together outside on the stoop, up in your room, and you ain't had the time to tell her?" I asked.

"Look," he said defensively. "She knows what she needs to know for now. I'll cross that bridge when I come to it. I mean, damn! Y'all ain't got nothin' else to worry about?"

"Actually, I do," I said. "I need to be looking over these cheat notes I got from Stretch, so I can get right for this biology midterm later. If a nigga don't pass this, it could be ugly for your boy."

"You've got the answers," Stretch said. "How hard can it be?"

Even though I had the answers to the test, I found myself going through the same pretest routine I'd performed since middle school—nervously nibbling my cuticles, looking around for someone to borrow a pencil from, and my trembling knees slightly rattling my desktop.

Timothy was sitting in the desk behind me, looking like he hadn't slept in days. His eyes were puffy, his hair was matted and he smelled like onions. I'd never seen him look so rough.

"Need a writing utensil?" Timothy asked, passing me a mechanical pencil. "I've got plenty."

"Good lookin' out, blood," I said. "What's wrong with you? Why are you looking so tired?"

"Long study session last night," he said, shaking his head. "I'm prepared to ace this exam, though. I'm almost certain I've studied everything."

Just as my palms were beginning to clam up, I felt a reassuring hand on my shoulder. It was Katrina.

"You'll do fine, baby," she said, bending down to whisper in my ear. "Just take a few deep breaths, focus and remember the things we studied."

I figured that was easy for her to say. She knew biology better than Ike's fist knew Tina's chin. Plus, her seat was toward the back of the class. Mine was right in the front. This wasn't the first test I'd cheated on, and I would've bet the thirty-eight dollars in my savings account it wouldn't be the last. But since it was my first time cheating in college, I figured I had to be extra cautious. As soon as Professor Obugata passed me my test and Scantron sheet and walked by my desk, I quickly looked around to make sure the coast was clear, then slid my answer sheet out of my pocket and underneath the test.

"Don't write anything until I tell you," he said. "Everybody should start this exam at the same time. You have fifty minutes to complete this midterm exam. It's worth twenty-five percent of your grade."

I felt a frog form in my throat. I was almost sure I could pass my other classes, but biology was the big question mark. Even though I'd dropped twenty dollars to secure a quarter of my grade, I still felt unsure about making the grade.

"Once you're finished with your exam," Professor Obugata said as he backpedaled down my aisle, "bring it to me, and you can go—ooohh!" he screamed as he tripped over my backpack and fell toward the floor.

The guy in the seat next to me grabbed one of his arms, and Professor Obugata grabbed on to my shoulder, to prevent the fall. But the guy in the seat next to me lost his grasp, most of Professor Obugata's weight leaned on me and my desk tumbled over, as I tried to hold him up.

With his back on the floor and legs straight up in the air, he said, "How many times have I asked you all to keep your shoulder bags off the floor?"

Everybody in the class busted out laughing like they had front-row tickets to a Comic View. Some of them laughed so hard they cried. Meanwhile, I squirmed around, trying to untangle myself from Professor Obugata, so I could get to my cheat sheet before he did.

"Let me help you with your things," he said, reaching for my Scantron and cheat sheet.

"I got it, Professor O," I said, my forearms battling his for possession.

"No," he said, scooting them away from me with his hand. "I insist. If it wasn't for you, I may have been seriously injured. I don't know how I will ever repay..."

He stopped in midsentence, and his eyeballs swelled. The laughter ceased.

"Don't mention it, Professor O," I said, reaching for my papers. "Just give me back my Scantron, and we can forget it ever happened."

"Not so fast," he said. "What is this?"

"What is what, sir?" I asked.

"What is this despicable piece of paper that I have in my hand right now?"

"That's a Scantron, sir," I said as candidly as possible.

"You know I'm not talking about the bubble sheet. I'm referring to this," he said, holding out the cheat sheet in my face.

"Professor, I don't know where that came from," I said, slightly trembling.

"I do," a voice behind me said.

"Who said that?" Professor Obugata asked. "Who is responsible for bringing this funny business into my classroom?"

"I am, sir," Timothy said, standing up.

My jaw almost hit the floor. Timothy was the last person on earth I would've expected to ever take the rap for me. I was floored.

"Well, I'll be..." the professor said, at a loss for words. "Mr. McGruden, you are one of my most prized students. What is the cause of this mischief?"

"I don't know," Timothy said. "I don't have an applicable excuse. It's just that things have been really hectic for me with my honors schedule."

"Spare me the malarkey, Mr. McGruden. You disgust me."

"I apologize, Professor."

"Well, I don't have time to accept your apology now," Professor Obugata said. "Now if you'll excuse me, I have an exam to administer to the students who took the time to study. You will receive a zero on this exam. You're free to go now."

"But, Professor," Timothy said.

"I said, you are free to go now! I'm trying to handle this without involving administration. Now please dismiss yourself from my classroom immediately."

"Let me explain," Timothy said, pleading with him. "I was just—"

"Flee!" he screamed, pointing toward the door. "Immediately!"

CHAPTER 16

HOMECOMING

The first time Todd called me to brag about how much fun he was having at homecoming up at Crampton, I figured he was probably putting a little extra tartar sauce on the catfish, embellishing his story a little to make his campus seem like it was more crackin' than mine, since his homecoming was one week before mine. But after all of the stories about the parties, the step show, the comedy show and the tales about how many fine women showed up for the pregame tailgate, I was convinced he was telling the truth.

Still, there wasn't anything anyone could've told me to adequately prepare me for the homecoming experience at an HBCU. Even though I'd been in school for two months, I was still in a state of awe when homecoming finally came around. By the amazed look on Dub-B's face, it was pretty safe to say he was feeling the same way. I don't think either of us even understood what going to an HBCU was all about until we saw the crowd of alumni gathered outside Panther Stadium on game day.

We were playing Lighthouse, the number one team in black college football, who just happened to be our cross-campus archrival. The game was so packed there wasn't an open seat in the bleachers, but it didn't matter, because the real party was going down outside the stadium. There were thousands of alumni tailgating, rockin' their old-school Greek paraphernalia. Vendors' booths cluttered the sidewalk on both sides of the street. There were people scalping tickets and vendors peddling bootleg CDs and DVDs, fresh fruit and homecoming T-shirts. Downtown-D mania was in full effect. There were people selling University of Atlanta football jerseys with Number One on the front and Downtown-D on the back, and game programs with his autograph on them.

After freeloading drinks and barbecue chicken from each of the frat houses, I headed over to the game with Dub-B to see what this Downtown-D hype was really all about. When I finally got inside, I spotted Fresh sitting in the bleachers sharing some nachos with his girl. Stretch was sitting on the other side of Fresh, tossing back his signature "water" bottle.

"What's crackin', y'all?" I asked.

"Man, y'all late as hell," Stretch said. "This boy Downtown-D is going hard."

"Yeah, he's going off," Fresh said. "Have I introduced you to my girl?"

"Nah, I've never met her," I said, extending my hand.

"Chantel, that's J.D. from Oakland," he said. "And that's my guy Dub-B over there."

"It's nice to meet you both," she said, with a smile.

By the time I looked up at the clock, there was only twenty seconds left in the game, and U of A had the ball near the fifty-yard line. We were losing by six points and needed a touchdown to win the game.

"I think I seen your girl in here, joe," Fresh said.

"Who?" I asked

"Katrina, who else?"

"It ain't like that just yet, blood," I said. "Where's she at, though?"

"Ain't that her right down there?" he asked, pointing a couple of rows down.

I looked down and saw a girl in a pink and green APA jacket. She was hoisting up a double-sided sign that read Downtown-D for MVP on one side and had a huge number one on the other. When the girl turned around to talk to one of her sorority sisters, I did a double take. I would've bet my refund check the girl riding Downtown-D's jockstrap was just some starstruck freshman. I was trippin' when I realized that the girl riding Downtown-D's bandwagon was indeed Kat. I wouldn't have expected that from her—especially after she'd told me that the two of them were "on the rocks."

"Yep, that's her all right," I said, slightly embarrassed.

Everyone in the stadium looked like they were holding their breath, waiting for Downtown-D to work his magic. They didn't have to wait long. He dropped back to pass, ducked underneath a Lighthouse linebacker gunning for his head, hopped over another diving at his ankles, spun away from an onslaught of raging defenders and threw a perfect spiral off his back foot to an open receiver in the corner of the end zone for the game-winning touchdown with no time remaining on the clock. Lighthouse players dropped to their knees on the sideline as the extra point kick sailed through the goalposts, giving U of A the 35–34 victory over our rival. Every Panther in a uniform on the sideline rushed the field, and the crowd went crazy. Their thunderous applause quickly gave way to an even louder, repetitive chant of "Downtown-D for MVP!"

"Oh, my God!" Stretch shouted. "Did you just see that?"

"Yeah," I said, gazing at Katrina, who looked elated. "I saw it."

Downtown-D took his helmet off and cockily stood on the sideline with his left hand on his hip, while holding up number one with his right hand high in the air. Maybe I was trippin', but for some reason it seemed like I could hear Kat cheering louder than everyone else in the stadium. She held her sign up high and jumped for joy like she'd won the lottery. Everyone in the stadium was happy. But for an average fan, she seemed overjoyed.

If someone would've asked me, at the start of the semester, which homecoming event I thought would be most memorable, I probably would've guessed either the football game, the coronation ball, the concert or maybe even the dorm step show. But I would've been wrong. I was chilling in my room, ironing my suit for the coronation ball, with my door open and music blasting, when the unforgettable took place.

"Okay, so who did it!" I heard a guy in the hallway scream at the top of his lungs. "C'mon, B, whoever is big and bold enough to do some nasty shit like this needs to fess up!"

Even with my Dr. Dre CD blasting, I could make out an East Coast accent that couldn't belong to anyone but Dub-B. When I walked out into the hallway to see what he was hollering about, I laughed so hard I damn near hit the floor. Dub-B was dripping wet, with a white towel wrapped around his waist, but was covered in runny, brown shit from head to toe. He smelled and looked like he'd accidentally fallen into a toilet, just after someone had taken a number two. He was so mad he was damn near crying. And so was I, because I was laughing so hard. I tried to hold it in, but I couldn't help it.

"Just admit it!" he said, in front of a growing crowd of hysterical onlookers. "Who in the hell is nasty enough to take a shit in their own hand and wipe it on each and every one of the showerheads in the bathroom? That is fucking disgusting, kid! Y'all better hope I don't find out who did this! Word to my mother, yo! That's some foul shit!"

Literally, I thought, as he walked toward the steps, boo-boo squishing in between his toes with his every step. No one could even think to take Dub-B's threats seriously. All anyone could do was laugh. The second Dub-B cut the corner, Lawry came running out of his room, laughing his heart out.

"Ha, ha!" he screamed. "I told you I was gonna get that boy!

Now that tattoo on his arm that says white chocolate really means something!"

"You a fool, blood," I said. "You gotta have some serious problem to even think to do some shit like that. I'm going to try to remember not to shake your hand for a while."

"Hey, shawty thought he was the shit anyway, right? All I did was make sure he lived up to it. Now he'll be the shit everywhere he goes. Hell, he can't help it!"

"Man, that had to be the funniest thing I've seen in hella long, blood. You're wrong for that."

"He had it coming," Lawry said. "But enough about that. I need to borrow your ironing board."

"Where you been at lately?" I asked. "How you just gonna pop up out of the blue on the night of our coronation ball, smearing dookee on showerheads and asking a nigga for his ironing board?"

"Man, I've been so busy studying for them midterms I ain't had time to do too much of nothing else," he said. "But speaking of your ironing board, that reminds me, I'm going to be needing your starch too."

"You're something else," I said. "The starch is over there in the corner next to the ironing board. I'm figna have to start charging you a fee, blood. You're killing me."

"Killing *you?*" Lawry asked. "You should be ballin' out right about now. Didn't you just get a refund check back for about a stack and a half?"

"It wasn't even a whole stack," I said. "It was only nine hundred dollars. And I've got to stretch that money out for the rest of the semester. I've gotta use that on everything from Christmas shopping to laundry money. Come to think of it, why are you all up in my checking account anyway?"

"All I'm saying is, if I'd gotten back that much money from my student loans, I wouldn't be trippin'."

"Cut the crap," I said. "I ain't ballin'. I'm falling. I need to be asking you if I can hold something."

I had to go up to the second floor to take my shower. After I hopped out, and threw on the light gray suit my mom had bought me for Easter several months ago, I headed over to Lawry's room. His door was closed, but I didn't bother knocking. I just walked right in. When the door flung open, it hit the ironing board, knocking his freshly pressed black slacks to the floor.

"My bad," I said, bending down to pick them up.

To my surprise, Timothy was in his room sitting on Lawry's bed, tying his shoe. He looked startled when I busted in. He quickly scurried to the floor to help me pick up the slacks, as if they were his.

"Damn, shawty!" he said, scrambling to his bed, seemingly trying to hide something. "You could've knocked."

When I picked the pants up, I noticed that they were way too big for him. They looked like they belonged to Stretch. Upon further investigation, I noticed that Lawry had over ten pairs of black slacks neatly folded on his comforter. Each pair of slacks had a freshly pressed white dress shirt and a gold bow tie laid out just above it.

"I'll take those," he said, grabbing the pair of slacks out of my hands.

"What's up with all the black slacks and dress shirts? You trying to run a bootleg cleaners?"

"I couldn't figure out which suit to wear, so I ironed all of 'em," he said nervously.

"What's the truth, cousin?"

"It ain't nothin', shawty," he said, nonchalantly grabbing his keys and passing me a fifth of Armadale. "Let's get out of here."

After Timothy helped Lawry neatly place each slack-and-shirt combo in separate garment bags, he threw them over his shoulder and we dipped out.

"You riding with us tonight?" I asked Timothy as we walked down the hallway.

"I suppose," he said. "Lawry told me that it would be a good way for me to get my mind off of that zero that I got on that biology midterm."

"Speaking of that exam, I've been meaning to thank you for that," I said. "I mean, you're a real nigga for looking out for me like that. I didn't know you had it in you."

"Well, I saw that you were in trouble," he said. "And I figured since my average in the class was around a ninety-eight, I could afford to take a fall on one exam. Especially since you're going to need to pass that class in order for you to come back next semester."

"That's what I'm saying," I said. "I mean, what made you do that for me?"

"I know we haven't been best friends or anything, but you are my roommate and I want to see you graduate. Besides, that advice you gave me after I screwed up on that First Year Seminar exam really helped me out."

"What did I say again?"

"You told me that all progress requires change, but not all change is progress."

"Oh yeah, that's right. I sure did kick that knowledge, didn't I?"

"Yeah, man. And hey, without it I might still be lost. For a second there, I was losing my religion. I was drifting pretty badly. I think I was receiving too many different doctrines at the same time, so I began to get confused. But for some reason, when you said that, it helped me put things in their proper place. And for that, I'm eternally grateful. So I figured I kinda owed you one. And at the end of the day, that's what brotherhood is all about, right? Stepping up for one another."

"Well, thanks a lot, *brotha*," I said, wrapping my arm around his neck. "We need more like ya!"

When we got outside, Fresh was standing in the parking lot, holding his girlfriend's hand. When I got close enough to see the green and gold tuxedo he was wearing, I laughed so hard tears came to my eyes.

"What's so funny?" he asked, as he pulled a brush out of his coat pocket and began stroking his waves.

"Oh no, the hell you didn't, shawty," Lawry said.

"I knew y'all wouldn't recognize pimpin' when you seen it. Man, my uncle Bishop Don Magic Juan gave me this suit. He wore it at the BET Music Awards show when he was onstage with Snoop."

"Well, keep it pimpin', then, pimpin'," I said as I downed my first cup of Armadale.

"You guys ain't figna be snappin' on my man like that," Chantel said, playfully pushing Lawry.

"*Your* man?" someone screamed from one of the windows in Turner Hall. "We're gonna see about that, bitch!"

"Let's get outta here," Fresh said, stuffing his brush back in his pocket and opening Lawry's back door.

"Who was that?" Chantel asked as she unscrewed the back of one of her earrings.

"Probably just a hater on some ol' bogus kick," Fresh said as he gave Lawry a look that said, *We need to get outta here right now.* "We ain't even figna be out here long enough to find out."

No sooner had Lawry stuck his key in the ignition than Alexis was standing outside Fresh's door, knocking on his window, trying to get him to roll it down. Chantel, who was sitting in the middle of the backseat, sandwiched between Fresh and me, was busy unscrewing her other earring. Fresh, obviously out of his element, locked his door and calmly asked Lawry to just pull off. After a few unsuccessful attempts to crank up the engine, it was clear Lawry's bucket was going to need some special attention to get up and running.

"It looks like I'm gonna have to get up under the hood and tap the starter first," Lawry said with a sigh as he got out of the car, locking the door behind him.

By that time, Fresh was sitting with his hands on his head and a blank stare on his face as his ladies exchanged verbal blows.

"What does that bitch got that I don't?" Alexis asked.

"Lamont Thelbert Mitchell! You'd better start talking quick, or somebody is 'bout to get their ass kicked!" she said. "You know I don't play that!"

"So if that's your girl, what am I?" Alexis asked.

"Well?" Chantel said, nudging Fresh with her elbow. "Who the hell is she?"

"Nobody," Fresh said.

"Lamont, if she is nobody, why the hell is she standing outside acting all crazy? And why are you just sitting here with your hands on your head? And why won't you let me out?"

"Just chill until Lawry gets the car going," Lamont said, sinking into his seat, taking a deep breath.

"You know, for you to be so *fresh,* you're full of shit, Lamont!" Alexis said, banging on his window with her fist.

"Hey!" Lawry said, poking his head around his hood. "I don't know what y'all got going on, but this is my car, shawty! You gonna have to be easy on my windows, baby."

Paying Lawry no mind, Alexis continued her tirade.

"I should've known something was up when you weren't answering the phone the past few days," she said. "And I'm tired of talking through this window. Why don't you get out of the car and be a man?"

Before I could blink, Chantel had hopped over the front seat and opened Lawry's door. Timothy tried his best to grab her, but once she knocked his glasses off, he was more concerned with finding them than holding her. By the time Fresh unlocked his door, the two girls were already nose to nose.

"So, how is it that you know *my* man?" Chantel said.

"To be honest, woman to woman, I didn't even know you existed," Alexis said. "I mean, me and Lamont have been fucking since we first met at orientation, and he never even mentioned you."

"That's strange because he didn't mention you, either," Chantel said, looking at Fresh.

"Alexis is lying, baby," Fresh said. "I wouldn't ever do you like that. I know you don't believe her."

"Well, somebody better believe somebody, because we're running late," Lawry said as he slammed down his hood. "Let's ride!"

"Wait a minute," Chantel said. "Alexis? That's your name?"

"Uh-huh," Alexis said.

"Does your number start with 404-555, something?"

"Yep," she said.

"Babe, everybody's phone number on this campus starts out like that," Fresh said.

"I'm in love with you, but I'm not that fucking naive," Chantel said. "When I was looking through your phone the other day, and saw all of those calls to A Lexus, you told me that your mom was thinking about helping you buy a Lexus next semester. But the whole time, you were really calling her?"

"I was going to get the car, but he wanted too much for it," Fresh said, stumbling over his words. "Plus, the mileage was too high."

"Stop lying to me!" Chantel said as she burst out crying. "I've been putting up with this shit since high school. I can't keep going through this with you, over and over again! I just can't."

"Well, one thing is for sure," Alexis said, just before she stormed off. "*Your* man can forget about ever hitting *this* pussy again. I don't even have time for trifling-asses like you."

The ride to the coronation ball was long and quiet. Aside from the fact that Lawry's radio was broken, Chantel hadn't made a peep since we'd left the parking lot. She just sat with her arms folded and lips poked out, making us all uncomfortable. The only thing that broke the silence was the fact that instead of rolling straight to the ball, Lawry made a few questionable pit stops along the way. First, we stopped by an upperclassmen dorm on the other side of campus, where he and

Timothy reached in the backseat, grabbed half of the garment bags and ran inside. They returned empty-handed.

"Who do you know up in there?" I asked.

"A couple of niggas I went to high school with," Lawry said.

"So who were all the suits for?"

"They play in the school orchestra..." Lawry said, seemingly pausing to think up the rest of his sentence. "I mean, somebody I went to school with is having a funeral. I'm the only one with a car, so when I picked up my suit from the cleaner's, I just picked up my homeboys' suits too. Damn, you nosy as hell, shawty!"

"You got us on a bogus mission, though, folk," Fresh said. "I've never known you to be so friendly. They got you runnin' errands like Jeffrey on *The Fresh Prince of Bel-Air*."

"I think the shuttle is still running," Lawry said sarcastically. "It's probably picking people up over in Elman's parking lot right now. If y'all want me to drop you off, I can."

Fresh and I looked at each other and busted out laughing. I had to keep it going.

"I know you trying to get your boys their suits and all that, but now can we make it to the party, Benson?"

"I got two more stops to make," he said as we pulled into an apartment complex right around the corner from campus. Again, he reached in his backseat, and grabbed a couple of garment bags, and Timothy helped him take them inside. At that point, I was so faded I didn't even ask any questions.

The last apartment we pulled up to was in the projects right across the street from Lighthouse. Again, Lawry and Timothy reached in the backseat, grabbed the last two garment bags and took them inside. Even though I was so tipsy I could no longer feel my face, I'll never forget the expression on Lawry's face when he came running out of the apartment toward the car, without Timothy. He looked like he'd seen a ghost.

"Man, shawty," he said, nervously rubbing his hands together, looking away from the car to avoid making eye contact with us. "We ain't even gonna be able to make it tonight. We're just gonna post up here over my boy's crib."

"What you mean, y'all can't make it, blood?" I asked.

"I can't really explain it right now, shawty," he said. "But look, y'all take my keys and roll down there. J.D., you done had way too much to drink already, so you just stay your ass right there in the backseat. Fresh, just follow this street all the way to Peachtree and hang a left. If you go down about three blocks, you'll see the spot on your left. You can't miss it."

"You sure you all right, folk?" Fresh asked.

"I'm straight. Y'all boys just make sure you put the pimpin' down for me. I'll holla at y'all tomorrow," Lawry said as he turned and ran back toward the apartment.

"Your boy Lawry and your roommate are on some 'ole other bullshit, G," Fresh said, before hopping out of the backseat to get behind the wheel. "I don't know what's up with them."

"Me neither," I said, taking another swig.

By the time we made it to the Convention Center where the coronation ball was being held, I'd already taken three cups of Armadale to the head. But I believe it was the fourth cup that really put me over the edge. At that point, I was liable to say or do anything to anybody.

After being patted down by security at the door, we walked down a red carpet into a huge ballroom of beautiful women dressed to kill. I smiled from ear to ear as I looked at females shake their bodies on the dance floor as if they were in street clothes instead of expensive gowns. I felt like I was at prom all over again. I was just about to take a walk around the dance floor, when I saw Katrina standing near the bar with a few of her girlfriends. She looked so good in her tight black dress from far away, I couldn't tell if she was wearing it, or it was wearing her. Without saying anything to Fresh, I staggered over toward her for a closer look.

"What's crackin', baby?" I asked, extending my hand toward hers. "Aren't you looking bootylicious this evening?"

"Well, thank you, sir," she said, looking me in my eye and flashing her Colgate-commercial-perfect smile. "You're looking quite suave yourself. J.D., let me introduce you to my—"

Kat's sentence was cut off by a voice with a Southern twang, coming from behind me.

"Damn, you didn't even tell me I looked good tonight," he said.

When I turned around and looked up, it was none other than Downtown-D, hulking over me.

"You are looking very handsome this evening, Deiondre," she said.

"You really think I'm looking fly in my suit?" he asked.

"Yes, Deiondre," she said. "I think you're looking fly in your suit."

"It's funny, but when I was looking in my mirror before I left the house, I was thinking the same thing," he said. "You look good too, baby."

"Thanks, Dre," she said.

"Well, now, that's more like it," he said, stepping around me, leaning on the bar. "As much as Downtown-D hates to interrupt your little small talk, he's trying to get some drinks flowing over here. You drinking tonight?" he asked.

No, he didn't just play me to the left like a sucka, I thought.

"I guess I could have a drink," she said.

He quickly motioned toward the bartender. By this time, Downtown-D had officially stolen my shine. At that point, I was just standing there, looking like a wanksta.

"What you drinking on?" he asked, smoothly grasping her by the waist with one hand and pulling her closer. "Moët? Patron? Gray Goose and pineapple?"

"Moët is fine," Katrina said.

"I'll have a glass of Moët for this beautiful young lady," Downtown-D said, gently stroking Katrina's elbow.

I couldn't just sit there and watch anymore. I figured if I wanted to prove to Katrina that I was worthy of just as much of her attention as Downtown-D, I couldn't be outdone. Since

I didn't have my own place, or a car, I figured my pride was all I had left. Once the bartender came over to pop the cork on the bottle, I stepped up.

"As good as she's looking tonight," I said, thumbing toward Katrina, "she deserves at least two glasses of Moët. Put that on my tab."

The bartender took out an extra glass, looked at me, and said, "That will be twenty-two dollars."

"No problem," I said, pulling out my fat wad of refund check cash.

"Hold up," Downtown-D said. "Make that *three* glasses of Moët."

"That will be thirty-three dollars," the bartender said, whipping out an extra glass.

"Make that *four* glasses of Moët," I said, whipping out a crisp fifty-dollar bill.

Katrina looked back and forth as Downtown-D and I went head to head, each of us trying to order more drinks for her than the other. In a matter of seconds we had worked our way up to ordering bottles of Moët instead of glasses. The more we ordered, the wider Katrina's friends' eyes got.

"I think each one of these ladies deserves their own bottle of Mo Mo," I said. "Just go ahead and put six bottles on my tab."

"Sir, that's going to be three hundred and sixty dollars," the bartender said. "Are you sure about that?"

"It's a small thing to a giant."

"Is that right?" Downtown-D asked. "In that case throw a couple more bottles on there, and throw it on my tab."

"That will be four-eighty," the bartender said, shaking her head as she bent down to get a few more bottles from the fridge.

As I stood there, contemplating whether or not my pride was worth upping the ante, Katrina chimed in with some encouraging words of wisdom.

"This is so stupid," she said. "You know you don't have to do this to impress me."

If she had stopped there, I could've easily walked away from the situation, laughing at Downtown-D for getting suckered into blowing almost five hundred dollars at the bar. But she kept going.

"I mean, Deiondre is competitive," she said. "He's not going to let you win."

"*Let* me win?" I asked in a drunken stupor. "Bartender, go ahead and ring up two bottles apiece for Katrina and her friends."

"That's going to be seven-twenty, sir," she said, with a smile on her face. "How did you want to pay for that?"

"Cash," I said, whipping out my entire wad of big-faced bills, without hesitation.

By that time, all of her girls were looking at me like I was the man. Katrina hadn't even introduced me to them yet, but I figured I'd already won them over with my showmanship and flossin'.

"This shit here is for the birds, man," Downtown-D said as he stormed off. "I'm outta here!"

"Thanks for all the drinks, J.D.," Kat said as she glanced at the twelve ice-cold bottles of Moët neatly aligned on the bar.

"Yeah," her friends said one by one, as I passed out glasses to each of them. "Thanks, J.D."

I didn't think twice about damn near blowing my entire refund check on Katrina at the bar that night. Where I would get money to wash my clothes, eat and go out for the rest of the semester wasn't important to me. I couldn't have been happier as I sat back sipping on my own glass of Moët, watching Katrina and her friends enjoying theirs. At the moment, I felt like I had just defeated Mr. Undefeated himself. Downtown-D had everything a guy in college could ever want—money, popularity, transportation, a sculpted physique and women. But at that moment, I figured I had him beat.

That moment didn't last long. One trip to the restroom ruined my entire ideology.

By the time I swung the bathroom door open, I'd damn near pissed my pants. When I looked up in the mirror, my eyes widened. I saw Downtown-D backpedaling into the bathroom, being pushed backward by a female. He was holding her wrists, but she kept her hands firmly pressed against his chest, shoving him into the first stall. I slapped some water on my face to make sure what I thought I was seeing was what I was really seeing. I was right. And Downtown-D was in the wrong. The girl he was in the bathroom with wasn't Kat. But she was a freak. As I used the urinal closest to the stall they were in, I heard Downtown-D groaning. I peaked underneath the stall, but all I could make out was the girl sitting on the toilet while Downtown-D stood over her. The smacking sound the female made with her mouth almost gave me a hard-on while I was using the bathroom. I zipped up my slacks and stumbled back to the dance floor, shaking my head in disbelief.

The more I thought about the situation, the faster the lump in my throat grew. I couldn't believe some chick was going downtown on D in the bathroom for nada, and I'd just spent my life savings on some girls I didn't know, and all I got was nada.

CHAPTER 17

UNHAPPY BIRTHDAY

Thanksgiving break couldn't have come at a better time. My classes were stressing me out, I was getting tired of eating the Cafeteria food, and ever since the shitty prank Lawry pulled on Dub-B, we hadn't been allowed to have female visitors in the dorm. V-Man suspended our visitation privileges until the guy he called the "Boo-Boo Bandit" fessed up.

Even though Kat always reminded me that she wouldn't be "caught dead" in Marshall Hall, even if we had visitation, the fact that she couldn't come over even if she wanted to further reminded her of my freshman status. Then again, if that was a problem for her, I couldn't tell. During the break, I hooked up with Kat almost every day. If I wasn't over at her place, she was chilling with me at my uncle Leroy's crib. For a week, we did everything together—the movies, the mall, the bowling alley. And when we weren't doing any of that, we were doing each other. We did it at Lenox Mall, in the dressing room at Victoria's Secret. We did it in the elevator on the way up to her room. Then we did it in the shower, once we got there. I was going through rubbers like tires at the Daytona 500. If you saw Kat, I wasn't far behind. She said she loved my spontaneity. And I loved just about everything about her.

Somehow, between our sexcapades, we even found time to study for our biology final together. The fact that I'd managed to somehow come up with a seventy-two on my midterm, without the cheat sheet, gave me the confidence that our study sessions were actually paying off. But more importantly, so was all of the quality time the two of us were spending together.

By the time we returned to school, Kat and I were officially "talking." Everyone knows that when two people are "talking," that generally means both parties are genuinely interested in each other and their feelings for one another are mutual. But the term "talking" to somebody is often used loosely, leaving an expansive gray area, and just enough room for excusable infidelity.

At any rate, being back on campus meant I was back to being "the man." There were only a couple of weeks of school left in the semester, and I had more schoolwork to do than I'd ever had in my life. I had a week to finish up two ten-page term papers that I hadn't started, in addition to studying for my biology, algebra and First Year Seminar finals. All of this pressure, with my nineteenth birthday just one day away. Luckily, my birthday fell on a Friday, so I planned on kicking it that weekend and buckling down on Sunday to study. I devised my plan while sitting in Dr. J's class, waiting to be dismissed. Since I only had First Year Seminar one day a week, that meant our class would be meeting again twice. He gave us a study sheet to complete to prepare for his test. Dr. J reminded the class of his motto, just before we left his class.

"And whatever you do, remember the five Ps," he said. "Proper preparation prevents poor performance. I know that all of you scholars have finals to study for in other classes, but I'm giving you ample time to study for this one. You've got two weeks until test time, so I don't want to hear any excuses. Now all of you scholars enjoy the rest of the week."

As I placed my notebook in my backpack, I heard Dr. J's Sidekick pager sound off. Just as the girl nearest the door was about to walk out of class, Dr. J stopped her.

"Wait," he said, a blank stare coming over his face. "Everybody have a seat."

Groans and murmurs quickly spread throughout the room. Dr. J solemnly sat on top of his desk, buried his chin in his chest and took a deep breath.

"Is everybody seated?" he asked.

"Yes," Lawry said in an aggravated tone.

"Please be patient. I know all of you have other classes to get to, but I believe your tardiness will be excused under the current circumstances."

He paused briefly, lifted his head toward the sky, then cupped his face in his hands. At that moment, I could sense that whatever he had to tell us wasn't good news.

"Look, there's really no easy way for me to say this. I just received a message notifying me that one of your classmates has passed on. He was actually a student in this very class. According to what I just heard, a student by the name of Shammond Salisbury, whom most of you all know as Stretch, passed away today."

A few of the girls covered their mouths in shock. Most of the fellas hung their heads. The expression on my face turned to stone. By the time I could think to say something, someone else in the class had already said it.

"No!" Fresh screamed.

"C'mon, man, you can't be serious," Lawry said.

"My teammate?" Dub-B asked.

"Yes," Dr. J said. "I'm sorry."

"This can't be happening," Fresh said. "It seems like we were just with him the other day. Where did this... When did... How did this happen?"

"I don't know much," Dr. J said. "All I know is that the police believe he may have been under the influence when he veered off the interstate. I don't even know how truthful that statement is. Like I said, I'm just getting this information for the first time myself. And again, I'm sorry that some of you all have lost a friend, or a classmate. Each of you is welcome to stay in here for as long as you need to."

At that point, I was pretty fed up with death. I thought that by going away to school, I'd left all of that behind me in Oakland. I'd made up my mind that I didn't want to hear about it, and I didn't want to accept it. Instead of sulking in it, I just grabbed my backpack, slung it over my shoulder and headed for the door, shaking my head back and forth in disgust. I was one step outside my door when I felt Dr. J grab me by my arm.

"J-Dizzle," he said, spinning me around. "Are you gonna be okay?"

"Yeah, Doc," I said. "I should be straight."

"Hey, man, losing a friend can be hard. Believe me. I know. But you've just got to keep pushing—if not for yourself, for them. You know?"

"Yeah, man," I said, wiping a tear from the corner of my eye. "I know."

After seeing all of the professors who came out to Stretch's candlelight vigil on campus, I could tell that most of them weren't just teaching for a paycheck. I came to the conclusion that most of them were probably there because they wanted to be. It wasn't until then, so close to the end of the semester, when I actually started to enjoy being a college student. The homework part of it never really grew on me. But for the first time in my life, going to class wasn't so bad. At the beginning of the year, my main reason for showing up was to see which girls were going to be there. But as time passed by, I noticed myself participating in the classroom discussions more often. Since I rarely studied in high school, whenever I was called on to elaborate on a topic, I rarely had anything meaningful to say. But since I'd actually starting hitting the books, I felt like my opinion actually meant something. Once they caught wind of my confidence, most of my professors encouraged me to speak my mind—but none more than Dr. J. What I respected most about him was that he stayed in my ear when I was in the wrong, but never failed to let me know when I was on the right track. Every blue moon, he'd throw in his two cents about things that had nothing to do with school.

"Hey, I don't want to hold you up," he said, one day after class. "But I just wanted to let you know that I see you coming up. You've come a long way this semester, but I knew you'd come into your own. I told you that when I first met you. Keep up the good work, man. Finish strong."

"Thanks, Dr. J," I said. "I will."

"And hey, watch yourself with those older women," he said with a laugh.

"What you mean?" I asked, looking around to make sure everyone else in the room had cleared out.

"What you mean, what I mean?" he said. "It looks like you've been doing more than just studying with Katrina."

I rolled my eyes, with a sly smile.

"It's cool," he said, giving me dap. "You ain't got nothing to hide, mack daddy. I've been in the game for a long time. Kat's a good girl. She's got a lot going for herself. I wouldn't normally suggest mixing business with pleasure, but you just make sure you don't mess up a good thing. You feel me?"

"Hey, you know I gotta make it do what it do, baby," I said.

"Well, by all means, do you, brotha. Just remember, in your lifetime you'll only get two women who will love you unconditionally. I mean, that woman who will bless you every time she hears you sneeze, wash your dirty draws and wipe your butt when you're too young or too old to do it yourself. One of them is your mama. When you find the other one…marry her."

"That's real talk, Dr. J."

"I'm just keeping it real," he said as I turned to walk out the door.

When I got to the bottom of the stairs outside, Kat was there waiting for me. She was sitting on a wooden bench just outside the door, digging through her bag. The second she saw me, she popped up, pulled me close to her and pecked me on my lips. I can't say that I'm one for public affection. Holding hands and being lovey-dovey has never really been my style. But Kat was so tight I didn't care.

"Are you okay, baby?" she asked.

"I think I'ma be all right," I said.

"Well, if you want to talk about anything, you know you can call me, and I'll be there for you."

"Thanks, boo," I said.

"Well, as long as you're okay, I guess I can get to my next class," she said, blowing me another kiss. "I'll give you a call later."

"Wait," I said, grabbing her by her wrist. "Before you go, answer this question."

"Don't you think it's a little soon to be popping the big question?" she asked, with a hint of sarcasm. "I mean, let's not rush things. We've still gotta finish school, J.D."

"Well, I guess I better return this eight-carat diamond ring I got from Tiffany's with my refund check."

"Whatever," she said, rolling her eyes and smiling. "What's up?"

"This might sound funny. But it's been on my mind since that night... Ahh, forget it. Go on to class. I'll ask you later."

"No, ask me now. I hate when people do that. If you weren't going to ask, why did you even say anything in the first place? I'm already late to class now. C'mon. Spit it out."

"Why me?"

"What do you mean, why you?"

"I'm sayin', on some real shit, you could have any dude on campus, if you wanted to. Why me—a freshman living on campus, without a whip? I mean, what got you? Was it my million-dollar mouthpiece, my smooth style, my overall studiousnessity or my magic stick?"

"Hmmm. Let me see. It definitely wasn't your hundred-dollar mouthpiece—"

"That was *million*-dollar mouthpiece."

"Can I finish? Now, where was I? Oh yeah, the ten-dollar mouthpiece… No, it definitely wasn't that. The fact that you've got a fly wardrobe was definitely a plus, but I wouldn't say that's what *got* me. I don't even think *studiousnessity* is a word, so I'm not about to even attempt to entertain that thought. And if I recall correctly, you weren't exactly Houdini the first time we got it on, Mr. *Magic Stick* man."

"Ssshhh," I said, putting my finger over my mouth. "There are people out here. Can we keep this convo between us? I mean, damn!"

"My bad," she said, giggling. "But honestly, I've been thinking about that myself. And I can't call it. I mean, you're sweet, you're cute and you treat me like I'm the most important thing in your life. I guess that's what I've been missing this whole time. You make me feel like I'm important. And I love that about you. Plus, you've always been confident, and I can appreciate that. If there's one thing I can't stand, it's an insecure man. That's the worst."

"All that's all good, but I'm sayin'…"

"You're saying what?"

"The magic stick ain't have nothing to do with it?"

"Didn't I just say I can't stand an insecure man?"

"Oh, I'm not insecure. Every now and then I just need to know that you know what you got."

"I know you've got everything I need," she said, pulling me close and pecking me on the lips again. "Gotta go to this doggone microeconomics class. It's kickin' my butt. I'll call you later, sweetie."

As I watched Kat walk away, I thought about how glad I was that we were "talking." But for me, "talking" to Kat meant I had grown feelings for her that I didn't have for any other girl on campus. Even though I'd just met her a couple of months ago, I was definitely thinking that she was the type of woman I could grow to love one day.

"Damn, I know that ass is fat but you kinda stuck, ain't you, joe?" Fresh said, throwing his arm around my shoulder.

"Look at him, yo," Dub-B said. "Son is mad pussy-whipped."

"Can you blame him, though?" Fresh asked, staring at Kat's ass switch as she walked away. "I ain't gon' lie. The Bayou Classic was off the chain! But if I had a chance to hit that, I would've stayed here over Thanksgiving break too."

I laughed, changing the subject as the four of us started walking toward the stoop.

"Where did you flip them tennis shoes?" I asked, looking down at Dub-B's crispy white Air Force Ones. "They don't even usually release the white ones until the spring."

"You talking about my sneakers, son?"

"Yeah, your tennis shoes."

"They're not called tennis shoes. They're sneakers."

"Where did y'all New Yorkers get the word 'sneakers' from anyway?"

"I don't know, but that's what they're called, son. And you can get these *sneakers* up north all year round."

"Those *tennis shoes* are the truth, blood," I said as I started to walk away.

"Where you headed, folk?" Fresh asked.

"To the ATM across the street at the Student Center."

"I could've sworn you went broke tricking off at the club before we left," he said. "Is what's her name paying your pockets too?"

"Nah, Moms slipped a nigga a lil' bit of cheese for his birthday."

"Today is your birthday, kid?" Dub-B asked.

"It's tomorrow."

"Oh, your birthday is on Friday?" Fresh asked. "We've gotta hit the club!"

"You already know!"

CHAPTER 18

IN THE CLUB

We were stuck in traffic, about ten minutes away from the club, when my heart shattered into pieces. I was on the shuttle, looking out of my window, watching a large crowd form outside the front door of Chicken 'n' Waffles, when I saw the one thing I wish I hadn't. Downtown-D was walking from the parking lot holding Kat by her waist. He whispered in her ear, and both of them started giggling. I didn't see the humor in the situation.

I couldn't believe my eyes.

Every time Downtown-D's hands touched Kat's body, my heart burned. I watched helplessly as he wrapped his arms around her, and she closed her eyes and folded her arms over his forearms, securing his grip.

My forehead became damp with sweat.

I felt like I was trapped on the eighty-sixth floor of a burning building with no windows. I was short on wind. I tried to swallow, but couldn't. I felt like I'd been punched in the stomach and stabbed in the back at the same time.

I didn't want to look, but I couldn't blink.

All of a sudden, my imagination began taking me places

beyond reality. I saw everything in flashes. I could see Downtown-D running his tongue across Kat's nipples. I could see him thrusting Kat on her back, lifting both of her legs with one hand and removing her panties with the other. I envisioned her slowly unbuttoning his jeans with her teeth, grabbing his manhood with two hands and placing it in her warm, wet mouth. I could see her caressing his balls with her hands, while licking up and down his shaft, then flickering her tongue across the top. The vision was surreal. It was as if I could actually hear her moan as he grabbed her by her soft ass, lifted her up and placed his bare shaft inside her warm glove. I could hear her calling his name over and over again. I cringed at the thought. My eyes teared up. My moment of despair was brought to a halt by a strong tug on my shoulder.

"J.D," Fresh said, tugging on my shoulder. "J.D.! C'mon, folk. What's wrong with you?"

"I must be trippin', blood," I said.

"Must be. I've been calling your name for the last two minutes, joe. Snap out of it. We're at the club."

"Let's do the damn thing," I said in a grim, low tone.

I tried not to wear my emotions on my sleeve, but I couldn't hide 'em. I didn't cry, but my anger was written all over my face. While everyone else on the bus took off on an all-out sprint to secure a spot in line, I slowly lugged myself toward the club with my head down. Fresh and Dub-B were the only two who waited on me.

"C'mon, fam-o," Fresh said. "Why are you dragging?"

"It's Katrina, blood."

"What about her?"

"I just saw her outside Chicken 'n' Waffles with Downtown-D. He was all hugged up with her...in front of my favorite restaurant!"

"You can't turn a ho into a housewife, kid," Dub-B said.

I must've looked at him like I was about to take his head off, because he walked behind me and stood on the other side of Fresh.

"So he took her out for dinner," Fresh said. "What's the big deal?"

"I don't think you're hearing me, fam. He had his hands all over her."

"He's Downtown-D. What do you expect?"

Fresh wasn't helping the situation by playing devil's advocate. Apparently, he knew that I was beginning to get fed up with his insincerity, because he quickly tried to change the subject.

"My bad, man. I'm just trippin' off how much you're feeling this girl. It's usually the other way around. They say a man can fake a relationship like a woman can fake an orgasm. You believe that shit?"

Fresh wasn't doing a very good job of taking my mind off the subject. I didn't say a word.

"I wouldn't trip if I was you, though," he continued. "I know the type of nigga you are. Ain't no slackin' in your mackin' and ain't no slippin' in your pimpin'." He patted me on my back. "I know you ain't about to let no brizzle ruin your birthday. I ain't even figna sit back and watch you turn in your player card like that, joe. We figna go up in here and juke with some dime pieces."

"I hear you talking," I said as we blended into the middle of the line. You would've thought they were giving out full scholarships to the first five hundred people, because we were a good football field away from the door—and standing in the male line. The female line was moving fast, but ours was at a standstill.

"To be honest, I really don't feel like standing in this long-ass line," I said. "I don't even know if I'm feeling this club thing at all. By the time we get to the front, they're gonna be charging fifty bucks to get in."

"Don't you see all the females waiting to get in this club? We're halfway to the front. We can't turn around now."

"You know they figna be charging hella, though, blood."

"If it's fifty bucks, I'll pay your way, folk. This latex party looks like it's juking."

"Why do they call it the latex party anyway?" Dub-B asked.

"Because the flyers look like condom wrappers," Fresh said. "Plus, everybody from Louisiana and Texas gets in for free with their IDs."

"I didn't even see the flyer for this party," Dub-B said. "I know it's probably gonna be bananas in there!"

"Man, this shit is for the birds, cousin!" I said. "Y'all can stay, but I'm outta here. Where's Fats?"

"Why is he bugging out?" Dub-B asked Fresh.

"Don't worry about all that," I said aggressively. "Where is he?"

"Whatever the problem is, it ain't that serious," Dub-B said. "Be easy. It's gon' be all right. I saw Fats hop out the back window as soon as the shuttle pulled up to the club. I think he did that so he could beat everybody to the front of the line."

"I'm ready to get outta here," I said.

"Personally, I feel like we've been waiting in this line way too long to even think about leaving," Fresh said. "But it's *your* birthday, joe. And since we came together, we're leaving together. Let me run in and get Fats."

"Hurry up, blood," I said.

We waited fifteen minutes for Fresh to come out of the club. He never did. So I decided to send Dub-B inside to find Fats and Fresh. After thirty minutes of standing outside waiting for the fellas to come back out, something told me they'd given up the search. I figured if I was going to be standing outside shivering, I might as well be warm, inside having a drink.

The club was separated into two floors—the DJ upstairs was only playing music by Louisiana artists, while the DJ on the bottom only spun songs by Texas rappers. Even though the party was crackin', I wasn't in a dancing mood. Besides, there were so many people in the club, you didn't even have to be dancing to work up a sweat. Just walking from one side of the room to the other would leave you drenched.

Finding Fats and the rest of my crew was like searching for

a needle in a haystack. By the time I'd rounded up Dub-B from the dance floor, the DJ was announcing last call for alcohol. That was right before he made the most embarrassing announcement of the night.

"If you're a freshman, and your mama ain't picking you up, and you ain't got no damn car, you better get outside because the last shuttle is figna leave yo ass! Last call for the shuttle!"

The freshmen without cars tried to play it cool, acting like they all had to go to the bathroom at the same time, when they were really rushing to catch the last shuttle. I wanted to go upstairs to find Fresh and Fats, but there were so many people rushing down the staircase it looked like somebody upstairs had started shooting. I stood on the steps with Dub-B, waiting on Fats and Fresh to come down. The DJ had finished playing another song before I saw Fresh and Fats running down the stairs.

"C'mon, joe," Fresh said, running past me. "We're about to miss the last shuttle back to campus!"

I hurriedly followed him outside. When we got to the parking lot, we had to pump our brakes. There were way too many fine-ass females in the parking lot to let them see us running for the shuttle. So we speed-walked instead. Except for Fats. He ran so fast you would've thought he was being chased by a police dog.

"I thought you were going in to find Fats," I said to Fresh as we tried to walk as fast as we could to catch the bus.

"I was. But you see...what happened...I spotted him. Then—"

"I ain't even trying to hear that shit, blood," I said, cutting him off.

By the time we made it out of the parking lot our speed walk had turned into a light jog. When we saw the bus close its doors our light jog turned into a fifty-meter dash. Just as we made it to the bus, it pulled off. But Fats was determined to catch it. He surprised all of us when he jumped up and held on to one of the windows on the bus. He was holding on for dear life, kicking his feet, trying to pull himself up as the bus pulled away. Everybody in the parking lot was cracking up laughing—from the bouncers to the people who were mad they'd missed the last shuttle.

"Oh, hell naw," Fresh said, pointing at Fats. "It's never that serious."

Just when it looked like Fats had gotten his footing and was about to heave himself into the bus, it picked up speed and he lost his grip. He was dangling off the bus with one hand for about half a block before he went flying off the side. He looked like an Olympic gymnast. First, he tumbled. Then he rolled, curling himself into a ball and tucking at the end. Everybody outside busted out laughing so loud you would've sworn Dave Chappelle was performing in the parking lot. Fats popped up quick and started walking back to the parking lot like nothing happened. But I knew that shit had to hurt. Other than a small hole in the knee of his blue Dickies, two buttons missing from his shirt and his hands being scraped up, he looked fine. But if I'd had a camcorder, I could've won a million dollars on *America's Funniest Home Videos* with that shit. I don't think I've ever laughed that hard in my life.

"I almost made it, cuz," he said, breathing hard. "I guess we gotta walk back to campus now."

We tried not to laugh in his face, but none of us could help it. I couldn't even look at him without cracking up. Our laughter infuriated him even more.

"Y'all thinking shit is funny now, cuz. But that walk home ain't no joke."

CHAPTER 19

ICING ON THE CAKE

The walk home from the club was long and quiet. Mostly because the club was about three miles away from the campus, it was about four o'clock in the morning and I didn't have shit to say to the clowns I was walking with.

"What's your problem, kid?" Dub-B asked.

"I just ain't feeling social right about now, blood."

"You've been flashing on us all night," Fats said. "What's wrong, cuz?"

I didn't want to talk, but I couldn't hold it in any longer. We were walking through the projects, three blocks away from campus, so I thought I'd better let them have it before we got back to our dorm.

"I can't believe you just asked me what's wrong," I said. "What's wrong? Everything is wrong. What's happened to us tonight that was right?"

"You can't be this mad about missing the shuttle, cuz," Fats said. "Is all of this really just about Katrina trying to play you?"

"Honestly, that probably has something to do with it," I said. "But looking for y'all for two hours in that hot-ass club didn't help. Neither did missing the shuttle. Come to think of it, this has just been one of my worst birthdays ever. It's like, what else could go wrong, blood?"

Cue more drama.

"Shut your bitch-ass mouth and stick your hands up, shawty," a muffled voice said.

"It's way too late at night to be playing games, blood."

"Didn't I just tell you to shut your fucking piehole, shawty?" the voice asked in a more serious tone.

"Lawry, where the hell you been at all night, blood?" I asked, spinning around slowly. "You need to quit playing like that."

Once I saw that Lawry was nowhere in sight, I froze up and closed my eyes. I hoped that when I opened them I would roll over on my pillow and awaken from a bad dream I was having. But this was no dream. I was staring down the barrel of a .40-caliber Glock, and we were getting jacked. The rest of the guys had stopped walking about five paces ago. Fats and Dub-B were standing at gunpoint, with their hands in the air. Fresh had already taken off his shirt, kicked off his Jordans and was ripping off his jeans as fast as he could. There were three guys dressed in all black, wearing black ski masks. They sounded like they were from Atlanta and all of them were strapped.

I heard one of the guys say, "You know what the fuck this is, white boy. Strip!"

Dub-B turned red. He was in his boxers and wife beater in about five seconds flat.

"You too, shawty!" the dude standing with his gun aimed at my hat screamed. "And take them earrings off too, fuck boy."

I tried to move but couldn't. I wasn't trying to be a tough guy. I was in shock. I grew up in one of the toughest hoods in Oakland, and I'd never been robbed. I couldn't believe I hadn't even been in Atlanta for four months and this shit was happening to me. I was stuck.

"Oh, you wanna play the hard role?" the guy said, cocking the hammer back on his strap. "I got an itchy trigger finger, nigga! Take that shit off! I want everything too—from your hat to your shoes. Break bread, bitch! And hurry your punk ass up." He flipped my hat off my head with the barrel of his gun.

As I slipped out of my brand-new jeans and kicked my Timbs to the side, I gazed down the street at the fellas. They were all on their knees with their hands on the back of their heads. One of the armed robbers was picking up all of their clothes and putting them in a large, black, plastic garbage bag. The other guy kept the fellas in check by waving his gun over their heads. It looked like they were preparing to murder them execution style. By the time I'd slipped off my last garment, I was convinced I wasn't about to go out like that.

"You thought I forgot about them earrings, huh?" he said, popping me in my temple with the butt of his gun.

I felt a stream of blood trickle from the side of my head as I fell to the ground.

"Not my earrings," I mumbled.

"Unscrew them mufuckas before I leave you lifeless! I should blast your neck off, throw your head in the bag and unscrew them mufuckas myself!"

I could barely see. The shot to my temple jarred my equilibrium. For a second I didn't even know where I was. But judging by his voice, dude was seriously about to kill me. Somehow I had the sense of mind to unscrew both of my earrings and lay them on the ground next to me.

"That's what I'm talking 'bout!" he said as he scooped the earrings in his hands and scattered into the dimly lit backstreets of the projects. "I'm figna be bling-blinging now, ya bitch, you!"

I'm from the hood where this type of thing happens all the time, so I know that the best thing to do in these types of situations is to play dead until it's cool to get up. I closed my eyes to keep the blood from seeping into my eye. I lay there shaking, with the tip of my head submerged in a puddle of mud until I felt a bunch of hands grabbing at me. At first, I shivered and started throwing wild punches, until I figured out that it was just Fresh and the rest of the guys trying to help me up. I found my cell phone lying in the middle of the street. I don't know how it got there, but I picked it up.

The four of us walked to Marshall Hall in our underwear, trembling. They had taken Dub-B's socks. None of us said a word. Dub-B walked straight into the Public Safety Office to file an incident report. The rest of us staggered back to our rooms. I felt like I was at my lowest point. But I was happy to be alive.

CHAPTER 20

THE FAULTY PHONE

I came back to my room and went through Timothy's first-aid kit in search of a Band-Aid. Luckily, the gun had barely pierced my skin, so the cut wasn't too bad. The worst part was the swelling. The side of my face was on sweezy, and my head was killing me. When I found the Band-Aid, I grabbed a couple of aspirin tablets too. I went into his emergency water supply and *borrowed* a bottle of Dasani to wash the pills down. I thought he would wake up when he heard me rumbling through it, but he was knocked out—snoring like a bear as usual. Except this time, for some strange reason, he was fully dressed in a suit and tie. After I'd applied the bandage and taken the medicine, my knees buckled. I was so tired I crashed down on my bed. Bad mistake. The impact of my body hitting the bed made me feel like I had just been hit in the head with a gun again. Timothy's obnoxious snoring problem didn't make things any easier for me. Just as I turned out the lights, the phone rang right next to my ear. Timothy had to have turned the ring volume up to the highest level, because it sounded like an elementary school bell. I didn't want to answer it, because I was dizzy and didn't feel like talking. But every time it rang, the dizziness worsened and my head pounded harder. I answered in a groggy "Why the hell are you calling here so late?" tone.

"Hello?"

"J.D.?" a soft voice asked.

"Yeah. Who's this?"

All of a sudden, Timothy popped up out of his sleep and jumped to his feet. It scared the hell out of me.

"Is it for me?" he asked, in a panicked tone. "Are you sure it isn't for me?"

For a second I sat there, looking at him like he'd lost his damn mind.

"Nah," I said, taking the phone down from my mouth. "It's for me."

"Oh, okay, then," he said, crashing back down onto his bed and instantly falling back to sleep. I always thought the dude was weird, but now he was taking his squareness to the next level. He was irking me. By the time I got back on the phone he was snoring again.

"H-e-l-l-o?" the person on the phone asked, sounding annoyed.

"Who this, blood?"

"It's Katrina, *blood,*" she said, mocking my slang.

I hadn't heard from her all day. I couldn't believe she had the audacity to even call my room.

"I'm sorry I didn't get a chance to talk to my baby on his birthday. I called you tonight because I wanted to do something, but you didn't answer your phone."

"Is that right?" I asked, trying to keep my composure. "Are you sure you called the right guy? I had my cell phone on all night and I didn't see your name on the caller ID."

"Oh, you know what happened? I put your dorm room phone number in my phone as the primary number to call. So that's the number I've been calling. I don't know what I was thinking. What did you end up doing?"

"I went to the club. How about you?"

"I had to help my grandmother move some of her things into her new apartment."

I figured today must be "everybody lie to J.D. day" or something, because she had turned into a compulsive liar—fabricating the truth for no reason. Who helps their grandmother move on a Friday night? Just thinking about her trying to get over on me was turning my headache into a serious migraine.

"I am so sorry we didn't get a chance to hook up, boo. Happy belated birthday anyway. You're going to have to let me make it up to you."

"Am I?" I asked sarcastically. Just when I was about to blow a fuse and tell her how sloppy her game was, somebody called on my other line. I clicked over.

"Hello?" I asked.

My mom answered in an excited voice.

"J.D.?" she asked.

"Hey, Mom."

Before I could finish, she started singing in her loudest choir voice. "Happy birthday to you! Happy birthday to you! Happy birthday, J.D.! Happy birthday to you!"

Something told me she had no idea I had a splitting headache or it was damn near five o'clock in the morning in Atlanta. You would've thought I'd just arrived at my third grade surprise party or something.

"Hold on real quick, Mom," I said, clicking over to give Kat a formal dismissal. The events that followed are questionable. I knew that cordless phone like the back of my hand. I could dial my Social Security number flawlessly without looking if I wanted to. And to this day, I believe I removed the phone away from my face and pressed the flash button on the phone to click over. But it was dark, and my eyes were closed. Apparently I hadn't when I thought I had. I just went off, holding the phone away from my mouth so I could get my aggression off my chest without being interrupted.

"Yeah, about that opportunity for you to make things

up...you should be good at that—you've been making shit up all night! I should've known not to fuck with no bootsie-ass ATL bitch like you in the first place. I should've treated you like what you are...a piece of loose-ass, weekend, groupie pussy. You can't play a player. But since you wanna kick game, you can kick rocks too!"

By the time I'd finished ranting and raving, my head was killing me again. I brought the phone back to my ear to hear her reaction.

"Excuse me!" an upset voice groaned.

I popped up into an upright position. Either I was tripping or the person on the other end of the line sounded just like my mom. I removed the phone from my ear, ran my hand across my face and put the phone back up to my ear.

"Hello?" I asked, returning to my drowsy voice.

"Excuse me! This is your *mother,* J.D.!"

"How long have you been listening?" I asked.

"Long enough to know that you done lost your damn mind! Who the hell do you think you're talking to?"

"I'm sorry, Mom. I'm gonna explain in a second. Hold on for a quick sec."

I put my head down and shook it back and forth. This birthday kept getting worse and worse. This time when I clicked over, I made sure. "Hello...Kat?"

"Yes," she said, sounding irritated.

"This is my mom on the other line. I'ma holla back when I get around to it."

Waiting a long time for somebody to click over and then getting hung up on by them is the worst. I figured it was the least I could do.

When I clicked back over my mom was still mad. After I'd explained my situation with Kat, she was a little more understanding.

"I'm gonna let you slide with all that street talk on your birthday," she said. "But you shouldn't be disrespecting women like that. I don't care what she did to you. I didn't raise my son to treat women that way."

I didn't want to tell her about the jacking incident, because I didn't want to worry her. But I've never been good at hiding things from my mom. So eventually I broke down and told her. I knew she'd overreact.

"Oh, my God!" she screamed. "My baby! Are you okay? Do I need to fly down there?"

"I'm cool, Mom. I'm just mad they got my earrings, my ID, and all my birthday money."

"You don't worry about that stuff, J.D. Those are material things. You can get all of that back. You need to be thanking God them no-good niggas didn't take your life! Did you call the police?"

"For what? They ain't gonna do nothing about it."

"You'll never know if you don't file a report. Now, do your mom a favor and go to the police first thing in the morning."

"All right, Mom. My head is killing me."

"You need to put some ice on your head, J.D. It will help take the swelling down. And put some Neosporin on that gash to sanitize it."

"I got you, Mom."

"Well, I'm so sorry to hear about your day, baby. I just thank God that you're alive. I don't have a lot of money, but I'm gonna put a hundred and fifty in your bank account tomorrow. That should last you until you come home in a couple of weeks."

"Thanks, Mom."

"You're welcome. Now say your prayers and get some sleep. Your mama loves you."

"I love you too," I said as I hung up.

My head was hurting so bad I didn't get on my knees to pray, although I probably should have. I just leaned back, closed my eyes and thanked God for letting me live to see my nineteenth birthday. I laid my head down, nestling the good side of my face into the pillow. Just when I started to doze off, the phone rang. Again! I picked it up on the first ring.

"You've got the wrong number," I said.

"May I speak with Timothy McGruden?" a deep voice asked.

"Hey, Mr. McGruden."

"This isn't Mr. McGruden. Tell Timothy his first cousin needs to see him on the baseball diamond in six minutes!" the voice said, immediately hanging up the phone afterward.

"First cousin?" I mumbled to myself.

Timothy popped up like a lottery ball.

"My first cousin called?" he asked hastily. "Did he ask for me? What did he say?"

"He said meet him at the baseball diamond, or something."

Timothy flipped on the lights. I squinted. I watched him slip on his muddy penny loafers and head for the door in a hurry.

"J.D.!" he screamed, stopping in his tracks. "What happened to the side of your face?"

"I got chased by a dog and slipped," I said sarcastically.

"Oh, I got you," he said. "You must be on line too?"

I was too delirious to make out what he was talking about. It felt like somebody was driving a nail into the left side of my head with a hammer. "Line two? What you talking 'bout, blood? We only got one phone line."

"Forget I even said that."

I was too tired to read between the lines. I wondered where the hell he was going in a church suit and muddy penny loafers at five o'clock in the morning. But I was happy to see him go. I could finally get some good sleep.

"Hey," I said.

"What's up?"

"Do me a favor and hit the light on your way out."

CHAPTER 21

FINALS

For the first time all semester, I went a whole week without smoking, drinking or partying. I had to buckle down. In order for me to pass my finals, I had to hit the books hard, and that's just what I did. Even though Kat and I weren't on good terms, she'd helped build my confidence to the point where I knew I could do it by myself, as long as I put in the effort.

The fact that I got tired of everybody asking me what happened to my face made it a little easier to stay inside. Isolating myself enabled me to accomplish my goals and do everything I had set out to do. By the end of the week I had knocked out both of the ten-page papers I had to write and mastered the cut-and-paste technique. I'd studied every assigned chapter and skimmed through every study guide. For the first time in my life, I felt like a real college student.

My independence included blocking Kat out of my mind. I'd purposely skipped all my study sessions with her. Even though she'd been calling me all week, I refused to return her calls. My pride wouldn't let me. When I walked into my First Year Seminar class, everybody was sitting down, nervously chitchatting with their textbooks open as they waited for Dr. J to hand out the exam. I felt Kat's eyes on me the moment I walked through the door. I intentionally avoided all eye contact with her. I never even looked her way.

The outfit Kat was wearing made it extremely difficult to pretend she wasn't there. She was wearing what had to be the sexiest outfit in her closet—a light pink blouse, buttoned down just far enough to expose the string of pearls that accentuated her sumptuous cleavage. I would be willing to bet half the guys in the class marked all Ds on their Scantron answer sheets because they couldn't take their eyes off Kat's tits. I even saw Dr. J sneak a peek.

A few seconds after I took my seat, I felt someone tapping me on my arm. When I turned around, a girl was shoving a letter on my desk. I looked up and read Kat's lips.

"Please read it," she mouthed.

I never even opened it. Instead, I looked at her, looked at the letter, balled it up, looked to the trash can in the corner and shot for three. Swish! I looked at her again. She was infuriated—damn near in tears. It was hard for me to empathize with her, but I knew her pain. I figured Kat was getting a taste of her own medicine. I avoided her painful expressions by turning toward Dr. J. As he administered the exam, he told us how to check our grades online.

After finishing my test, I walked toward Dr. J's desk to hand in my Scantron. I looked at the floor all the way there, checking to make sure my shoes were tied to avoid any incidental eye contact that might have occurred along the way. When I got there, I slipped my Scantron onto Dr. J's desk, looked him square in the eye and shook his hand. It was the first time in a long while I actually felt confident turning in a test. It was as if I knew the studying had paid off.

"Thanks for the knowledge," I said. "Have a nice winter break."

Kat was sitting right next to him, staring up at me with a pouty face.

"You're welcome," he said. "And you do the same. Are you going back to Cali?"

"You know it."

"Well, be safe and remember what I told you."

"What's that?"

"All progress requires change—"

I finished the sentence for him. "But not all change is progress. I got you."

I walked right past Kat and headed for the door. When I closed it, I took in a deep gasp of air. It had taken everything I had in me not to look her way. But as far as I was concerned, I'd jumped the first hurdle. I had no idea how I would clear the next one though. I still had a biology final to take the next day, and our seats were close to each other's.

I tried to put Kat out of my mind once and for all, but she didn't make it easy for me. That night, she blew my cell phone to smithereens, leaving message after message. She told me that she needed to talk because it was an emergency. I was starting to get under her skin, but at least she knew how I felt. I wanted to call her back but figured the emergency she had to discuss was probably just another one of her lies. She had a sense of urgency in her voice on the message, but then again, she had a sense of sincerity in her voice when she told me she was *helping her grandma move* on a Friday night. I tossed and turned in bed all night, thinking about what Kat could've possibly had to tell me that had her calling my cell phone like she'd lost her mind, even though I hadn't called her back.

As I dozed off, looking across the room at an empty bed, I thought that aside from the day we took our final exam in Dr. J's class, I hadn't seen Timothy all week. And come to think of it, when I saw him in class, he was taking the First Year Seminar final standing up next to his desk. In fact, when Dr. J asked him to have a seat, Timothy damn near begged him to let him take his exam standing up. He was acting so strange I almost felt like calling his mama. For a second, I thought somebody might've slipped ol' Timmy a mickey in his Capri Sun.

CHAPTER 22

THE GRILL

"Are you going?" Fresh asked.

"Going where?"

"To the probate show."

"A pro-gay show?" I asked. "You know I ain't into that funny shit."

"You're crazy, G," he said, laughing. "I said a *probate* show!"

"I hadn't planned on it," I said as I sat down on the stoop next to him. "I really need to study for this final for my biology class tomorrow."

"You're still taking finals?"

"Yeah. I've only got one left to take, though. Thank God! Hey, what's a probate show anyway?"

"You know, when a Greek fraternity or sorority brings a new line out on the yard for the first time," he said. "It's kind of like a step show, but it's outside. I went to see the Delta Delta Thetas probate show at Chicago State last spring. It was off the chain, folk! And that ain't even an HBCU."

"Like that?"

"I'm trying to tell you, joe. They had niggas coming out of

the woodwork to see that probate show. Man, it was so packed out there I could barely see what was going on."

"They're having one tonight on our campus?"

"Yes, sir!"

"Who? The Delta Delta Thetas?"

"Nah. Alpha Mu Alpha."

"I ain't even trippin' on going to see no niggas stepping and all that," I said.

"You know who their sorority sisters are, right?"

"Nah. Who?"

"The sweet 'n' sexy ladies of Alpha Pi Alpha."

"So, what time are we going?"

"That's what I thought," he said laughing. "What time is it now?"

"Seven o'clock."

"That means the probate starts in six minutes," he said. "We need to be on our way right now."

"Where is it at?" I asked, as I followed Fresh.

"Over there in the quadrangle, next to the Greek plots."

"No wonder I've been seeing so many people walking down that way. I was wondering where everybody was going. I guess I can go over there for a minute and check it out. I've gotta get back to study for this biology test, though, blood. My final grade in that class might be the difference between whether or not I come back next semester. Hold up," I said as we walked up toward the crowd. "Are you telling me that this is the probate show?"

I'd never seen that many people in the quadrangle in my life. Mostly everybody had either a gold plastic cup in their hand or a black plate with barbecue chicken on it. I could hear the DJ's music blaring over the speakers, but I couldn't see any farther than five feet in front of me. People were standing shoulder to shoulder on the large, grassy area. Before we could make it to the grill, a huge surge of about twelve guys dressed in black three-piece suits and gold masks bulldozed the congregation of people, splitting the large crowd into two sides.

"You said you've never been to a probate before, right?" Fresh asked.

"This is my first one," I said. "What are they about to do?"

"You'll see," he said, pointing to the single-file line of guys standing upright with their heads to the sky like military cadets. I lifted my empty wrist to check the time on my watch, but was reminded that my watch was another one of the items stolen from me at gunpoint a week ago. I checked the time on my phone instead. It was seven-oh-six on the dot.

"You wasn't lying about the show starting in six minutes," I said. "I wonder why they didn't just start it at seven o'clock instead of seven-oh-six."

"Because their fraternity was founded in 1906. And 1906 is seven-oh-six in military time," he said.

"How you know all that?" I asked. "I mean, damn! You would think you were on line."

"You still going to Harvard for grad school, right?" he asked sarcastically.

"Whatever, nigga," I said. "I see you got jokes."

I quickly returned my attention to the ceremony. Upperclassmen Alpha Mu Alphas wearing their black and gold jackets paced up and down both sides of the single-file line, pumping the pledges up. Then they ripped their gold masks off, and everybody in the crowd started screaming like they were at a rap concert.

Without hesitation, the guys standing in the line began reciting some shit that sounded like gibberish. I knew that they were saying something important, because the crowd became silent all of a sudden. But their words sounded muffled, because they were breathing so hard and talking so fast. They were speaking as loudly as they could, but they were spitting their sacred words so rapidly it was hard to understand them. I heard bits and pieces.

The guys were lined up in order, from shortest to tallest. The probate show kicked off with each of the guys stating a historical fact. They started at the front and worked their way to the back. The closer they got to the back, the more I heard. The second to last guy in the lineup sounded hella familiar. I couldn't see his face, but I knew that voice. I stepped around to the other side of Fresh to get a better view and damn near fell off the bench when I saw who it was. It was my roommate. I immediately spotted Timothy's parents in the crowd cheering him on. His father was wearing a black and gold A-Mu-A T-shirt with his 1978 line jacket. He looked proud.

"Go on, baby!" his mom screamed.

"That's my boy!" his father yelled.

Timothy spoke with an intensity I never would've guessed he had in him. From where I was standing I could see that his bottom lip was slightly swollen and both of his cheeks were a little puffy. I knew that he could hear his parents screaming. He fed off their energy.

"Alpha Mu Alpha!" he shouted. "A-Mu-A was the first intercollegiate Greek-letter fraternity!"

I'd never really given joining a fraternity much thought. If anything, I figured I'd probably get along with the pretty boys of Kappa Nu Psi the best because they were known around campus for being smooth with the ladies. But aside from all the rumors I'd heard about fraternities, I'd never really done any research of my own. I always looked at Greeks like they thought they were too good for everybody else. But surprisingly, the ceremony was full of humility. And the more Timothy spoke, the harder I listened.

"Brother T-Mac's frat was founded December 1, 1906, on the campus of Cornell University in Ithaca, New York, by seven distinguished college men who recognized the need for a strong bond of brotherhood among African descendants in this country!"

The expression of dignity and honor on Timothy's face was mirrored on his father's. Looking at them was enough to make me wanna join. I guess it was a rite of passage for Timothy. The Alpha Mu Alphas hurried up and down the line of pledges with water bottles, giving them a squirt here and there. I tripped out looking at the faces of the guys in line. I'd seen all of them eating together in the Caf, studying together in the library, but never really put two and two together. As I stared harder, I noticed that something was missing. Actually, somebody. Every time I'd seen them together, there were eight guys. Now there were only seven. Somebody was definitely missing. I just couldn't put my finger on who it was.

After thirty minutes of watching the pledges recite more historical information, clown other fraternities and get their step on, I was in awe. As I stood on top of a bench, I noticed the great lengths people had gone to just to get a good seat. Everybody was taking pictures with their cameras and videotaping the probate show. One guy had climbed a tree so he could tape the show from an aerial view with his handheld camcorder. A few girls perched atop the shoulders of guys to get a better view, while others hung their heads out of their dorm room windows, snapping pictures with their disposable cameras. And just beyond the chaos, about fifty feet away, a guy was sitting on a bench by himself with his head down. At first, I couldn't make out who it was, but the silhouette looked familiar.

"Don't that look like Lawry over there on that bench?" I asked, nudging Fresh.

"It's hard to tell from here," he said, squinting. "Hold up, joe. Damn, you got some good eyes! That is him. I wonder what he's doing over there."

"Me too," I said. "I'ma go see what's up with him."

"All right," Fresh said. "I'ma watch the rest of this show. I'll be right here."

As I made my way through the crowd, I took note of Lawry's body language. He was slumped over, his elbows resting on his knees and his face nestled into his hands.

"Lawry?" I asked cautiously. "Is that you, blood?"

"Yeah, it's me," he said, in a low, groggy tone.

"What's good with you?" I asked, extending my hand toward his, while sitting down next to him. "How come you ain't watching the probate show with everybody else?"

When he lifted his head to shake my hand, I immediately wished I hadn't. He was wearing shades, but they didn't do his face any justice. He looked like he'd sparred three rounds with Mike Tyson—before dinner. His face was covered with fresh cuts and bruises.

"Whoa!" I said, instinctively leaning away. "What happened to your face, blood?"

"I'm figna hop in my ride and shoot to the gas station and pick up a White Owl so I can roll up a blunt," he said, completely avoiding my question. "I finally got that raggedy mufucka fixed, shawty. The engine still shakes a little, because I gotta change the timing belt, but I got a new radio. I get all the stations now. You tryna ride?"

"I ain't trying to smoke," I said. "I gotta stay focused while I'm studying for my finals. But I'll ride with you. What happened to your face, though, blood?"

For the first time since I'd met him, it looked as if Lawry was struggling with what to say. Every time he tried to speak, he froze up.

"It's my pops," he said, returning to his slouched position. "He don't know. He think he know, but he don't."

"What you mean?"

"You know I was s'posed to be on line, right?"

"Damn, that's crazy. I was just over there at the probate show. I had a feeling somebody was missing. What happened?"

"My pops, shawty."

"What about him?"

"You know he's a Q, right?"

"That's right, you did say that."

"When he found out I was pledging Alpha Mu Alpha, he damn near had a heart attack. My mom has seven brothers and five of them pledged A-Mu-A, so I didn't think he would trip like that. But he said he ain't wanna have nothing else to do with me if I crossed. And he's dead serious. He told me I wouldn't even be welcome at home if I did."

"Damn, that's deep. I didn't even know people take pledging that serious, cousin."

"It's crazy, 'cause I done put up with so much shit this semester. I really humbled myself, shawty. I mean, these dudes were on some real ignorant shit. I done did some shit that you couldn't even imagine, just to be accepted."

"Sounds like your pops is on some other shit."

"It's to the point where even if I wanted to pledge Q, I couldn't because they're suspended for the next five years for hazing."

"How come you ain't tell him that?"

"I did! He still wasn't trying to hear it. He's just stubborn as hell, shawty," he said, burying his face in his hands and shaking his head.

"Don't you have to be at least a sophomore to pledge anyway?"

"You're supposed to, but I already had enough credits from those classes I took in summer school."

"Oh yeah, that's right. I forgot all about that."

"I just can't believe I went through nine weeks, thirteen days, eight hours, thirty-five minutes and twenty-two seconds of bullshit, just to drop line one week before we crossed. I just came out here because I wanted to be there for my line brothers. Well, I guess I can't even call them that anymore. But we went through a lot together. I just wanted to show up, so I could show them that I still had love for them. I tried to go over there, but this is as close as my feet would take me, shawty. I couldn't even look at that probate show. I can't lie. A nigga probably would've broke down."

"You said nine *weeks?*"

"Nine weeks, thirteen days, eight hours, thirty-five minutes and twenty-two seconds, shawty. That seemed like forever to me. I don't know how the rest of 'em made it through hell week alive."

"It was that bad?"

"We got worn out so bad the night before, niggas couldn't even sit down. My ass is still swollen."

"Hell naw," I said, shaking my head. "Y'all had to get beat in? I always thought that was some movie-type shit. I never knew that's how it was really going down. That sounds like joining a gang. Did y'all do something wrong or is that just part of the initiation?"

"To be real with you, I don't even know," he said. "Half the time it was on some trick-question-type shit. I think they just liked to play mind games with us."

"Like what?"

"I really shouldn't even be telling you no shit like this," he said. "You my boy and all, but that shit is sacred. You gotta swear to God you won't say nothing, if I tell you."

"C'mon now," I said. "Don't even play me like that. You know I ain't gonna say shit to nobody. That's on my mama."

"All right. Well, this one time we at the spot, and one of the niggas asked me some shit like, 'If your mama, Jesus and an Alpha Mu Alpha man were in a burning building, and you could only save one, who would you save?'"

"That's a rough one," I said. "I'd definitely have to go with my mama, though."

"That's what I said, shawty! I figured if Jesus could walk on water, he could find his way out of a burning building."

"So, what did they say?"

"It ain't what they said, it's what they did!"

"It was that bad?"

"Don't you remember how I was taking the final in Dr. J's class? I was standing up!" he said. "My ass was so sore I couldn't sit down! My ass is still swollen."

"Oh yeah," I said, scratching my head. "That's right. Come to think of it, Timothy was standing up too. They must've really fucked you guys up."

"Pledging ain't no joke," Lawry said.

"Damn," I said. "So, what was the right answer to the question they asked you?"

"What's so cold is, I don't even think there was a right answer, shawty."

"On some real shit, if I would've gone through all of that to rock them letters, a nigga like me probably would've had to just go ahead and finish."

"I wanted to, shawty," he said, wiping a tear off his cheek with his sleeve. "Believe me. I wanted to."

I'd never seen him cry. Nine weeks, eight hours, thirty-five minutes and twenty-two seconds—all for nothing, I thought.

"C'mon, let's make a move, shawty," he said, using his white tee to wipe his face. "Sitting out here is making me sick to my stomach now."

"We can make it happen. Let me go over here and let Fresh know we're bouncing."

"I'll come with you," he said.

As we made our way back toward Fresh, a huge crowd began to form in a circle across the yard. There were hella people leaving the probate show to see what was going on. When I saw Fresh jump down from the bench and head in that direction, I followed. When Lawry and I pushed through the crowd to see what all the fuss was about, I saw Downtown-D standing in the middle. I thought to myself, *Why am I not surprised?* There was a girl standing on her tippy-toes pointing her finger in his face, but I couldn't see her face because she was standing with her back to me. She was hella animated and obviously pissed off about something. I jumped on top of the bench I was standing in front of, and Fresh followed.

"Ahh, shit, joe," Fresh said. "Ain't that your girl Katrina?"

"Is that her?" I said, taking a closer look. "Damn. That sure is her, blood."

At that moment, Downtown-D started walking toward the bench I was standing on, attempting to walk away. Instead of letting him leave, Kat ran around his back, grabbed him by his forearm and pulled as hard as she could, spinning him around. When I saw that Kat was doing the finger-pointing, I wasn't surprised. But when I saw the agony in her face and heard the despair in her voice, I became concerned.

"I need to talk to you in private," Kat said in a disturbing tone, inching closer to Downtown-D. He was standing in a cocky, bowlegged stance, with his back straight and feet spread wide apart.

"I think you need to chill out, baby," Downtown-D said in a relaxed manner. "Chill out. Can't you see me Kool-Aiding with my patnas? We'll talk later."

"This can't wait!" Kat shouted, as moisture welled up in her eyes and she fought back tears. "I need to talk to you now!"

The crowd surrounding their argument continued to grow. The word must've spread that Downtown-D was about to publicly call it off with Kat, because a majority of the crowd were females.

"Be easy, baby," he said, maintaining his cool. "I'ma rap with my boys, and then I'll holla at you, all right?"

In the middle of the heated argument, Downtown-D unsnapped his Sidekick from its holster on his hip, switched on the backlight and held it up to his face as he read an incoming message. He wasn't paying Kat any attention. He started chopping up game with some of the other members of the football team who were standing behind him. But by keeping his composure and playing Kat to the left, Downtown-D was actually further irritating her. Misery loves company.

"Deiondre Randolph Harris!" she said, grabbing his wrists and pulling his Sidekick down from his face. She was laughing, but tears were streaming from her eyes. "I can't believe you're playing me in front of everybody like this. I've got something really important to tell you."

"Randolph?" somebody in the crowd asked jokingly. Everybody who heard started busting out laughing. For the first time since I'd met him, Downtown-D looked embarrassed. He was human. He was also frustrated and increasingly angry.

"Can't we talk about this another time?" he asked.

"We need to talk about this right now!"

"Well, talk."

"Not in front of all of these people. In private, Dre!"

"Whatever you've got to say to me, you can say it right now!" He motioned toward the football players standing behind him. "These guys are my family. Whatever you've got to tell me you can tell them too."

"This is already hard enough for me as it is," she said, bursting out in tears. "Why would you make it harder? You know what? Since you want to act like an ass, forget I even tried to warn you. I guess you'll just have to find out for yourself."

She tried to wipe the tears from her eyes, but they kept falling. Downtown-D returned his attention to the text message on his two-way.

"She must be pregnant!" somebody in the back of the crowd blurted out.

An uproar of "oohs" and "aahs" came from the crowd. Then, suddenly, a somber aura fell over the onlookers. I think it's safe to say most people felt sorry for her—but not everybody. I saw more than a few females perk up at the sight of Kat's despair. I looked at them and shook my head.

"That's bogus," Fresh said. "He didn't even have to play her out like that, G. You think she's pregnant, though?"

"I hope not," I said, taking a deep breath.

Kat had been in such a rage I don't think she realized she'd drawn such a large audience. Her eyes quickly surveyed the crowd, eventually landing right on me. That's when it seemed like Kat's condition went from bad to worse. Her eyes teared as if she'd eaten an onion whole. Anguish riddled her body. Her bottom lip quivered and her nose was running. I'd never seen her look worse. She just stood there with her arms wrapped around herself, rocking back and forth, trembling uncontrollably. She looked like she had more to say. If she was pregnant, I'd never seen someone that broken about it before.

With tears rolling down her cheeks, Kat took off running toward her dorm. I wanted to chase her, but my legs wouldn't move. I wanted to call her back, but my mouth wouldn't open. I didn't know whether to stay mad at her or feel sorry for her. At that point, the only thing I knew for sure was that my heart was with Kat. The only reason I'd gotten so upset with her in the first place is that my feelings for her were so deep. I couldn't conceal my emotions anymore. She obviously had some things to say to me, and I didn't want to fly home without getting some things off my chest. I had questions. I decided to head over to Kat's place for answers. I didn't want to end my first semester with a heavy conscience.

"After we hit the gas station, you mind dropping me off at the Heritage Commons?" I asked.

"You know somebody who stays up in there?" Lawry asked.

I never answered. I just looked at him again. I didn't have to tell him who I was going to see. My facial expression said it all.

CHAPTER 23

TESTED

I couldn't convince Lawry to wait for me in the car. He said that he hadn't been in an upperclassman dorm all semester, and there was no way he was going to winter break without at least seeing what the inside of their dorms looked like.

"Man, it's nice in here," Lawry said once we were inside the elevator, sounding like an underprivileged child from a Third World country. "You didn't tell me they had elevators."

I paid no attention to Lawry's ignorant comments. I was focused. As the elevator slowly ascended to the third floor, I tried my best to clear my mind of all the bullshit I'd been through the last few weeks. I went over what I was going to say to Kat in my head and convinced myself that I would be quiet long enough to listen to what she had to say. When I stepped off the elevator, my heart rate increased like I'd just sniffed ten lines of uncut cocaine. I could literally feel it thumping through my linen shirt. Nervousness had officially sunk in. I placed my thumb in my mouth and started nibbling at my fingernail. Apparently I was incoherent, because I hadn't moved since I stepped off the elevator.

"Which way, shawty?" Lawry asked, nudging me on my

shoulder. "You're gonna have to snap out of it. She's got you whipped like that?"

"Never that," I said, regaining my essence. I started walking toward Kat's room. "It's this way, blood."

The stretch of hallway leading to Kat's room had never looked so long. Her door looked like it was a mile away. My stomach was doing backflips. But these weren't your average butterflies—they were full-grown pigeons. It was the longest hallway I've ever walked down in my life. Kat's door was getting closer and closer, but I was in no rush to get there. Lawry didn't even know which room we were walking to, and he was a half hallway ahead of me. He turned around when he realized I was walking at a snail's pace.

"When are you leaving to go back home?" Lawry asked.

"I'm leaving tomorrow afternoon. Why?"

"If you keep walking that slow you're gonna miss your damn flight. C'mon!"

I sped up from snail to turtle. I thought about walking faster but my head and my legs weren't on the same page. I felt like a serial killer, condemned to capital punishment, walking that last mile to the electric chair. I was just waiting for someone to yell out, "Dead man walking!"

When I got to Kat's door, I had a sudden change of heart. I hadn't called, and didn't quite know what to expect. I'd completely forgotten everything I'd prepared to say to her in my head. So instead of knocking I stood there, staring at the room number on her door. As I stood there, a barrage of questions ambushed my psyche. What would I say? How would she react? What if the baby was mine? What if Downtown-D was already inside? Apparently, my moment of insecurity was as obvious as my heartache.

"Are you gonna sit on the pot or shit on the pot?" Lawry asked impatiently. "I mean, is it barbecue or mildew with you? I could've stayed in the car for this."

I started to remind him of the fact that nobody asked him to come in the first place. Then I thought about just turning around, walking back to my dorm and packing up my things.

By the time I thought about knocking on Kat's door, Lawry had already beaten me to it.

"Hey, if you won't, I will," he said. "I didn't ride the elevator all the way up here for nothing."

Before I could utter a reply the door swung open. Some short, big-boned, dark-skinned girl wearing a red do-rag, gray sweatpants and a white T-shirt with a yellow mustard stain on it opened the door. I had no idea who she was. I wasn't thinking sensibly. I tried to push the door open and walk by her, but she stuck her plump forearm out and stopped me.

"Excuse me," she said, rolling her eyes with an attitude. "Can I help you?"

"I'm here to see Kat," I said.

"Could you be referring to Katrina?"

I wasn't in the mood for entertaining her sarcasm. I just stood there, looking at her like she was slow.

"H-e-l-l-o?" she asked in a joking manner. She started talking hella slow, wiggling her fingers like she was doing sign language. "Did you want to see K-a-t-r-i-n-a or not?"

Lawry must've known I was figna tell shorty doo-wop about herself, because he spoke up before I could, with desperation in his voice.

"Yes, shawty. Is she here?"

"That depends on who you are. What's your name? And what happened to your face?"

"Who are you, the police? I mean, damn, shawty, you ask more questions than Oprah. What yo name is?"

"You're trying to come up in my room, nigga," she said, putting her hand on her hip. "Name please."

"I'm Lawry," he said.

The girl laughed. "*Lawry?* That is so country."

"Well, what yo name is?" Lawry asked, sounding offended.

"*What my name is?*" she asked, mockingly. "I know you're from Atlanta, talking like that. I'm Jessica."

"Well, Jessica, we're here to see Kat," Lawry said.

"Y'all smell like weed. You been smoking?"

"Can you just please check and see if Kat is here?" I asked.

"Hold on. Let me check," she said, closing the door.

She was so lazy she didn't even walk to Kat's room. She just stood there, yelling from the door. We could hear every word.

"K-a-t-r-i-n-a! Kat! There are two guys at the door who want to see you. One of 'em is named Lawry—he's the one with gold teeth, a black eye and bad breath. The other one is cute, but I think he's crazy!"

Two seconds later, the door flung open again and a cloud of smoke seeped out. I didn't see the little tree stump who'd initially opened the door. This time she just pulled the door open and ran to the kitchen.

"Close the door behind you," Jessica said. "Y'all got me burning my pork chops!"

I walked inside, fanning the smoke with my hand. I tried to close the door with my other hand, but struggled. I tried to push it with both hands, but it wouldn't close any faster.

"What's wrong with your door?" I asked.

"The hinges are broken," Jessica said, trotting back into the kitchen. "That thing takes forever to close, no matter how hard you push it. Y'all almost made me burn my kitchen down." She was fanning smoke with her hand. "Lawry, if you want, you can have a seat in the living room."

"I think I'll do that," he said.

"I'll be right back," I assured him.

The door to Kat's room was closed. That wasn't a good sign. If she knew I was coming in, why didn't she have it open? I took a deep breath before I knocked.

"Who is it?" she asked.

"J.D."

"Hold on."

It took about twenty seconds before the door finally squeaked open. I took in another deep gasp of air, bigger than that of an Olympic swimmer before jumping off the high dive into the deep end of a pool. At the time, I had no idea I would need all of the oxygen.

The second I stepped into Kat's room my phone rang. It was

Todd. I quickly answered, told him I'd hit him back in a few. It wasn't until I hung up the phone that I noticed how out of place Kat's room looked. I felt like I was in *The Twilight Zone* or something. Her TV, radio and computer were off. All the pictures of her family and sorority sisters on her nightstand were now lying facedown. Her backpack was wide open and her textbooks were scattered all over the floor. She was sitting on her bed, her legs folded Indian style. She was holding a box of tissues. Her hair was pulled back into a rough ponytail. Both of her eyes were swollen, black and puffy. She looked like she'd just come from her mother's funeral. There was a piece of paper lying at the foot of her bedspread. When I touched the paper to move it aside so I could sit down, her entire body shuddered. Before I could move it, she quickly pushed it aside herself. She was sniffling and tears dripped continuously. Her trembles sent sinister vibrations down the bedspread toward me. Her body shook relentlessly, as if she was suffering from hypothermia. She couldn't even look me in the eye.

"So, I guess you heard the news, huh?" she asked in the solemnest of voices, in between sniffles.

"Nothing specific," I said, tossing my phone onto her bed and plopping down next to it. "What's up?"

"Please don't look at me, J.D.," she said. "You're going to make this harder than it already is."

At that moment I contemplated the worst-case scenario: I was going to be a teenage father and have a baby with good hair. I'd have to drop out of school to work full-time at FedEx lifting boxes to buy Pampers and baby food.

"Make *what* worse than it is?" I asked, hesitantly.

"Well, remember when I said I had something to tell you?" *Here it comes*, I thought. "Uh-huh."

"Well, I've been feeling a little under the weather lately. So I went to see a doctor a little over a week ago to get checked out...and... I don't even know how to say this," she said, putting her hands over her face. "J.D., I'm... I'm..."

"You're pregnant?"

Kat didn't respond. Instead, she just sat there, her face still collapsed in her palms.

"Hey, nobody is perfect," I said, wrapping my arm around her and rubbing her shoulder. "I mean, don't get me wrong. I'm not exactly ready to be a father, but everything happens for a reason. We all make mistakes. We just have to be grown enough to take responsibility for them."

"I didn't want anything from you, J.D.!" she said, completely flipping the script. "I just needed a shoulder to cry on—somebody to talk to. And you couldn't even call me back. You hurt me!"

For a second, I wondered what the hell that comment had to do with her being pregnant. Then I figured she was just being emotional. And as much as I hated to show my vulnerable side to females, somehow in the heat of the discussion it leaked.

"Hey, you hurt me too," I said, putting the guilt trip right back on her shoulders where it belonged. "I thought we had something special, but I guess I was wrong."

"What are you talking about?"

"I'm talking about the night you were supposedly helping your grandma move, but I saw you hugged up with your guy outside my favorite restaurant."

Evidently she didn't see that one coming. She just sat there for a few seconds, with this dumbfounded look on her face.

"How did you—"

I cut her off like a car going too slowly on the freeway. "Don't worry about how I knew that. I ain't new to this, I grew to this. C'mon now, I was born at night, not last night."

"I'm sorry you had to find out about that," she said, with sincerity in her voice. "I really am. But you could've called me back and given me a chance to apologize and explain."

"Call back for what? At that point, I figured an apology was useless. I just assumed it was over between us. Plus, I didn't know you were having my baby. It is mine, right?"

"That's not even the reason I was calling you," she said, abruptly avoiding my question once again. "I'm not pregnant, J.D."

"You're not?"

"No."

"Well, you were blowing me up for some reason, passing notes in class and all that. What could've been so important?"

The shivering returned. Her hands and legs quivered uncontrollably, and she nibbled her lip. I noticed beads of sweat congregating atop her forehead. It looked like she could go into a full-blown seizure at any second. She hadn't looked me in the eye since I'd been in her room. She was seriously starting to scare me.

"What's wrong with you?" I asked.

"I got my test back, J.D.," she said, grabbing the piece of paper that she'd moved to let me sit down on her bed.

This time when she touched the paper, her fingers fluttered so vigorously she dropped it. I watched it slowly drift from her hand back down to the bedspread. When I reached for the paper, her hand covered mine and she pressed down as hard as she could. My hand trembled underneath hers. When I tried to move it, she tightened her grip. When I looked up into Kat's eyes, I didn't see the glow that I'd fallen for—the radiance that I would have given anything for to wake up next to every morning for the rest of my life. Instead, I saw fear. It was warm in Kat's room, but her palm was ice-cold. It wasn't the same hand that I'd dreamed about holding while walking through the mall. Her hand felt the same way my grandfather's did as I held it just before he died of cancer. I felt a hopelessness that preceded death.

"Is this about that microeconomics class you're always complaining about?" I asked. "I know you're on the dean's list and all that, but you can't be this upset about a stupid test grade."

"You don't understand!" she screamed as tears began to flood her cheeks. She grabbed both of my hands and held them firmly in hers. Then she got up from the bed and stood in between my legs as they dangled off the side of her bed.

"Whatever you got, it couldn't be that bad," I said, pulling one of my hands away to wipe the dampness away from her face. "C'mon, just tell me."

"J.D.," she said, looking down at the floor. "I didn't pass."

"It's really not that big of a deal. You're a straight-A student.

Show the professor your transcript. I bet you he'd let you take the final again if you told him about your situation."

"You don't understand!"

"Kat, it's just a test. I'm sure you passed the class."

"I'm not worried about passing a class."

"Well, what are you tripping about?"

"It was a blood test," she said, in a dismal tone. "J.D., I'm... I'm... I'm..."

"You're what?"

"I'm HIV-positive."

At that moment, I felt my heartbeat stop. Then, suddenly, it increased to a pulse ten times its normal speed, as if a state trooper had just pulled behind me on the highway, and I was driving in a stolen car with no license, twenty pounds of cocaine in the glove compartment and a dead body in the trunk. My mind went blank. I couldn't think. I blinked. While my eyes were closed I saw my life flash before my eyes. Tears drowned my pupils. My eyesight faltered, but my other senses were enhanced. All of a sudden I could smell the scent of scorched pork chops in the air, and I could hear the tears that fell from Kat's eyes nestling into her carpet. The second time I blinked I saw my casket. From that point on I was afraid to close my eyes.

"Wait a minute..." I said in a low, portentous tone. "So you mean to tell me..."

I took my hand and wiped it slowly from the top of my forehead to the bottom of my chin, in hopes that by the time my fingers rolled off my face, I would awaken from the worst dream I'd ever had. When my fingers reached my Adam's apple, she was still standing there and so was I. I cleared my throat.

"So you're telling me you've got AIDS?" I screamed at the top of my lungs.

My sentences were fragmented. I tried to speak, but couldn't complete a thought.

"Why didn't you...? Where did you...? How long have you known?"

"The test results took a while to come back," she said, sobbing in piercing shrieks. "I tried to call you, though. You know I did!"

"So, what exactly are you trying to say? Are you trying to tell me that I might have AIDS too? Is that what you've been calling me for? I'm not one to put my hands on a female. But, Kat, I'm telling you right now, if you gave me that shit—"

"J.D., please," she pleaded. "I really need someone to be here for me right now. I just... I don't know what to do. I don't know who I can turn to. I feel lost...confused."

"You should! I know I am. I mean, here you are, Miss AIDS Awareness herself—sponsoring STD-free rallies on campus, reciting all of the HIV statistics, wearing red ribbons and you mean to tell me you've got the shit? You can't be serious right now. This is not why I came to college. I swear, I didn't sign up for this. This just can't be happening to me right now."

"J.D., I said I was sorry."

"*Sorry?* Bitch, sorry don't cut it! We're talking about life and death here. Of all people, I would think you would take this more seriously. If anybody is sorry, it should be me. I'm sorry I ever met your ass!"

She put her hands on my shoulders and tried to talk, but couldn't find the words. I felt one of her tears drop onto my linen pants. That's when I grabbed her wrists, forcefully removed her hands from my shoulders, hopped off her bed and bolted toward her door.

"Wait!" she screamed, grabbing me by my shoulder with one hand. "Please, J.D., don't leave me right now. I don't know what to do. I don't know if I can go on. I really need someone to talk to."

"You wanna talk? Okay, cool. Let's talk. Let's talk about who else you've been fucking this semester. Let's talk about all the times you told me you were hanging with your line sisters or *helping your grandmother move,* when you were really with your boy, Downtown-D. Nah, you know what? I've got a better name for him. How about STD? How 'bout that? I can't believe I actually thought you were the genuine, sincere, wifey type. I guess that's what I get for thinking, huh?"

"I mean, if that's how you really feel about me, then I don't know what to say," she said as she looked up at me, still crying.

"When I went out with Deiondre without telling you, that was a mistake. I should have been honest with you, and I apologized for that. But I just found out I'm HIV-positive, and I'm scared to death. Don't kick me when I'm down! I mean, you're acting like this is all my fault. I didn't ask for this. And I didn't ask you to have unprotected sex with me, either. That was your choice."

"Man, I'm not even figna sit up here and listen to this bull-shit, blood. I'm outta here!" I said.

With that, I attempted to make a peaceful exit. I was almost out the door, but then it happened. Somewhere between me trying to remain levelheaded and sane, she tried to grab me with her other hand. And that's when I lost it. I went berserk.

"Get the fuck off of me!" I yelled as I put the palm of my hand on her forehead and pushed as hard as I could. Her head snapped back so fast that for a moment I thought I might have accidentally broken her neck. Her arms flew up in the air and the force of the shove made her feet backpedal until her spine crashed up against her drawer, sending her collapsing to the floor. She let out a loud scream and whimpered like a baby. Her door swung open and Lawry stormed in with Jessica.

"I knew your ass was crazy!" Jessica said, pushing me out of her way.

When Jessica tried to help Kat up from the floor, she resisted violently. Without looking up to see who was trying to help her, she started windmilling her fists wildly, catching her roommate on the chin by mistake.

"Get away from me!" Kat screamed in her loudest voice. Veins popped out of her neck as she grabbed her head with both hands and pulled out two fistfuls of hair. She repeated herself three times in a row, without intermission. "I just want every-body to get the fuck out of my room! I need to be alone."

"C'mon, let's get outta here, shawty," Lawry said, grabbing me by my shoulder and pulling me out of the room. "Baby girl definitely needs some time to herself."

"Let me help you up, Kat," Jessica insisted.

Kat refused the help for a second time.

"*Everybody!*" she shouted.

"C'mon!" Lawry screamed, dragging me to the door. "Let's go!"

Kat's roommate came running out of the room toward us. Lawry ran out of the room, pulling me along with him.

"Yeah, y'all better run!" Jessica shouted. "I'm calling Public Safety!"

We weren't even two doors down from Kat's room before my conscience kicked in, and I stopped in my tracks. Something about pushing a girl down like that just didn't sit right in my heart. The fact that Kat was already in between a rock and a hard place made it even worse. I'd kicked her when she was down. I suppose growing up in a household with my mother and sister may have had something to do with it, but even when I was in the middle of cursing Kat out, it just didn't feel right—even if she deserved it. Lawry was halfway down the hallway before he even noticed I'd stopped walking.

"What you stopping for?" he yelled. "Let's get the hell on!"

"I need to go back," I said, trying to think up a good excuse to give Lawry as to why.

In the process of thinking up a good reason, I found that I actually had a legit one. "You know what?" I asked, patting my pockets frantically. "I think I might have…"

"Think you might have what?" he asked.

"Did I have my phone with me when I came up here?"

"I think so. Why?"

"I think I left my phone on Kat's bed, blood. I'm going back to get it."

"Man, hell naw. You heard her say she was figna call Public Safety on us. Later for that phone. You can come back and get that another time."

"*Another time?*" I asked. "Nigga, please. I need my phone. I'm figna grab it real quick and then we can get up outta here."

Luckily, I made it back to Kat's suite door before it closed.

"You're lucky this door was nigga-rigged," Lawry said as he followed me inside. "Ain't no way Kat's roommate was figna let us back up in here."

Aside from Lawry's endless banter, Kat's suite was eerily

quiet, especially for a room that was full of commotion less than a minute ago. All of a sudden, I had a really bad feeling about the whole situation, like something wasn't quite right. The closer I got to Kat's bedroom door, the worse I felt. A thick cloud of smoke coming from the kitchen fogged up the living room area. The water on the stove was boiling over, yet neither Jessica nor Kat were anywhere in sight. When I looked at Lawry, I could tell that he was just as leery about the situation as I was.

"I tried to tell you to come back and get your phone later," he said, fanning smoke away from his face with his hand. "These girls are tripping up in here."

Just as we cut the corner, the fire alarm sounded off. The siren made both of us flinch. But the sound that followed was one I could never forget.

"Aargh!" a female voice shrieked. "Oh, my God, Katrina, no!"

Even with the fire alarm sounding off, you could hear it loud and clear from under Kat's door.

Instinctively, I froze for a second, before opening the door. Lawry hesitantly followed me inside. I hadn't taken three steps inside the room before I stopped dead in my tracks. The sight of Kat balled up in a corner stuffing the barrel of a chrome-plated 9mm pistol in her mouth caught me off guard. It made Lawry take a few steps back.

"You really don't have to do this, Kat!" Jessica said as she stretched her hands toward her, tears flooding her eyes. "I mean, you've got so much to live for. Kat, please don't do this!"

After scanning the room, looking first at Jessica, then Lawry, then me, Katrina closed her eyes and started rocking back and forth, all the while sobbing profusely. At that point, my stomach fluttered. I thought she was going to kill herself in front of my eyes. Each breath she took was deeper than the previous one. I was afraid each one would be her last. Her fingers were fidgety. One second she'd wrap her finger around the trigger, the next she'd remove it.

A million things ran through my head as I stood there looking at Kat. I went back and forth in my mind, trying to think of the right words to say. But at that point, I was still furious about the possibility that I might have contracted HIV from her. I wanted to tell her, "Go ahead, do the world a favor and pull the trigger." But before I could fix my lips to say a word, I thought about how I thought the first time I laid eyes on Kat during orientation, and how I thought she was the most beautiful female I'd ever seen in my life.

Then the selfish side of me took over, and I thought about what *my* mother would say, how *my* friends would react, how *I* would go on with *my* life, if *I* found out that *I* was HIV-positive.

Even as the anger resurfaced, I never said a word. Instead, I just kept thinking. I thought about whether she *really* went straight home all of the late nights she dropped me off at my uncle Leroy's during Thanksgiving break, or whether she made a pit stop at Downtown-D's place on the way. I thought about all of the times she might have sucked his dick in the morning and French-kissed me the same night.

I thought about all of the late nights we'd spent together studying, and all of the times she'd helped me study for my tests, when she had term papers to write for her own classes. I thought about how if it hadn't been for her, I probably never would even have had a chance of passing Dr. J's class—not to mention the other five. As I looked around her room, I couldn't help but remember the first night she invited me there, and how excited I was just to be in her room.

Then, for some strange reason, as I looked down at Kat, my hands nervously gripping the seams of my pants, I thought about Robyn. I pictured my little sister in Kat's shoes—balled up in a corner, holding a gun to her head, all because she was ashamed to go on with life. I thought about what I would say to get her to choose life. Then, I said it.

"Think of all the people who love you," I said. "What about your mom? What about your dad? Kat, you mean too much to too many people to…"

In the middle of my sentence, I could tell I'd said enough. I didn't want to go overboard. I'd said enough to take her mind off her problems and think about how her actions would affect those who loved her most. Slowly she loosened her grip on the gun and removed it from her mouth. As the gun dangled from her hand, her head drooped in between her legs, she spoke softly, in between sniffles.

"But how am I going to… How am I supposed to… I don't know if I can…"

"You can," I said. "Can we have a moment?" I asked, looking at Jessica, then Lawry.

Jessica gave me an "I'm not going anywhere" kind of look.

"Please?" I asked.

"Are you sure?" Lawry asked.

"Yeah, blood."

"I'm gonna be right outside, if you need me," he said as Jessica hesitantly followed him out.

With just the two of us in the room, a feeling of calm came over me. I figured if she'd really wanted to kill herself, she would've done it already. But judging by the way she hesitated, I could tell she didn't really want to do it. She just needed someone to remind her why she shouldn't.

"Look, Kat," I said, cautiously making my way over to her, hands raised slightly in an unassuming position. "I don't think I've ever told you this, but when I first met you I thought you were the most beautiful girl I'd ever seen in my life."

"J.D, you tell me that all the time," she said, cracking a slight grin.

"Well, you know what? I still do. But more importantly, you're smart, you're funny and your attitude is on point. I know this may seem like the end of the world, but it's not. Believe me, you can beat this thing. Now, please, give me the gun."

"But how am I supposed to tell my mom that I'm HIV-positive?" she asked, tears streaming from her eyes. "And what about my sorors? Here I am, organizing safe-sex rallies, and I end up like this. Everyone is going to think I'm a hypocrite."

"Honestly," I said, squatting so that Kat and I could speak eye to eye, "what other people think of you isn't even important, Kat. It's what you think of yourself that matters most. And I know that you know you're better than this. If anybody is strong enough to beat something like this, it's you."

"I'm scared, J.D.," she said. "I'm so scared."

Me too, I thought. The verdict was still out on my health status. But at that point, I figured I couldn't let her see my fear.

"Hey, I felt the same way about taking tests before I met you," I said. "I know it's not the best comparison in the world, but it's true. When it came to taking exams, I was terrified. Truthfully, as soon as I heard that I'd have to keep a 2.5 GPA to stay in school, I figured my first semester would be my last. My whole intention was to have as much fun as possible before I went back home. But then I met you, and everything turned around for me. After studying with you, I actually believed I could pass my classes on my own, without cheating. You gave me that confidence. Now it's my turn to help you. And I'm asking you to give me that gun." I slowly extended my trembling hand toward hers.

"Thank you," she said in a whispered tone as she placed the barrel of the gun in my palm.

I quickly retracted my arm and stood to my feet. As I looked down at the gun in my hand, then Kat, I felt like I'd done the right thing, for once. It had been so long since I'd actually done something that I could be proud of for someone else that for a moment I didn't know what to say.

"You're welcome," I said, exhaling a deep sigh of relief.

CHAPTER 24

EXIT EXAM

Tossing and turning all night kept me from getting any sleep. Every time I closed my eyes, I pictured Kat sitting on the floor crying with that gun in her mouth. Once, I actually dreamed she pulled the trigger. That time, I woke up in a cold sweat.

I tried to turn on some music to get some peace of mind, but it didn't help. I just kept hearing the same words in my head over and over again: HIV-positive. By the time I finally got to sleep, my alarm clock was going off to wake me up.

My original plan was to wake up early in the morning and squeeze in a little more reviewing before the big test, but it was no use. I couldn't focus to save my life. Studying for biology was hard enough without the mental strain of worrying about whether or not I'd live long enough to put my degree to use. So, with that on my conscience, the task at hand seemed impossible. I couldn't even hold my pencil steady, let alone distinguish a prokaryote cell from a eukaryote. After scrambling to study what I could, I got dressed and left for class.

Wouldn't you know it? Kat was the first person I saw when I walked through the door. She was sitting at her desk, doing some last-second cramming, her eyes hidden behind a pair of large shades. Even though I'd saved her life less than twenty-four hours before our biology final, it was still hard for me to even glance in Kat's direction without feeling disdain. While I was glad to see her alive, part of me still hated her guts. Sitting near her would make it almost impossible to stay focused. When she looked up, I mustered a fake smile, then headed for a seat in another row.

"Your final grades will be available for your review on the school Web site in a few days," Professor Obugata said in his heavy African accent. "Remember that your grade is not a reflection of you, but the effort that you put into this class. Good luck. And no cheating!"

As I flipped through the hundred-question test, I noticed something different about myself. I wasn't the same student who had left an entire test blank in Dr. J's class at the beginning of the semester. This time around, I'd brought my own pencil. There was no need to apprehensively bite my fingernails, because I'd studied. Even with the uncertainty of my HIV status in limbo, I felt confident. Aside from operating on a few hours of rest, I was prepared.

I got halfway through the test without incident. And then it happened.

Kat coughed.

To everyone else in the class, it was nothing more than a harmless indication that she either had some phlegm in her throat, might have slept with her window open or might be coming down with a cold. But to me, it was a deathly cough—surely one of the many symptoms she would have to treat with a buffet of antibiotics and drug cocktails in years to come. The thought of it sent my stomach into convulsions. Within seconds, I felt nauseated. One minute later I was hovering over a toilet in the men's bathroom, spitting up just about everything I'd eaten in the last twenty-four hours.

When I made it back to the classroom, Katrina's desk was vacant. With her gone, finishing the exam was harder than starting it. I had a headache, my breath stank and I felt like crap. Still, I pressed on. After filling in the last bubble on my answer sheet, I just sat. This might be my last time ever sitting in a desk at the University of Atlanta. So for a moment, I just cherished it.

I stretched my arms to the sky and took a deep breath. At that moment, I felt a huge weight fall from my shoulders. Pass or fail, I'd finished my last final exam. I had completed my first semester.

EPILOGUE

THE AFTERMATH

Todd picked me up from the airport when I got back to Oakland. He was the only person I'd told about my dilemma, because he was the only person I could trust not to tell anyone else. Plus, he was one of the few people I could depend on if things didn't turn out so well.

Ever since I found out Kat was HIV-positive, my own status was the only thing I could think about. I thought about it when I was packing my bags. I thought about it when Uncle Leroy was driving me to the airport. And when I fell asleep on the plane, I dreamed about it. As Todd drove down the highway, he tried to talk about everything he could think of to take my mind off it.

"You know Keisha's been asking me about you," he said.

"Is that right?" I asked blandly.

"Yeah," he said. "Her cousin Latrice is pregnant again."

"Damn," I said, sounding disinterested. "Like that?"

"Yeah, bro. Three kids by three different dudes. I don't even think she's twenty yet. Can you believe that?"

"That's crazy, blood."

"It's good to see you back in the Town, boy! You gonna be

all right, my nigga," he said, sensing my distant demeanor. "Don't even trip."

"Yeah, I know, right," I said.

"Hey, did I tell you about what happened to my room the day before we left?"

"Nah, blood," I said, still peering out my window. "What happened?"

"My suite mate was talking to this one breezy all semester, right... J.D.," he said, nudging me with his elbow. "J.D.!"

"Oh, yeah," I said. "Yeah. I hear you. You said your breezy was talking to your suite mate all semester. And what?"

"No! I knew you wasn't listening, blood. I said my suite mate was talking to this female all semester. Anyway, he wound up making her his wifey, and giving her a key to our suite, right?"

"Uh-huh."

"Man, I guess she found out he was cheating or something. All I know is, I come back to our dorm room after I finished my last final, and there was water creeping from under my door all into the hallway. Man, you know I walked inside my dorm room and the whole thing was flooded. I mean, water up to my ankles, bro. It looked like Hurricane Katrina. The furniture in our living room was completely ruined. I'm talking 'bout turds floating by my bedroom door and piss all on the living room carpet, blood."

"No!" I said.

"Yes! That nigga's breezy had the nerve to come flood the toilet in the suite on purpose."

"Hold up. Y'all had bathrooms and living rooms in your dorm rooms?"

"Yeah," he said. "But you know I was staying in the honors dorm, though."

"Oh yeah, that's right. How do you know she was the one who flooded the room, though, blood?"

"Because she wrote 'Ha, Ha' on the mirror in the bathroom, and signed her initials under it. My suite mate saw it when he got in the shower and the steam fogged the mirror up."

"That ain't even cool, blood," I said as we pulled off the exit. "Say, where you going, bro? This ain't my exit. Where you gotta go?"

"I ain't gotta go nowhere," he said as we pulled into the parking lot of North Oakland Medical Clinic. "But you do."

"What you mean, blood?" I said, sitting straight up and looking him in the eye for the first time since I'd gotten into the car.

"You've gotta do this, bro," he said. "If you don't find out now, you'll drive yourself crazy worrying about whether or not you're cool. And with you being like my brother, I can't even see you going through that."

"I don't know, blood," I said, sinking back into the seat. "I mean, I know I need to go ahead and find out. But damn. It's like a nigga really don't wanna find out. You know? It's like I'd rather not know. I mean, say I got that shit, blood. Then…"

"C'mon, man. You can't even think like that, bro. You don't have it. I'm speaking that into existence right now. And after you take this lil' test, you'll know for sure. For good. Now let's go," he said as he opened his car door. "And speaking of tests, how did you do on that biology final?"

"I don't even know," I said as I got out of the car. "I ain't checking that grade on the Internet until I find out these test results first."

"Why not? Didn't you say you had to pass that class in order to stay in school?"

"Yeah, but none of that matters if this test don't come out right. There's no way I'm going back to ATL if I got the package."

"You don't!" he said, pounding his fist in his open palm. "Damn, would you quit talking like that, blood? I told you you're gonna be straight."

"I can't believe I put myself in this position!" I said, banging my hand on the hood of the car. "I should've known something was up with that bitch, blood. She was just too good to be true."

"Whoa!" Todd said. "I know you're not still hanging this situation over her head. You've gotta let that go, my nigga."

"So you're taking *her* side?" I asked aggressively.

"C'mon, now. You know we're brothers from another mother. Why would I do that? This ain't about picking sides. All I'm saying is, you really can't blame this situation on anybody but yourself, because at the end of the day you knew about the high STD rate down there in Atlanta before you left. That's why your mama left you with all those condoms."

"So, what you trying to say?" I asked.

"Look, you know I ain't even figna preach to you, blood. I probably need to get a checkup my damn self. As a matter of fact, I will. That way, we can get our results back together. My whole thing is, I don't want to see you pin the blame for this on somebody else, because if you do that, then you're liable to be in this same position again. But if you take responsibility for your actions, and think about how you could've handled the situation differently, then you will make wiser decisions in the future. Feel me?"

"You've got a point there, blood," I said. "I feel you."

"Remember, you've still got a promise to keep."

"What promise?"

"The one you made to T-Spoon at the party that night. You remember that, right?"

"I wish I didn't."

The doctor told me that he would call me within seven days if he had any bad news.

The following week was the longest 168 hours of my life.

For the first couple of days, I gagged and hyperventilated damn near every time I heard the phone ring. I never left the house and rarely wanted to even get out of bed. I was battling depression. By the third day I'd chewed my fingernails away and had begun nibbling at what was left of my cuticles. I was a nervous wreck.

That week, I did just about everything I could to keep my mind off that blood test, but it seemed like there was a reminder everywhere I turned. When I watched music videos on BET, every other commercial was "Know Your Status." One of the few times I left the house to grab a bite to eat, I just happened to roll up to Magic Johnson's Burger King. The final straw came four days after my visit to the clinic, when I was chilling on my living room sofa, checking out ESPN—the one station I felt safe watching.

I never thought that my favorite sports anchor, Stuart Scott, would deliver the worst news report I'd ever heard in my life. I wanted to change the channel but my fingers were numb. All I could do was listen.

"I've had the esteemed pleasure of being the voice you've heard narrate some of the phattest highlights in sports history. But this is, by far, one of the most heartbreaking reports I've ever had to give. University of Atlanta quarterback and Heisman-award-winner Deiondre Harris has tested positive for HIV. After leading college football in touchdown passes thrown, total passing yards, maintaining the highest quarterback rating in the country for the last two years, being projected to go as high as number three in this year's NFL draft and putting athletes at HBCUs across the country on the map, the quarterback likened to Michael Vick and Steve McNair will never hear his name called in an NFL stadium or see it printed on the back of an NFL jersey. Harris had visited three different NFL combines, passing all of their physical workouts and agility drills with flying colors. He was notified of his positive HIV status after taking a blood test during a physical examination for the Dallas Cowboys. Again, Deiondre 'Downtown-D' Harris has tested positive for HIV and will not enter the NFL draft as expected. Harris was not available for comment. My prayers go out to Deiondre and his family."

As I sat on the edge of the couch, my mouth half-open and heart half-broken, I couldn't help but think about all of the girls I'd seen Downtown-D around campus with—from the toned-up cheerleaders, to the supersexy sorority chicks, dime-a-dozen groupies and the girl he was with in the bathroom at the coronation ball. I wondered which one gave him the virus. Then I wondered which ones he'd given it to, and how many of them would find themselves in the same situation as Kat. I thought about how, at one point, I'd have given anything to be in his shoes. And now I'd do just about anything to be as far away from them as possible.

Six days after my visit to the clinic, I received a call around seven o'clock in the morning. I rolled over, took a deep breath and picked up the receiver sleepily.

"Hello," I said groggily.

"Yes," the guy on the other end of the phone said. "May I please speak with James Dawson?"

"This is him," I said, sitting up straight, my heartbeat doubling in speed. "Speaking?"

"This is Timothy. Timothy McGruden."

"Timothy who?" I asked.

"Timothy McGruden. Your roommate."

"Oh! Whoa! You scared me for a minute there. What's up, T?"

"That's funny," he said, giggling. "Why were you frightened?"

"Man, I'm not used to getting calls this early in the morning, blood."

"Oh yeah, I completely forgot you guys are three hours behind out there."

"Yeah, man. What's up with you, though?"

"Hey, I'm just relaxing. Enjoying the life of an Alpha Mu Alpha man."

"An *Alpha Mu Alpha* man, huh? So, what does that mean exactly?"

"I haven't figured that out yet. For now, I'm just delighted that I can finally feel comfortable just being myself. I can love God without being viewed as lame. And believe it or not, people have started to just accept me for who I am."

"I can dig it," I said. "I heard that pledging shit was no joke."

"I totally abhorred it. I was suffering from sleep deprivation and malnutrition all at the same time. I wouldn't ever do it again. But I'm glad I did it."

"They said y'all were getting beat down like Rodney King. I don't see how you did it."

"I got a lot of help from my line brothers," he said. "But halfway through the process, I just completely zoned out. I really got into the Word and came to the conclusion that fear and God don't occupy the same space. They're never in the same place at the same time. So as long as I knew He was with me, I figured I didn't have anything to worry about."

"So I probably don't have nothing to worry about, then, huh?"

"Why would you have anything to worry about? What are you talking about?"

"Oh, nothing," I said. "I'm just tripping. I don't know what I'm talking about, blood. It's so early in the morning. Hey, let me give you a call back a little later."

"That's fine. I was just about to start reading a new book anyway. But hey, before you go… Have you checked out your grades online yet?"

"Nah. I didn't even know they'd posted them yet. How did you do?"

"I would've had a perfect 4.0, but Professor Obugata gave me a C because he thought he caught me cheating on that test."

"I'm sorry to hear about that. I'm gonna call you back a little later after I check mine."

Shortly after I hung up with Timothy, my phone was ringing again. I took a deep breath before I answered.

"It wasn't worth it," a guy on the other end of the phone said.

"Huh? Who is this?"

"C'mon, joe. You ain't even been back on the West Coast for a week yet. I know you ain't forgot about me that fast. This is Fresh, nigga."

"Well, today must be call J.D. day."

"Why you say that?"

"I just got off the phone with Timothy a second ago. What's good with you, bro?"

"Nothing, man. Absolutely nothing."

"What you mean? What's the problem?"

"It wasn't worth it, joe."

"What wasn't worth what? Quit talking in parables and speak English, blood."

"It's Chantel."

"What about her?"

"She won't take me back, folk."

"And what? I know this can't be Mr. 'I don't chase 'em, I replace 'em' sounding all depressed."

"That rule doesn't apply to wifey, G. You know that."

"Damn, blood. I don't even know what to say. You must've really loved that girl."

"I still do."

"Well, what have you done to get her back?"

"Man, I done tried just about everything I know to do. I tried to call her, but she won't answer my calls. I sent her text messages, but she won't return them. I bought her an early Christmas present from Victoria's Secret and tried to take it by her crib, but her mama told me that she didn't want to see me. I think she's got somebody else. She probably linked up with him when I was at school."

"There you go, jumping to conclusions," I said. "You're probably overreacting, blood."

"I mean, don't get me wrong, she's said she was through with me in the past, and she always came back. But, man, I think she's really, seriously for real this time. I ain't never felt like this before in my life."

"All I can say is, if she's the right one for you, she'll be back. If I was you, I wouldn't even call her anymore. She's probably just acting like that because she knows you're on her. Ya know? She's probably just playing those mind games that girls like to play. As soon as she realizes you ain't stuck on her like that and she starts to think you've moved on, she'll be back like a Frisbee. Mark my words."

"Yeah," he said. "You know what? You're probably right."

"I know I'm right. I did the same thing with Keisha, and it worked. She broke up with me right before I left for U of A. It hurt at the time. But then I just decided to flip the script. As soon as she suspected I'd moved on, she was blowing me up like a balloon at a first grader's birthday party."

"See, that's exactly why I had to call, my man," he said. "I can always count on J.D. to keep it real. Speaking of keeping it real, did you hear that shit about your boy Downtown-D? When all of those NFL scouts were saying he had the total package, I didn't know they were talking about AIDS," he said, laughing halfheartedly.

Before I could answer, I heard a beep on my phone, letting me know I had an incoming call. When I looked down at the caller ID, my fingers turned cold. It read: North Oakland Medical Clinic.

Then I accidentally dropped the phone.

"Hello?" Fresh asked. "Hello?"

"Yeah," I said. "I dropped the phone. My bad."

"I thought I told you about trying to talk on the phone and take a shit at the same time, folk."

"Ha, ha," I said sarcastically. "That's real funny, man. Hey, look, I've gotta take this call on the other line. I'm gonna call you back."

"That's cool. I gotta get off the phone anyway. Ever since Chantel stopped paying my phone bill, Nextel has been real bogus on the daytime minutes, joe. If you don't pay that bill, they'll cut your phone off in a second. So, shit, if you're planning on calling me back, wait till after nine, when my minutes are free."

"All right, blood."

With that, I clicked over and faced my destiny like a man. It had been five days—113 hours to be exact—since I'd left the doctor's office, my entire future waning on the brink of this one phone call. I'd made my bed; I figured I was as prepared as I'd ever be to lay in it if I had to.

"Hello," I said solemnly.

"Yes, hello," a familiar voice said. "May I please speak with a Mr. James Dawson?"

"This is him."

"Oh, hey there. This is Dr. Goldstein. How are you?"

"I'm okay."

"Good. Well, I know you've probably been on pins and needles these last few days, so I don't want to keep you waiting any longer than you already have. Are you sitting down?"

When he asked that question my heart rate increased to that of a marathon runner's. All the times I'd seen the show *ER*, the only time a doctor asked a patient if he or she was sitting down was when the doctor had bad news to deliver. I closed my eyes and braced myself for the worst.

"Yeah," I said, my heart racing.

"Okay, cool," the doctor said nonchalantly. "So here's the deal—I've got good news and bad news. Which would you prefer to hear first?"

"Give me the bad news."

"Well, the bad news is that, after analyzing your mental health status, I've determined that you're suffering from post-traumatic stress disorder."

"That's the bad news?"

"Yes, sir. Judging by the things you shared with my assistant, this could have resulted from your close friend dying in the car accident while you were at school, being robbed at gunpoint or you finding out that you may be infected with HIV. The side effects include nightmares, flashbacks, difficulty sleeping—"

"Excuse me, Doc."

"Sir?"

"If that's the bad news, then what's the good news?"

"Oh, well, the good news is that your HIV test came back negative. You are not infected with the virus."

After six days of listening to my mom constantly nag me about finding out my GPA, I finally turned on the computer and faced my fate. When I first sat down at the computer, my fingers became jittery, and I could barely keep them hovered over the home keys. After I'd checked my e-mails, read an article about Downtown-D on ESPN.com and checked my e-mails again to make sure I hadn't missed anything the first time, I figured I was ready to log on to my school Web site to check my final grades. By that time, my mom was a nervous wreck, pacing back and forth in the kitchen.

"So, what did you get, J.D.?" she asked.

"I don't know yet," I said. "I'm about to log on now."

"About to log on?" she asked. "You've been sitting there for about forty-five minutes! What have you been doing the whole time? I mean, how long does it take to find out? I could've called the school and found out for myself by now. What's the number?"

"Mom, I'm checking right now," I said.

"Well, what do you think you got?"

"I don't know, Mom. All I know is, as long as I passed my biology class, I should be straight. That's the only class I'm really worried about."

By the time I typed in my password—the last step before finding out my final grades—I'd come to the conclusion that if I could be man enough to face my HIV test results, finding out whether or not I'd be allowed to return to college shouldn't be too tough to swallow. After all, those test results were a matter of life and death. But judging by the way my mom was acting, I had a feeling my final grades could prove to be just as deadly.

"Okay, J.D., this is taking way too long. Is there something you want to tell me?"

"Mom, it's loading now. Hold on."

"Oh, good!" she said, scampering around the dining room table to look over my shoulder. "Okay, here they come."

At that point, I couldn't take it anymore. I looked away as my mom read my grades off the screen.

"All right, here we go," she said, clapping her hands, then placing them on my shoulders. "First Year Seminar, A. Good. Okay, we can work with that. Music Appreciation, B. That's what I'm talking about! English, C. We can work on that. African-American History, B. Yes! That's my baby! Algebra, C. Oh, my goodness, J.D.! So far, I think this is the best report card I've seen you bring home in a long time! I haven't gotten to the bottom, but the way this is looking, you would've had to fail your last class in order for you not to have at least a 2.5. Let's see what you got." She grabbed the mouse to scroll down. "You got a C! J.D.!" she said, gyrating my shoulders. "You passed, baby! Look at that! You got a C in biology. You go, boy!" The tears were streaming from her eyes. "Let's see. That brings your GPA to a 2.67! Oh, my God! I am so proud of you. I knew you could do it! Where is the cordless phone? I've got to call your sister and tell her the good news!"

Now that I look back on my first semester, of all the frivolous banter tossed around by Dub-B, Lawry, Fresh and Stretch, and the wise, philosophical statements made by Timothy and Dr. J, none of it sticks out more than the words uttered by the disgruntled woman who helped me in the registration line. She said I'd never get a second first semester—and she was right. But after all I'd been through, I was just glad my first semester wasn't my last.